LUTON L...

D0755587

BOOKS SHOULD BE RETURNED BY THE LAST DATE STAMPED

"Are you certain?" she asked softly.

"Look at me, Artemis."

Whatever she saw in Darrel's eyes apparently frightened her, and she almost bolted. But he grabbed her hand, and she settled down again, panting and trembling. Her teeth penetrated his flesh. She moaned as his blood began to flow, and he felt desire take hold exactly as he had prayed it wouldn't. He reached out to clasp his hands around her waist. He found the hem of her tunic and slipped his fingers beneath, sliding his palms over the skin below her ribs.

Then he paused, because she hadn't asked for his touch, because he knew that she was not a vampire. But Artemis gripped his wrist and held his hand where it was.

She was too far gone to stop. And so was he.

NIGHT QUEST

SUSAN KRINARD

MILLS & BOON

First Published in Great Britain 2016
By Mills & Boon, an imprint of HarperCollins*Publishers*
1 London Bridge Street, London, SE1 9GF

© 2016 Susan Krinard

ISBN: 978-0-263-92162-5

89-0216

Printed and bound in Spain
by CPI, Barcelona

Susan Krinard has been writing paranormal romance for nearly twenty years. With *Daysider*, she began a series of vampire paranormal romances, the Nightsiders series, for Mills & Boon Nocturne. Sue lives in Albuquerque, New Mexico, with her husband, Serge, her dogs, Freya, Nahla and Cagney, and her cats, Agatha and Rocky. She loves her garden, nature, painting and chocolate… not necessarily in that order.

With special thanks to my editor, Leslie Wainger,
for her patience and editorial expertise;
and to Serge, who will never give up on me.

Prologue

Some thirty years after the signing of the Treaty between human and Nightsider, or Opiri, forces, human Enclaves and Nightsider Citadels maintained a sometimes uneasy peace. Territories were well established, and the neutral Zones between were regularly patrolled by Citadel and Enclave agents.

The agents were of two specific genetic types. The half-breed Daysiders, or Darketans, day-walking Opiri, were born of human fathers and Nightsider mothers. Previously considered mutants, they had human coloring and extra-human speed and strength, but possessed the standard need for blood.

The half-blood dhampires, offspring of human mothers and Opir fathers, were of a different genetic type, with "cat-like" eyes and the ability to walk in daylight, while also possessing full Opiri speed, strength and acute senses. A percentage were dependent on blood, while some were able to digest human food.

Though both Daysider and dhampir agents were charged to prevent potential enemies from entering their respective territories, they could not prevent the establishment of illicit colonies.

In California, humans and progressive Opiri founded mixed settlements in which humans and Nightsiders could live in peace and cooperation. These new colonies were for the most part left alone by both Citadels and Enclaves. Farther north, in the former states of Oregon and Washington, humans established heavily guarded compounds inhabited by militias more devoted to killing stray Opiri than maintaining the peace.

Their victims were primarily exiled Opiri known as Freebloods. Most Freebloods were humans who had been bitten and turned into Opiri by powerful Bloodlords and Bloodmasters after the beginning of the ten-year War, first serving as vassals to their sires and then, after being replaced by other vassals, released from the bond created by the process of conversion.

Freebloods within the Citadels were forced to compete for human serfs in order to establish a Household and gain rank. But though, by treaty, the Citadels were compelled to send convicts to their former enemies, the supply of such convicts began to dwindle, and competition for the serfs became a significant problem.

As a result, hundreds of Freebloods were exiled from the Citadels to survive in any way they could. These Freebloods, running in packs, became a significant threat to human and mixed colonies, often stealing humans or killing Opiri colonists.

At the same time, certain Citadels began to see the necessity of changing the Opir way of life in order to deal with the ever-shrinking supply of accessible human blood. Some Opiri spoke of the need to abandon the taking of human blood in favor of animal blood, while others favored a new war. Meanwhile, the mixed colonies continued to grow and spread, offering a new alternative of peaceful coexistence based on the voluntary sharing of blood.

It was, of course, inevitable that these competing philosophies would come into conflict.

—from the Introduction to *The Armistice Years:*
Conflict and Convergence

Chapter 1

Timon.

Garret Fox knelt beside the footprints scattered in the dirt, tracing the smallest with his fingertip. They had paused here, the kidnappers, and the little person to whom the footprint belonged had briefly touched ground before being swept up again.

Still alive, Garret thought. He dragged his hand across his face, scraping against the four-day beard he hadn't had time to shave off, and got to his feet. Fear for his son made him ignore the deep ache in his muscles, the rawness of blistered feet, the heavy autumn rains that penetrated his coat and pried icy fingers under his collar. He hardly noticed the sting of the scratches across his face and hands where branches from trees and bushes had scraped his skin.

Speed had been far more important to him than caution. He wasn't interested in concealing his trail. Neither were the rogues ahead of him. They felt safe now, nearly two hundred miles away from the colony they had raided. Safe because they had left complete chaos in their wake, and every adult human or Nightsider had been needed to clean up the mess and protect the other children.

The rogues believed they had nothing to fear from a single human.

Garret adjusted his pack, reassured by the weight of the VS-134 rifle—the highly effective and notorious weapon known as the "Vampire Slayer," whose use was strictly forbidden except in cases of extreme emergency.

And that was why this had happened, Garret thought bitterly. Timon had paid for the colony's philosophy of non-

violence and indiscriminate acceptance of every potential settler. Garret had no compunction about using deadly
force to save him.

If Roxana had been alive, she would have done the same.
Timon was all he had left, the only thing in the world that
gave meaning and purpose to what remained of his life.

I will get him back, Roxana, he promised.

He set out again, though dawn was still hours away.
Rain turned to sleet with the unseasonable cold. The moon
was bright enough for him to see by, but he didn't need to
rely on it completely. He'd spent years not only honing his
body and skills to fight enemy Nightsiders, but also in developing his senses of hearing and touch to help him move
in darkness. The night would never be his element, but he
had long ago reached a truce with it.

As darkness gave way to sunlight, he moved more
quickly. As each day passed, the trail had led him deeper
into wild country that seemed to grow colder with every
mile, far from any human Enclave, Nightsider Citadel or
free colony.

Time and again, he lost the trail and then picked it up,
losing ground by night and gaining by day. Along the way
he found the bodies of solitary humans drained of blood,
their hollow shells cast aside, and each time he spoke a
few brief words over the dead before he forced himself
onward. His supply of dried foods shrank steadily, but he
didn't dare search for some isolated homestead or settlement to replenish his stores. He sought clean streams to fill
his canteen, gathered edible greens and caught whatever
game he could find.

At the end of the second week, his stomach hollow and
his gait uneven with exhaustion, he knew he had fallen far
behind. Still he drove himself on. He began to see more
human settlements—not mixed colonies, like Avalon, but
high-walled, paramilitary compounds with heavily armed

militias whose sole purpose seemed to be hunting down and killing rogue Freebloods. Garret avoided them, as he had avoided the less warlike settlements he passed.

Fifteen minutes before dawn on the first morning of the third week, near what used to be the city of Eugene, he heard the distant sound of a woman's scream.

He didn't pause to think. Dropping to his knees, he shrugged out of his pack and removed the components of the VS. With shaking hands he assembled the rifle and looped its strap over his shoulder. If the woman was being harassed by Nightsiders, the Vampire Slayer might be all that stood between her and an ugly death.

The sound of a twig snapping brought Artemis to attention. She grabbed her bow, her hunt unfinished, and ran toward the denser forest and one of the many refuges she had built for herself in the area she had chosen as her territory.

If it hadn't been for her hunger, she might have been clearheaded enough to notice the humans before she ran into them. If there had been one less human, she might have taken them down before they trapped her.

But there were five, all armed with automatic rifles, and they had thrown the wire netting over her before she could do more than raise her hands. Each segment of the weighted net was razor sharp, and though a thousand small cuts couldn't kill an Opir, the damage would prevent her escape.

"You were right, Coleman," one of the men said. "Never would have believed we'd find a female bloodsucker living alone out here." He looked at the sky. "Just about sunrise. We might still get her back—"

"Why?" a younger man asked, holding his section of the net with thickly gloved hands. "She ain't no spy."

"Dean's right," a third human said. "She wouldn't be out

here alone near sunrise if she was. She won't have no useful intel. Might as well take care of her here."

Artemis barely heard their voices. The wire burned
wherever it touched her skin and sliced through her clothing, but she tried to focus on calculating her best means
of escape. One of these humans would surely be careless
enough to loosen his grip on the net, giving her a few seconds to fight her way out. Blood loss might be great, but if
she could grab even one of these monsters…

"Watch out!" the first male said as she lunged toward
the loosest part of the net.

"Burn her!"

Something jabbed against Artemis's neck, and a paralyzing shock jolted her nerves and froze her muscles. She
felt her useless body being dragged across the ground and
through the mud, the wires cutting deeper as the humans
found a patch of dry earth far from any hint of shade.

The sky had grown pale in the east. The sun was minutes
away from rising, and her body ignored every command
her brain tried to send it. She was aware of increasing pain
as the humans jostled the net and anchored it to the ground,
driving stakes into the earth to pin its edges so tight and
close that she wouldn't find even the smallest opening.

Still, she tried. The paralysis broke, and she flung herself
up and against the stinging web, cutting what remained of
her clothes to ribbons and shredding the skin of her hands
while the guttural laughter of the humans echoed inside
her skull.

Then they stepped back, denying her what little shelter
their shadows might provide, and watched the first rays of
the sun strike her bleeding fingers.

She didn't intend to scream. She fought it with all the
discipline and self-control she had learned both in the Citadel and as an exile in the wilderness.

But her own cry deafened even the laughter of the humans, and the last thing she saw was the bright hair of a man with green eyes blazing like emeralds in the rising sun.

For a few fleeting seconds Garret considered the possibility of leaving the Opir woman to her fate. There were five men, all carrying modified assault rifles, and numerous knives and bladed weapons. It would be impossible to approach them without being seen.

He'd faced similar odds before and met them head-on. But he had expected a human woman, not a Freeblood. For all he knew, the female might be among the most vicious rogues in this patch of wilderness, as bad as those who had taken his son.

And if anything were to happen to him now, there would be no one to look for Timon. No one to save him from whatever fate the rogues intended for him.

But the militiamen were torturing the woman, and that was far beyond the pale of what Garret could accept. He had no doubt of what Roxana would have done if she were here.

Kneeling behind a screen of shrubs, Garret separated the VS into its component parts and returned them to his pack. Raising his hands above his head, he walked out into the clearing. Almost as one, the militiamen lifted their rifles and pointed them at his chest.

"Human," Garret said in his mildest voice, trying to ignore the muffled moans of the Opir woman in the net. "Peace."

Two of the men lowered their rifles. The others held steady. The eldest of the bunch, grizzled and scarred, stepped forward.

"Who are you?" he demanded, his hand on the butt of his hunting knife.

"My name is Garret Fox," Garret said. "I'm looking for my son, who was taken by rogue bloodsuckers." He glanced at the Freeblood in the net. "Have you seen any children in the area?"

The leader looked at his comrades. They shook their heads.

"We ain't seen no kids outside our compound," he said, his eyes narrow with suspicion. "Or any bloodsuckers except this one." He kicked at the body curled up on the ground, and Garret fought the instinct to stop him. "Your son, you said? Where you from?"

Garret estimated that he had no more than a few minutes before the sun was high enough to kill the Nightsider woman. He didn't have time for conversation.

"South," he said. "I've traveled a long way."

"Looks like it," one of the younger men said. His eyes were small and cruel. "If bloodsuckers took your kid, he's probably dead."

"Shut up, Dean," the grizzled man said. "How'd it happen?"

"We were out hunting," Garret said, staying as vague as possible. "Maybe this female knows something. Will you let me question her before you kill her?"

There were murmurs of protest, but the leader silenced them with a wave of his hand.

"Get her out of the sun," he ordered his men. He met Garret's eyes. "You got five minutes. Here." He tossed a shock stick to Garret, who snatched it out of the air. "Use this if she don't cooperate."

Garret edged closer to the leader as the other men dragged the net into the scant shade of a nearly leafless bush. "She probably won't respond to more pain," he said. "Let me tell her that you'll give her a quick death if she cooperates."

"Why should she believe you?"

"I was the interrogator in my compound," Garret said. "Even with *them*, persuasion can be effective."

"Why should I give her a quick death?"

"I didn't say you had to keep my promise."

The grizzled man bared his teeth in a grin. "Five minutes, like I said."

"Thanks." Garret turned toward the net, but the leader grabbed his arm with a callous hand.

"You got guts to travel out here by yourself," he said, "and you look like a good fighter. You married?"

The grief was almost as fresh now as it had been four years ago. "No," he said.

"Then you might be welcome to join us if you decide not to go back south again."

"After I find my son, I may take you up on your offer."

"My name's Claude Delacroix. Find the old town of Melford and wait by the bridge over the creek. Someone'll find you and bring you to the compound."

"I'll keep that in mind." Garret pulled free, firmly but politely. "If you can keep your men away, I'd appreciate it."

"Will do." Delacroix gestured to his crew, cast Garret another assessing look and followed them.

Well aware that the militiamen were watching every move he made, Garret crouched by the net. The Opir woman's pale skin was striped everywhere with narrow lacerations, her jacket and pants were little more than scraps of fabric held together by a few threads, and the hand tucked half under her chest was blistered and red. Her hair, a rich shade of ivory, was just long enough to cover her face.

No matter what she was or what she might have done, Garret thought, she didn't deserve *this*.

"Listen to me," he said, leaning as close to the net as he dared. "I can help you get out of here, but you'll have to do exactly as I say."

Slowly she lifted her head. Her eyes were dark amethyst, unexpectedly and extraordinarily beautiful. Her body was slender, her face delicate and fine-boned, but there was nothing weak in either. The defiance in her eyes told him that anyone who made the mistake of thinking her fragile would quickly regret their assumption.

"I heard what was said," she said. "You are lying."

The misery in her voice cut straight through Garret like the razor wires that cut her body. "Where I come from," he said, "we don't leave people to be tortured to death."

"People?" she said with a brief, hoarse laugh. "Is that what you think I am, human? A *person*?"

"*They* obviously don't think so," he said, tilting his head toward the militiamen.

"You wish to interrogate me, but I have nothing to tell you."

"Do you live in this area?"

Her full lips remained stubbornly closed.

"You don't know anything about a pack of rogues with a human child?" Garret asked.

"No."

"I know his kidnappers came this way, but I lost their trail. You must have sensed them."

"I did not."

"Where is the rest of your pack?"

"I have no pack." She coughed, turning her face away. "If you have any of your supposed human mercy in you, let me have the quick death the other humans will never give me."

"Is that what you want?" he asked. "To die?"

"I cannot help you. Why would you offer me any other alternative?"

He glanced over the top of the net. The militiamen were muttering among themselves. Garret's five minutes were almost up.

"You have two choices," he said. "Trust me, or force me

to hand you over to them. And I don't want your death on my conscience."

She tried to brush her hair out of her face, but the movement cracked the burned skin of her hand, and her expressive eyes blurred with pain. "What do you want me to do?"

"What's your name?"

"If it matters… Artemis."

He showed her the shock stick. "Artemis, you'll have to pretend I'm using this on you. Be convincing. I'll flip the net back. You come out, grab me and drag me into the woods."

"You believe I will not kill you?" she asked with obvious astonishment.

"Will you?"

"They will shoot both of us."

"It's possible. But I think I've persuaded them to believe that I'm one of them."

"Yes. You are *human*."

Garret held her gaze. "I hope you'll choose to live."

With another quick glance at the militiamen, Garret raised his voice in a harsh question and pretended to jab the stick into the net. The Opir woman began to convulse very convincingly, and as she did Garret grabbed two of the weights with his gloved hands and flung the net back over itself, leaving a narrow gap at the bottom.

Artemis was injured and in great discomfort, but she moved very fast, scrambling out from under the net, grabbing him by the shoulders and half dragging him toward the woods. He dropped the shock stick. Sunlight struck her, and she swallowed a cry. The weakness of her grip told Garret that she wouldn't be able to keep up the pretense for long, so he made a show of helplessness, struggling as if she had complete control of him.

A bullet whizzed past his ear when they were still a few yards from the woods' edge. Garret shouted and raised one hand in a plea as the woman continued to tug at him, her fingers beginning to slip from his coat.

"A little farther," Garret said. "Once we're inside the woods, run."

Artemis stumbled, and Garret twisted to push her toward the trees. The militiamen were jogging after them now, deadly silent and ready to shoot. Garret and the Freeblood reached the shade, and she staggered, her breath sawing in her throat.

"Go!" Garret said.

"They'll kill you," she said hoarsely, refusing to move.

"For being an idiot and allowing you to escape? I don't think so."

She didn't have time to answer, because the men were almost on top of them. Artemis grabbed him around the neck and dragged him deeper into the shadows. He could have escaped easily, but he played along, gasping for air and digging his heels into the dirt.

"Come no closer!" she shouted. "I will kill him!"

Chapter 2

The militiamen slowed to a walk. Delacroix signaled a halt. He met Garret's gaze.

"I'm sorry," he said, "but I can't let her escape." He lifted his rifle and aimed at the center of the woman's forehead.

"She knows where my son is!" Garret rasped. "Let her go, please!"

Delacroix hesitated. "Your son is no more important than the people this bloodsucker will kill."

"I will release him if you give me five more minutes before you follow me," Artemis said.

Bending his head toward the man next to him, Delacroix spoke in a low voice, listened to his comrades and nodded.

"Five minutes," he said, checking his watch.

Without warning, Artemis released Garret, pushing him toward the men, and sprang into a run. Almost immediately the militiamen started after her.

"Wait," Garret said. "I thought you said—"

Delacroix signaled a halt. "You think we'd keep a promise to one of *them*?" he asked. "Don't you want the info you say she has?"

"Yes, of course," Garret said, rubbing his throat as he got to his feet. "But if you go into those woods after her, she'll have the advantage."

Two of the men aimed their rifles at him. "Who *are* you?" Delacroix asked again.

"A former serf from the Citadel of Erebus," Garret said. "Do you know what that's like? Any of you?"

The men exchanged glances. One lowered his gaze. Another spat.

"This is my fault," Garret said. "Give me one of your weapons and I'll get her myself."

"She'll have even more of an advantage over one hunter," Delacroix said. "Why aren't *you* carrying a gun?"

The VS seemed to burn a hole through Garret's pack and into his coat. "I had one," he began, "but—"

"Take off your pack," Delacroix said.

"Why?"

"You're hiding something, and I want to know what it is."

Garret lunged at Delacroix, grabbed the man's rifle in both hands, yanked it away and slammed the butt into the leader's face. Without slowing, he struck the next man in the neck and then reversed the rifle.

Two of the others began to shoot, but Garret had already moved out of their path. He shot one of the men in the hand, forcing him to drop his rifle. The youngest one yelled and charged at Garret wildly. His heedless rage gave Garret the chance to kick the weapon out of the boy's grip before he could pull the trigger.

But another rifleman and the one he'd struck in the neck were almost on top of him. Someone flashed by him, a small figure who took the two men down so quickly that Garret couldn't see how she'd done it. He didn't take time to think it over. Shrugging out of his pack, he uncoiled the rope hanging from the metal frame and cut it into five lengths. By the time he turned back, all the militiamen were on the ground—alive, but weaponless and either unconscious or disabled.

He met Artemis's gaze briefly and knelt beside Delacroix, who was moaning as he began to wake up. Garret rolled him over and tied his hands securely. The Opir woman helped him with the other men, her face and body shielded by an oversize hooded daycoat that was thick enough to protect her from the worst of the sun. She wore equally heavy gloves. Garret could only assume that she had kept the day clothes close by in case she was caught out of the woods after dawn.

He checked on each of the men when he was finished. Two of them were already struggling and cursing, while Delacroix and his second-in-command were bleary-eyed and disoriented. The youngest glared at Garret with undisguised hatred.

"Listen to me," Garret said, crouching in front of him. "I'm going to set you free. You go back to your colony and tell them to come fetch their people."

The boy pulled hard against the ropes around his wrists. "You gonna leave them out here for the rogues to eat?" he demanded.

Garret glanced at Artemis. "Are there any other Opiri in the area?" he asked.

"No."

"You *believe* her?" the boy said, his face twisted in amazement.

"No Opiri are going to attack you in sunlight. Your people should be able to return with plenty of time to spare before dark."

"Traitor!" the boy spat, tears running down his cheeks. "We'll hunt you down."

Garret moved behind the boy and cut through the ropes. "Take your pack," he said, "and go."

For a moment he thought the boy would stay and try to fight, but even *he* had enough sense to realize he didn't have a chance. He grabbed the pack and ran off, his pace much too fast to maintain for more than a few minutes.

"You will pay for this," Delacroix said, his words a little slurred. "We kill sucker-lovers around here."

Garret ignored him. He gathered up the weapons and backed away until he was in the woods again. Artemis went with him. He noticed that she was carrying a bow in one hand and a quiver full of arrows in the other.

"Thank you," Garret said roughly, trying to adjust the rifles' straps so that he could carry them all at once to a place where the militiamen wouldn't find them. "You can go."

"You saved my life at the risk of your own," Artemis said, her eyes reflecting crimson under the hood of her coat.

"I told you—"

"That you would not leave someone to be tortured," she said. "But I still do not understand why you would turn against your own kind to help one of mine."

Anger and grief clogged Garret's throat and tore at his heart. "I knew an Opir who did the same for us."

Her brows drew down and her lips parted as if she were about to ask how such a thing could be possible.

And then she collapsed.

Artemis woke to pain. Tiny filaments of agony circled her limbs and waist, her chest and neck. And her hands…

"Easy," the human said as she tried to sit up. He eased her back down to the bed of fallen leaves on which she'd been lying.

Instinctively she resisted, irrational panic flooding her body. But he refused to let her up, and she realized that he was strong enough to impose his will.

Human or not, he was dangerous. She had seen him fight. He moved almost as fast as an Opir.

"You're already healing," he said, his brows knitting in a frown, "but if you push yourself, you'll slow it down. We don't want to stay here any longer than we have to."

She disregarded the "we" and compelled herself to relax. "Where are the men?" she asked, casting about for their rank scents.

"It's only been a few hours." He glanced over his shoulder, and for the first time Artemis saw that they were far into the forest under a thick canopy of cottonwoods, protected on two sides by boulders that stood beside a small creek. She realized that she was wearing unfamiliar clothes that were much too large for her, carrying the oddly pleasant smell of the human who had saved her. Her daycoat and gloves lay neatly folded within reach; her knives, bow and quiver were farther away. It would take some effort to get them.

She might have just enough strength to surprise the human, grab her things and run.

"You don't have to be afraid of me," the man said, his eyes tracking her gaze.

"I am not afraid of you…*human*."

"My name is Garret Fox," he said, seemingly indifferent to her mockery.

"There is no need for you to stay," she said. "It would be best if you did not."

"Why? Are you planning on attacking me when my back is turned?"

The question seemed hostile, but his face was impassive. Too impassive to be credible. "If you believed that," she said, "you would never have brought me here."

"That's right," he said, dropping back into a crouch. "Saving my life just to kill me wouldn't make much sense."

She began to formulate an answer, but all at once she found herself lost in the extraordinary green of his eyes, like the moss clinging to the sides of the boulders. His dark red hair brushed the back of his collar, as if he hadn't cut it in some time, and there was a shadow of darker hair on his jaw and upper lip. His features were strong but not coarse, his mouth mobile but decisive.

By human standards he was very attractive. And Opiri appreciated human beauty well enough to seek out serfs that bore the same qualities this man exemplified, such as his lean, fit body, broad shoulders and easy grace.

Artemis had never owned such a serf. She had never owned a serf at all, though she had been strong enough to stake out her own Household in Oceanus, if that had been her intent.

Now, in a haze of pain and caught in the snare of this human's gaze, she wondered what it would have been like to own a man like this. What it might have been like if he were her Favorite, and they—

The man jerked away, and she realized that she had been touching his hand with her raw fingertips. His reaction had been so violent that she expected to see distaste on his face, but there was only confusion, as if he had been taken unaware by more than just the touch itself.

Artemis, too, was bewildered. Her fingertips tingled, and a series of small shocks ran through her arms and deep into the core of her body. Physical sensations she hadn't experienced in many, many years.

And through that touch she felt something else. Something that she thought she'd been rid of for a very long time. An emotional aura flared briefly around Garret Fox, as red as his hair, fed by all the anger and passion his expression concealed.

The aura vanished quickly, but her shock lingered. The ability she had worked so hard to erase—the ability to sense and feel the emotions of others—had returned with a vengeance, and a human had reawakened it.

But how could that be possible, when her brief dealings with her own kind since her exile had had no effect at all?

Fight it, she told herself. *If it takes hold again...*

"Lie still," Garret said, as if nothing had happened. "And keep that hand covered."

She lifted her chin, hoping that he hadn't noticed her bewilderment. "I am not accustomed to taking orders from your kind."

"Call it a suggestion, then." He cocked his head. "Why *did* you come back for me?"

"Do I not owe you my life?"

"Most of your kind wouldn't feel bound by a debt to a human."

"You said another Opir had helped you."

Artemis could hear the steady rhythm of his heartbeat break and then resume at a slightly faster pace. "She was a remarkable person," he said.

She. "What was her name?" Artemis said, trying and failing to control her curiosity.

"Roxana." He shifted his weight and looked away. "Which Citadel did you come from?"

"Why does it matter?" she asked. "Do you plan to interrogate me now, where you will not be interrupted by my untimely death?"

"You *are* an exile, aren't you?"

She wondered why he had chosen that word when he might as easily have called her a "rogue bloodsucker." It was how he had spoken of her to the other humans. And how most humans thought of Freebloods, or Opiri in general.

Opiri. Nightsiders. *Vampires.*

"What else would I be?" she asked.

Her supposedly rhetorical question provoked a raised eyebrow and a keen look. She knew what was going through his mind: the same thing that was going through hers, but in reverse.

Both sides in the ongoing conflict between humans and Opiri had scouts and spies in the vast, supposedly uninhabited areas between human and Opir settlements, usually known as "Zones." Most of the human colonies' scouts and agents were mixed-breed Opiri, called dhampires. But a few pure-blood humans were skilled enough to survive in the Zones, even against Nightsider opponents.

Garret could easily be one such human. But he was too far from the nearest human Enclave to be one of their scouts, and she would bet her life—again—that he didn't work for any of the militias.

"I am not an operative for any Citadel," she said, answering his unfinished question.

"I believe you," he said. "You were alone when those men found you?"

"I told you I was."

"You also said you knew nothing about a human boy in this area."

"I do not." She hesitated. "This boy is your son?"

"Timon," he said.

"I am sorry," she said, realizing that she truly meant it. "I would help you if I could."

He met her gaze. "You can."

Alarmed by thoughts of what he might ask of her, she forgot her pain. "I am leaving," she said, propping herself up on her elbows. "Do not try to stop me."

"You aren't going anywhere," he said, getting to his feet.

"I may be injured," she said, "but you appear to be unarmed except for a hunting knife, and even now I am stronger than any human."

"I wouldn't bet on it. Sit down, before you—"

Artemis climbed to her knees. Agony like a spear of sunlight drilled into her skull. Her mouth was dry, though she suspected that Garret must have given her water. She swayed, and all at once he was beside her, supporting her, holding her. He was warm and solid, and she could hear the steady beat of his pulse, the throbbing of his blood in his veins. The shock she had experienced earlier returned with his touch, a raw electric current that attacked her mind and body as if she had literally been struck by lightning.

"I said you weren't going anywhere," he said, gripping her more tightly when she tried to jerk away. He eased her down to the ground. "You'll need blood or you won't fully recover."

His matter-of-fact statement gave her a very different kind of shock. Humans didn't despise Opiri only because of their attempt to conquer the world but also because the very idea of feeding on blood was an abomination to their kind.

He did not offer you his *blood*, she thought wryly. But where else did he think she would get it, in her condition?

"Wherever you lived," she said, "it must be very unlike the human compounds in this area."

He pulled his pack close so that he could reach inside, and she caught a glimpse of a rifle stock, a kind she didn't recognize. It wasn't one of the weapons he'd gathered from the militiamen, then hidden. Apparently he wasn't unarmed, after all.

"I assume the local militias kill every Nightsider they find," he said.

"Yes," she said. "They consider it their divine purpose to hunt down as many Opiri as possible. Do you find that strange?"

"The militia compounds see packs of vicious predators, and the rogues only a source of food. An eye for an eye."

Now she heard in his voice what she'd sensed in his mind and seen in his aura: simmering anger fed by a deep fear that was not for himself.

Don't think about his feelings, she reminded herself. *Don't let them get inside you again.*

But she knew it wasn't that simple. Her shields had fallen, and she had to build them back up again. As quickly as possible.

"What was it that your famous peacemaker once said?" she asked, forcing herself to remain calm. "'An eye for an eye makes the whole world blind.'"

His laugh reflected his obvious surprise at her knowledge of human philosophers. "Very clever," he said. "Most

Opiri don't have much interest in human wisdom. Are you one of those rare Nightsiders who see humans as more than barbarians, killers like the militiamen or potential serfs?"

"How else should I regard them?"

"Forgive me for my foolish question. Tell me—why don't you live with other exiles?"

"It is not in the nature of Freebloods to live in packs," she said.

He searched through his pack, and the scent of his skin—his blood—drifted toward her. "Not in the Citadels," he said.

"And how do you know so much about our lives inside the Citadels?"

"Inside the Citadels or out," he said, "Freebloods spend most of their time struggling constantly for dominance, so they can build Households of their own. That's the entire basis for their existence."

"It is not the basis for *my* existence," she said.

"Because you don't want to fight?" He withdrew a wrapped object from his pack. "Somehow, I don't think you live apart because you're afraid of being killed by your own kind."

"I am not."

"Then there's something else about your fellow Freebloods that you don't like. Do you hunt humans?"

The direct question startled her. "No," she said, without thinking.

"That would explain it, then." He opened the package to reveal several strips of dried meat, and Artemis's stomach clenched with hunger. "I knew you were different when I first met you."

"How would you know that?"

"Instinct."

The same kind of instinct, she wondered, that had made *her* trust *him* so quickly? "And if you had determined that

I was like every other Freeblood," she asked, "would you have let me die?"

His very green eyes met hers. "But you aren't," he said. "I've met Opiri who didn't believe in living on human blood on principle, and others who just didn't believe in taking it by force. Which type are you?"

He spoke, Artemis thought, as if he had engaged in long, philosophical discussions with other Opiri, and that idea was flatly ridiculous. Wasn't it?

"Many Freeblood exiles do not know how to live without human blood," she said. "But most do not kill."

Garret offered her a piece of jerky. "Too bad the ones who don't kill can't—or won't—stop the ones who do."

She pushed the offered food away. "Are you so certain they have not tried?"

"Have *you*?" he said, searching her eyes.

"I want what is best for my—" She broke off and took a deep breath. She had no reason to tell him what she had attempted and failed to achieve in Oceanus. He would never believe it was possible.

"You hate us, just like the militiamen do," she said, covering her confusion with anger.

"*Us* is a very big word," he said. "I don't hate *you*."

He was right, she realized. She couldn't sense any personal hostility from him. To the contrary, he was intrigued by her, genuinely interested in knowing more about her life. She was afraid to look any further.

"I am still a Freeblood," she said.

"But you're no rogue," he said, setting the knife down on a flat rock beside him.

She was almost tempted to let him go on thinking that she was superior to her own people. *Different*, as he claimed. She found that she wanted his good opinion.

But if she let herself believe that she was better than the rest, she would betray her own principles. Freebloods only needed to be shown, guided, by one who had seen a little way beyond the bars of the prison they so blindly accepted as the limit of their lives.

Guided not by emotion, but by rationality. She didn't need her unwanted empathic ability to tell her that Garret was controlling feelings that might have paralyzed him if he set them free. In that, they were frighteningly alike.

"Where do you come from?" she asked. "From all you have said, it cannot be anything like the local compounds."

"I live alone."

"Without the protection of your own kind?" she asked. "Is that how you lost your son?"

Her cruel question had been meant to provoke an unguarded response—any response that would help her understand him—but all it did was open her mind to the ache of his sadness.

"It is my fault," Garret said quietly.

The red aura flared around him again, and Artemis covered her face. It made no difference. She wasn't seeing it with her eyes but with her heart. And now all she could feel was his pain, his sorrow, his terrible sense of loss.

She had known loss, too. But nothing like this. Not since she had been human herself.

"I am sorry," she said, dropping her hands from her face. "Have I convinced you that I know nothing of this abduction?"

Staring at the dried strip of meat he still held in one hand, he gave a ragged sigh. "Yes," he said.

His simple answer almost made her doubt his honesty. But the "talent" she'd tried to bury insisted otherwise.

If she was wrong…

A fresh stab of hunger caught her unaware, and she sank back to the ground with a gasp. Garret set down his scanty meal and leaned over her.

"You've spent too much time talking and not enough resting," he said.

"And whose fault is that?" she whispered.

"I should have been more careful."

She did her best not to notice the concern in his voice, his worried frown, the compassion he should not feel for one like her. Whoever and whatever he was, son or no son, she had to get away from him. The temptation to feed was terrifyingly strong in the wake of her injuries. If she should hurt him…

"You should continue your search," she said, turning her face away, "and I must return to my shelter to collect my things and move on before the other humans find me."

He ran his hand up and down his left sleeve. "Your physical state is obviously deteriorating. How far do you expect to get this time?"

"Far enough."

"And then?"

Shivering with animal desires she could barely contain, Artemis moved to gather her things. "I am going. Do not follow me."

"It won't work." His footsteps were almost silent as he moved behind her. "In a few minutes you're going to collapse."

"Then what do you suggest?" she asked, spinning to face him. "I see no other—"

"I obviously didn't make myself clear," he said. He pushed up his left sleeve. "I'm offering an alternative."

Chapter 3

His meaning was terrifyingly clear, and suddenly Artemis was furious—at her own helplessness; at his inexplicable generosity, in spite of his valid reasons for despising her kind; at a world that had created such a bizarre set of impossible circumstances. Her mind and emotions and physical senses reacted all at once, making her excruciatingly aware of the body she had so admired.

Even thinking of taking his blood aroused not just her hunger for nourishment but for other things, as well. Her imagination began to spin scenarios that could never be. Her empathic talent burned more brightly—extending fingers of amethyst light, *her* light, toward Garret—and he began to breathe more heavily.

Vivid images sprang into her mind: lying beside Garret, naked in his arms as she sank her teeth into his neck; moaning in pleasure as the blood flowed over her tongue and he guided her down on top of him; urgency building as her hunger exploded into an unbearable need to feel him inside her, giving as she took, taking as she gave...

She came back to herself, her body hot and throbbing, to find him looking at her with that steady gaze, his eyes so clear that she could see every shadow passing beneath the surface. No pain now, no anger, no sorrow. Only need. And desire.

Desire for a Freeblood. For *her*. She looked from Garret's hungry eyes down to his broad chest and lean waist, and then below, where the evidence of his response was so readily apparent.

And *she* was responsible. *She* had to put an end to it.

"How can you do this?" she asked. "How can you bear to let an Opir take your blood? Is it because of this Roxana?"

"I've done it before," he said, his hunger still burning in her mind. "I have no reason to fear it."

She wondered again where he'd come from. He hadn't always been alone, not with such a casual attitude about donation. But if he had ever lived among Opiri…

"If I take your blood," she said, "what do you expect in return?"

"Your help in finding my son."

His blunt response took her aback. She felt the completely unexpected and irrational disappointment of realizing that he was being generous only because he wanted something from her. Something he had probably wanted from the very beginning.

If she gave in now, she would be throwing away the very principles she had worked so hard to establish since her exile.

"I cannot accept," she said. "I must go."

Garret's expression changed again, as if he were waking from a deep sleep and had forgotten where he was. His aura folded in on itself and vanished. He rolled down his sleeve, returned to his pack and began to shift things inside it, clearly pretending to keep himself busy so that he wouldn't have to deal with her. She watched him, her muscles frozen, knowing she would never see him again.

"I will lay a false trail," she said, pulling on her daycoat with clumsy hands. "If the humans do find our tracks, they will follow mine. I'm sure they would far rather kill me than you, traitor though they may name you." She stumbled a little as she took up her bow. "As your own people say, good luck."

An instant later she was running…throwing all her energy into every step, hoping that the initial burst of speed would carry her beyond his reach before she lost her breath.

She knew it was time to abandon the area completely, and not only because of Garret. She had to get away from the possibility of any human or Opir contact, and lose herself in a place so remote that not even the most desperate Freeblood exiles would claim it.

True to her word, she laid a false trail, though it took a good deal more of her energy than she could afford. When she reached her temporary shelter, a small cave in the side of a hill, she gathered up her few possessions and left as quickly as she could, dizzy but still able to maintain a regular pace.

Every step carried her farther and farther away from the human who had inexplicably saved her life, then turned it upside down. Her heart seemed to drag several feet behind her.

By the time she left the woods a few hours later and reached the narrow path that paralleled the old northbound Interstate 5, a cold, driving rain had begun to fall. Normally it would not have bothered her; Opiri had lower body temperatures than humans, but their efficient metabolisms and greater strength enabled them to bear adverse conditions for longer periods.

But her energy was draining away a little more with every hour that passed. Hunger gnawed at her constantly. The weather didn't make her attempt to find game any easier, and she soon discovered that something had frightened away most of the local wildlife…a situation that might suggest an Opir pack in the area. She needed to avoid such packs at all costs.

As sunset approached, she sat down on a boulder under a stand of pines at the edge of a wide meadow and simply waited. The light began to fade. Nocturnal creatures would soon be venturing from their dens and hiding places, giving her another chance. Whatever came, she would have no choice but to take it.

Something large moved through the undergrowth on the other side of the meadow, an animal powerful enough to disregard any need for stealth.

A bear and her half-grown cubs emerged from the trees. The sow rose up on her hind legs, nostrils flaring, while the cubs tumbled about and cuffed each other in play.

Artemis caught her breath. She had seen plenty of bears before, but something in the scene touched her in a way she hadn't expected.

She rose slowly, careful not to attract the bears' attention, and prepared to set off again, feeling as if she had become detached from her body. Pebbles rolled on the ground behind her. She spun around, lost her balance, and then righted herself as she belatedly grabbed at the waterproof case of her bow.

Garret was standing a few feet from the boulder. He had thrown back the hood of his coat, and his wet auburn hair had darkened to a deep brown. His strong face seemed sculpted out of the rain itself, but he seemed no more disturbed by the weather than the bears were.

What disturbed Artemis was that he had approached almost as silently as an Opir. Once again she was surprised at his skill. Surprised—and furious that she had been caught off guard.

The only thing she had to be grateful for was that she perceived him only through her physical senses, not her mental ones. There was no aura to distract her.

Is that truly all you have to be thankful for? an inner voice demanded.

"What are you doing here?" she asked aloud. "Were you following me?"

"Did you finish your hunt?" he asked.

"Leave," she said, taking an aggressive step toward him. "Leave this place, before I must force you to go."

He looked her up and down with those keen eyes. "Why

are you so afraid?" he asked softly as the rain continued to pelt down on his head and shoulders. "Is the prospect of helping me find a lost child so repugnant to you?"

A human child, she wanted to cry out. *Why should I care?*

But how could she lie to him, and to herself?

"You would ask me to hunt my own people," she said.

"They're barely 'your people' at all."

"But they are. And I believe they have a chance at a better future than what they face in the Citadels or as exiles."

He arched a brow. "You didn't mention this before."

"Why should you listen?"

"What does this 'better future' involve, Artemis? Teaching the rogues to follow your example and refuse to take human blood? Convincing them that humans aren't animals, aren't just another form of prey? How would they consider that an improvement on their lives now?"

She shook her head sharply. "There is so much you cannot possibly understand."

"I understand that you follow an ethical code of conduct that stretches to include humans, and that you live alone because you won't share your life with barbaric killers."

"I will not debate this with you," she said, knowing that she'd made a mistake in bringing her philosophy into the argument. "If our positions were reversed," she said, "would you lead me to humans *I* might choose to kill?"

"When did I say that I planned to kill anyone?"

"You have made your feelings about Freebloods very clear," she said, "and you will not hesitate to use any means to save your son."

"You're right," he said, matching the challenge in her voice. "But I'm not seeking revenge. If I can get Timon safely back without resorting to violence—" He broke off and took a deep breath, his gaze shifting to a point somewhere behind her.

She glanced over her shoulder. The bear had obviously seen them and had reared up again. Her formidable teeth flashed in her brown muzzle.

"Is that what you were hunting?" Garret asked.

Artemis licked the moisture from her lips. "I had no plans to attack them," she said, grasping eagerly at the change of subject.

"But you haven't found anything else."

"That is not your concern."

Garret set his pack down against the boulder. "I think you need my help," he said.

Growing sick with hunger and the scent of the blood pumping beneath his skin, Artemis stopped herself from falling against the boulder by a sheer act of will. "You cannot help me," she said.

"Do you object to taking human blood, even if it's freely given?"

"Freely given—at a price," she whispered.

"You live in the wilds. I'm well trained, but you're faster and have keener senses than I do. Even if you won't come with me, you can point me in the right direction. That's all I ask."

His voice began to fade in and out, the sound replaced by a thrumming behind her ears. She tried to convince herself to hold to her convictions, her vow never to take human blood again.

But philosophy would always fail when survival was at stake.

"Come with me," he said, holding out his hand.

No longer able to resist, she stumbled toward him. He picked up his pack and kept just ahead of her, leading her under the shelter of a stand of close-growing alders. Without quite knowing how she got there, she found herself on the damp ground beside him.

Garret removed his coat and then his shirt, neatly folding both garments and laying them across his pack. Her head began to pound, and she found herself staring at the muscles of his shoulders, arms and chest—an ideal image of human masculinity. There was nothing vulgar in the way he displayed himself, but she felt need pulsing not only in her belly but also between her thighs.

As she struggled with growing delirium, he removed a rubber cord from his pack, tied it around his arm above his biceps and flexed his hand into a fist, raising the veins in his wrist. His forearm was corded with muscle, the kind achieved only through hard manual labor.

But then she looked up at his face and noticed the pulse beating in his neck. Her mouth watered. She knew that he was no serf to be taken by the throat, though the desire to bare her own body, press it against his and sink her teeth into his neck was nearly more than she could endure. She looked at his mouth, the lips slightly parted, and wondered what it would be like to kiss him.

She hadn't kissed anyone in over a century.

"Are you certain…this is what you wish?" she asked, her voice raw with thirst.

He didn't seem to hear her. He ran his finger along the length of the most prominent vein in his arm and met her gaze.

"Are you ready?" he asked.

A thread of sickness coiled through her belly like a parasitic worm. "I should not—"

"Are you afraid you'll hurt me? I promise that won't happen."

She licked her lips. "I can't."

Garret held her gaze. "You're afraid of losing control, aren't you? Whatever you think you might do, I'm prepared for it."

"Perhaps… *I* am not."

"You've run out of options, Artemis. Take my blood— or die."

His words were more than merely a warning. They were certainty, and Artemis knew he was right. It was a kind of blackmail, but he must know that in her desperation she might still overpower him and take what she needed.

He *trusted* her.

One time, she told herself. Then she would be strong again, and she would have learned from her mistakes.

Unable to fight her instincts, she grabbed his arm just below the elbow and bit into his wrist, barely remembering to temper the force of the bite before her teeth pierced his skin. He didn't so much as flinch, nor did he look away.

As his blood flowed over her tongue, Artemis felt something quite extraordinary. It wasn't at all like taking blood from the Citadel's public serfs, provided to Freebloods solely for the purpose of keeping them alive…barely. Nor was it similar to the times she had been compelled to feed from humans before and during the War, before the establishment of the Citadels.

That had been necessity. *This* was a far more intimate act, not merely a bargaining chip.

Intimate. That was the word, the sensation, the emotion, that overwhelmed her. Her body grew warm with the rush of vital nourishment and the headiness of lust.

Only after she was sated did she dare to look up. Garret's aura was alive, a scarlet halo visible only to her mind. His eyes were like faceted emeralds, cool and hot all at once. His chest rose and fell quickly, and she could smell a distinctive change in his earthy, masculine scent.

Lust. It was happening again…his emotions were invading *her* mind, feeding her desire as hers fed his in an endless cycle.

Bending to his arm again, she sealed the wound. Her tongue lingered on his skin, tracing a line down to his palm.

He made a sound deep in his throat, and she felt herself being pulled toward him. Her heart seemed ready to leap from her chest into his. She closed her eyes and pressed herself against him, her breasts exquisitely tender. He adjusted her to straddle him, and she could feel his hardness thrusting against her through his camouflage pants.

Then he turned his face aside, pushed her away and jumped to his feet. She did the same, trembling when she should have been at her strongest, and wiped her mouth with the back of her hand.

Wrong, she thought, *all wrong*. Garret had knocked her so far off balance that she wasn't sure she would ever find her footing again.

"That should be enough to help you finish healing," he said, reaching for his shirt as if nothing had happened. "But we'll need to move soon."

"We." For a moment, she had almost forgotten.

This was a bargain. Now she had to fulfill her part of it.

Chapter 4

Artemis's lovely face turned utterly cold.

Garret wasn't surprised. She justifiably believed that she'd been blackmailed into helping him. She'd taken his blood only because she knew she had no other choice, and he would have done nearly anything to get her help.

But he also knew that she had been struggling ever since he'd rescued her...struggling with the same impulses and emotions he'd been feeling almost from the moment of their first meeting. Emotions most Nightsiders denied, believing them to be the bane of inferior humanity.

Yet when she'd taken his blood, he had experienced the kind of intense physical attraction he hadn't felt since Roxana's death. He'd been painfully aware of Artemis's petite but generously curved body, the quickness of her breathing, the deep mystery of her dark eyes. He had held her against him, feeling the heat of her arousal matching his, imagining her soft moans as he stroked her naked skin...

He cut off the thoughts before they could carry him into dangerous waters. In the end, he'd rejected his own lust. As the leader of Erebus's human Underground, he had always striven to be disciplined, watchful and patient. Roxana had made it almost easy.

Artemis didn't. What was it about her that stirred his body and soul to such an inexplicable degree? Knowing that she was different from other Freeblood rogues couldn't account for this strong, almost uncontrollable reaction. What had started out as a compulsion to save an intelligent being from an act of barbarism had quickly evolved into something else, something he didn't want any more than she did.

If he were making the decision only for himself, he would go his own way and let her go hers. It would be far better for both of them.

But Timon came first. His well-being was a thousand times more important than the relief of any small discomfort his father might experience along the way. No price was too high.

He had to gain Artemis's trust and keep it. Until Timon was safe.

"I'm sorry," he said, grabbing his coat. "I should have remembered that we'll both need to recover before we move on." He pulled on the coat and zipped it up with slightly numb fingers, aware that he had begun to tremble from loss of blood. The ground seemed to tilt toward him. He'd forgotten what it was like to give so much blood at one time.

"Are you ill?" Artemis asked, a little of the coldness leaving her eyes.

"Nothing that an hour of rest won't cure," he said. "And if you move too fast after taking so much blood, you're likely to have problems yourself."

She studied him with a frown. "I am in no danger," she said. "But I see that you are not steady enough to travel. You had better sit down."

With a brief nod of acknowledgment, Garret slid to the base of the tree and leaned his head back against the trunk, grateful that they'd independently made the decision not to mention what had happened during the blood-taking.

"I don't expect you to stand guard for both of us," he said. "Wake me if I start to drift off."

Artemis chose a tree a little distance away and sat beneath it, holding herself erect and alert. "You are a strange human," she said.

"I thought you'd reached that conclusion when we first met," he said, closing his eyes.

"I know why you saved my life and shared your blood, or at least why you claim you did. What I do not understand is why you are so willing to reveal weakness."

Garret wondered if she was trying to make him angry. She didn't know him well enough to realize that he'd been through far too much to let pride influence his actions.

"I've already put my life in your hands many times over," he said. "If I didn't trust you—"

"No," she interrupted. "I have always heard that free human males believe themselves to be stronger than females in every way, and will do anything to avoid revealing any physical or mental impairment before one of the opposite sex."

Garret opened one eye a crack. "How do you know?"

"It is common knowledge."

"The same way it's common knowledge among humans that all Nightsiders are vicious killers?" He laughed shortly. "Not all human males feel the need to prove that they're invulnerable."

Artemis reached for her own small pack and unhooked her canteen. "It would be foolish to attempt it with a female Opir."

"I'd like to think I'm not a fool," Garret said.

"Would you have begged for my help, if I had been unwilling to give it?"

"Would that have made you feel better?"

"It would only have proven how much you wish to find your son."

"Then you have no more interest in having power over me than I do in having it over you. Which makes you exactly what I judged you to be."

"I still do not accept your 'judgment.'"

Garret rolled his head to observe the bears, who had apparently determined that the human and Nightsider were no threat and resumed their search for food. "Why didn't you go after them when you needed blood?" he asked. "It wasn't fear that stopped you, was it?"

"I was not afraid," she said, indignation in her voice.

"But something about them made you hesitate." He straightened, wishing he could sleep but determined to keep Artemis engaged. "They are a family."

She shrugged, though he could see that he had struck true. "Many creatures belong to what you call 'families,'" she said. "I cannot spare all of them."

"Do you know how long the female black bear protects her cubs?"

"I am not ignorant about the behavior of the creatures that live in the wild."

"One and a half years," Garret said. "These cubs are less than a year old. They'll go into torpor with her pretty soon, and then they'll be with her through the spring. No one can fault a bear's skill at parenting." He met Artemis's gaze. "When were you converted?"

"What has that to do with—"

"Did you have children?"

Her body stiffened. "I don't remember."

"You don't remember, or have you chosen to forget?"

"Even humans leave the past behind," she said.

"We try," he said, thinking of Roxana. His throat felt thick and full. "Do you remember what love is?"

"I…"

Garret unfastened his coat's padded chest pocket, withdrawing the battered photograph in its transparent envelope.

"This is Timon," he said. He rose and reached out to hand her the picture, and she accepted it with obvious reluctance. It had been taken before Roxana's death; Timon was smiling, a ball in his hands, and his best friend and cousin, Alessa, at his side. With his red hair and violet-gray eyes, Timon looked human.

There was softness in Artemis's face as she gazed at the picture, a softness that Garret had glimpsed only once or twice when she was at her most unguarded. Now she touched the picture with the tip of her finger, her lips curving in something like a smile.

"This picture was taken in a time of peace," she said. "Who is the other child?"

"Her name is Alessa. She's the daughter of my sister Alexia and her husband, Damon." He tucked the photo back into his pocket. "Alexia is half Opir. A dhampir."

Artemis stared at him. "Your father was a—"

"We had different fathers. I assure you, I'm fully human."

"But your sister—"

"Was born in the Enclave of San Francisco, after our mother found refuge there. She married a human in the Enclave, and I was the result."

Wrapping her arms around her chest, Artemis looked away. "I know…" she began. "I know it is an ugly thing, what our males did to your females during the War."

"It wasn't my intention to bring up the time before the Armistice," Garret said, regretting his slip.

"But surely Alexia was an agent for the Enclave, like all those of mixed blood."

"She left that life long ago. All I want for Timon is the freedom to live as he chooses, when he's old enough to make that decision. I'd hoped this would help you to understand."

"I always understood," she said in a near whisper.

"Then help me track the rogues who stole my son, and then return to your life. I won't trouble you again."

Her mouth tightened. "You will not expect me to fight for him?"

"I won't ask what you can't give."

They both fell into an uncomfortable silence, and Garret knew that it didn't matter whether or not they talked about what had happened between them. It was there, hanging in the air, haunting them, mocking them. An odd sensation seemed to tickle the surface of his brain, and all at once he was reliving the endless moments of lust and desire, hopelessly entangled with Artemis's need for blood and the memories of saving each other's lives.

"Artemis," he said, desperately resisting the urge to touch her, "I swear on Timon's life that what happened today won't be repeated."

It was clear that she understood him. She felt for the tree trunk at her back, fingers digging into the rough bark. Her breath came in short, sharp bursts.

"No," she said. "It will not."

They both looked away at the same time, and Garret released his breath. She said that now, and she must truly believe it.

But the connection between them couldn't simply be explained by the sharing of blood. He had wanted her in a way he hadn't wanted any woman since Roxana, and she'd wanted *him*. The blood was only the catalyst.

His mind refused to speculate further.

"I think we should go," he said, pushing himself to his feet. "If we walk slowly for a while, I'll be back to normal in a few hours."

"Surely you are not ready," she said. "It is nearly dark."

"As long as I stay close enough behind you, we can travel at night. It'll be harder for you by day, and we need to keep moving as long as we can." He hesitated, choosing his words carefully. "You can hunt along the way, and I'll do whatever I can to make things easier for you by keeping my distance."

Easier for both of us, he thought. But Artemis had al-

ready turned her back on him and was self-consciously examining her arrows, leaving him to wonder if they could
both hold to their promises.

They started north in silence, setting out along a woodland trail commonly used by both men and Opiri passing
through the region once known as the Willamette Valley.
Artemis took the lead, casting her senses wide for any trace
of Freebloods. The rain had obliterated most animal tracks
in the area, and she knew it would perform the same ser-
vice for any two-legged creatures.

However, she didn't have to rely only on sight. The
scents of the wet forest were almost overwhelming, and
she could track the movements of every animal—reptile,
bird and mammal—that passed anywhere near them. Ironi-
cally, now that she no longer needed to hunt, she could hear
tiny feet pattering over the pungent earth, and through the
weeds and fallen pine needles, the rustle of wings in the
undergrowth and deep among the branches.

But no Freebloods, and no humans.

As good as his word, Garret remained some distance behind. Yet he might as well have been clinging to her back;
she could hear his rough breathing, the muffled tread of
his boots, even the beat of his heart. And she could smell
him, a pleasant scent that seemed to complement the aroma
of freshly washed vegetation.

She could also smell his blood. As full darkness fell and
he moved closer to take advantage of her night vision, she
realized that the situation would not become any easier.
One taste of his blood had been enough to make her crave
it again. If she didn't find a way to ignore him, the journey
would soon become intolerable.

As intolerable as the memory of other cravings...and the
way he had turned her own unwanted emotions against her

by asking her about her former life. About children, and loss, and forgetting.

And love.

As she walked, she concentrated on rebuilding the crumbling barriers inside her mind. By dividing her consciousness between observing their surroundings and reconstructing her mental shields bit by bit, she could almost forget Garret for minutes at a time.

After several hours of unceasing rain, stillness fell over the woods. Artemis slowed her pace. She knew this area well; after her expulsion from Oceanus she had lingered here, well outside the borders of the Citadel's territory, hoping that she might locate other exiled Freebloods and persuade them to accept her philosophy. She'd soon discovered that the outcasts had no interest in anything beyond survival.

She looked over her shoulder as she and Garret passed through a clearing where a cluster of ruined buildings stood, relics dating to sometime before the War. Garret was moving unsteadily, though his pace had never flagged. She came to a halt and waited for him to catch up.

"It's after midnight," she said as he drew level with her. "We should stop so that you can rest and eat."

He met her gaze from underneath his hood. "I'm not tired," he said.

"Nevertheless, you must have food. Wait here. I will hunt."

Before he could protest, she slipped away into the darkness where he couldn't follow. She brought down two rabbits in rapid succession and carried them back to the abandoned buildings.

Garret looked up, his eyes shadowed with exhaustion. "The goddess of the hunt returns," he said.

There was a complex note to his statement, not mockery but something more lighthearted. Belatedly, she remembered what it was. Teasing. And there was real admiration behind his words.

Admiration that deeply unsettled her.

She laid the rabbits down on a broken chunk of concrete and crouched beside it. "If I were a goddess," she said, "I could guarantee that a fire would be safe. As it is, I can only suggest that maintaining your strength is probably worth the risk."

"My future strength is worth nothing if we attract a pack of Freebloods or militiamen," he said. "Did you see or hear anything?"

"Freebloods *have* passed this way, but not in many nights."

"Then I'll risk the fire."

He removed a lighter from his pack and began to gather kindling. She went to look for fallen branches, and by the time she returned he had a small fire going. With quick, efficient movements, he skinned and cleaned the rabbits and suspended them from a long sharpened branch over the fire.

"You're welcome to share this with me, if you have an appetite for meat," he said, the firelight dancing in his eyes and carving his face out of the shadows.

"There is little enough for you, and I am not hungry," she said. "Eat, and I will patrol the area."

"Thank you, Artemis."

She ducked her head and pretended to examine her bow. While he finished cooking his meal, she paced out several wide circles around the ruins, listening as much as watching. By the time she returned, the fire was out, the remains of the rabbits had been buried and Garret was fast asleep.

He trusts me, she reminded herself with more than a little wonder. It was likely that he hadn't intended to sleep, but his body had insisted, and his instincts…

His instincts told him that she would be there to wake him if any danger threatened them.

Squatting beside him, she studied his face. Now that he was asleep, she was even more aware that his usually calm demeanor was only a kind of mask. He mumbled something that sounded like a name. She couldn't quite make it out, but his muscles were tense, and she could feel distress radiating from him along with his body heat. Grief beat against her new and fragile mental barriers.

"Garret," she whispered. "It is only a dream."

His eyelids fluttered. He expelled a short, harsh breath and then relaxed into normal sleep. The pressure inside her head disappeared, and she realized that learning to block him was no longer a matter of mitigating the uncomfortable turmoil his emotions created in her thoughts. It had become a necessity.

Still, a part of her longed to stroke the damp hair from his forehead, to tell him that all would be well and there was no need for bad dreams.

If she surrendered to such impulses, anything that happened afterward would be entirely her own fault.

An owl hooted somewhere above her and glided out of the trees. It dived into the tall brown grass, and something squealed. The strong taking the weak. The world fell into a deep hush, as if in mourning for the fallen. Another sound came faintly to Artemis's ears. No animal had made it.

She entered the woods on the other side of the ruins and listened for a repeat of the cry. It came again, softer than before, a moan of someone in pain.

Unbearable pain, forcing its way into Artemis's mind. She paused to brace herself and searched for the source.

She found the Freeblood lying half tangled in a mass of blackberry bushes, one arm caught in the brambles and his body twisted awkwardly. There was a gaping wound in his neck, too severe to heal on its own. The bite of another Opir.

Dark eyes rolled toward Artemis as she approached cautiously. He made a sound in his ruined throat. Most Opiri maintained the appearance of the age they'd been when they were converted, and this one appeared to have been turned in his late teens. Perhaps, she thought, after the end of the War.

"I will not hurt you," she said, though she knew such an assurance would probably mean nothing to an exile. He jerked as she drew nearer, his hands clenching and unclenching.

She didn't try to ask him what had happened. She could guess well enough. He might have been dying for hours, and his body's attempts to heal would have driven him to starvation.

"Brother," she said, dropping to her knees beside him. "Can you hear me?"

If he did, she thought, she had a feeling that things were going to get a lot more complicated.

Chapter 5

The boy's mouth opened, but all that emerged was another groan.

"I know you suffer," she said. "But I can ease your discomfort." She laid her hand on his cool forehead and bent over him. She placed her mouth on his neck, releasing a little of the healing chemicals she had used on Garret. He tried to resist her, but he didn't have the strength to fight for long. After a few moments he relaxed and closed his eyes.

Artemis withdrew and sliced her wrist with her smaller knife. While the blood of a pure Opir could not nourish another full Opir, it would temporarily ease his raging hunger. She offered her wrist and let him take what he could.

When he was finished, she pressed her palm to her wound until it began to close, and then touched his forehead again. It was slightly warmer, but she knew he had little time left.

"Listen," she said, stroking the boy's pale hair out of his face. "I am seeking a pack of Freebloods who might be carrying a human child with them. Have you seen such a pack?"

Confusion crossed the young Freeblood's face. "Human?" he mumbled.

"A child, who never did any Opir harm."

"Why...you care?" he whispered.

"Because I believe that it is not our true nature to kill each other over humans, or take life, even human life, simply because we can."

With unexpected strength, the Freeblood grasped her wrist. "I...saw...the child," he said. "I was...with..."

She covered his hand with hers. "Where?"

Both she and the Freeblood heard the approaching footsteps before he could answer. The young Opir flinched. His fear nearly paralyzed Artemis, and only her rational assessment of Garret's essential character permitted her to keep her objectivity.

"Stay back," she called to Garret without looking away from the Freeblood's panic-stricken eyes. "He won't hurt you," she said to the boy.

Disregarding her warning, Garret circled around the bushes to stand just on the other side. "He was with *them*?" he asked. There was no pity in his voice.

The young Opir pushed against her, the urge to flee warring with his body's need for blood. Artemis held him down.

"What is your name?" she asked him.

"P-Pericles," he croaked.

"Pericles," she said, "this human is called Garret Fox. He saved my life from other humans who would have killed me."

"Where is my son?" Garret demanded.

"Garret," Artemis said sharply. She cupped the dying Freeblood's head in her hands. "Pericles, where did you see the child?"

Pericles closed his eyes again. "Make the human go."

Ruthless in his suspicion, Garret moved to stand behind her and gazed down at the boy with his hand on his knife. "Where is he?" he repeated.

Shifting her body, Artemis placed herself between human and Opir. Garret felt like a looming thundercloud at her back.

"Don't come any closer," she warned.

"Answer me," Garret said, stepping around her.

Artemis stood and turned, her face only inches from

his. "It would be very foolish if you and I were to fight now, when we may learn something of use to us," she said.

They stared at each other until the Freeblood gurgled in a way that sounded very much like death. Darkness swirled up in Artemis's mind.

The boy's time had run out.

Pushing all thoughts of dying aside, Artemis knelt beside him again. "It's all right," she said gently, cradling his head in her arms. "Garret, if you provide him with a little blood, he may be able to speak."

She expected refusal. Instead, he crouched beside her and gazed at the boy, his jaw working. He began to draw his knife from its sheath. Artemis caught his arm.

Garret jerked away and cut his wrist. "Tell me where I can find my son," he said to Pericles.

"Take it," Artemis urged. "His blood cannot cure you, but if you help us, at least one of your people will remember you with honor."

Licking his dry lips, the boy stared at the dripping blood in fascination. "North," he said. "Beyond…Oceanus's territory, across the…Columbia River." He choked. "Wa-Washington."

"Why?" Garret asked. "Why are they taking my son so far away?"

"I…" Pericles closed his eyes, beginning to lose consciousness. With a quick glance at Artemis, Garret offered his wrist to Pericles. The young Freeblood's mouth clamped on his flesh. Garret winced but held steady, and Artemis found herself battling both her own unexpected hunger and Garret's heightened emotions.

After a minute the boy's head fell back onto Artemis's arms, and he went still. The echo of his pain faded from Artemis's mind. Then there was only an emptiness where he had been for such a short while.

Somewhere in the darkness, an owl hooted. Perhaps, Artemis thought, the same owl as before. She laid the boy's head on the ground and closed his eyes with a sweep of her palm.

"Thank you," she said to Garret. She took his arm and sealed the wound. Garret hardly seemed to notice.

"He was with the ones who took my son," he said, his voice hoarse with anger.

"And they left him here to die," she said.

"They are rogues, and so was he."

"Yet you showed him mercy."

"To find out what we needed to know. It's unlikely he'd have done the same for me."

Garret had not felt the boy's very real fear of him, Artemis thought. She wished *she* had not. She lifted the boy in her arms and carried him to a place under the trees. She laid him out there, his hands folded across his chest, and stood over him for a few moments. Garret waited silently behind her.

"I know you don't believe it," she said, "but this boy was also a victim. I do not think he has been Opir for more than a few years."

"That makes it worse," Garret said. "He doesn't have the excuse of having had decades or even centuries to forget what it was like to be human. He chose to join a pack of rogues and kidnap a human child."

"Did it occur to you that he might have needed to join a pack in order to survive?"

"Like *you* did?"

His sarcasm bit hard. "It is because I am older that I could do what he could not," she said.

"You can't make excuses for every rogue who commits crimes against humanity."

"Many of your kind would say that I have committed such crimes merely by existing."

Garret gripped her arm and turned her to face him. "Those humans would be wrong," he said.

"How many would have saved *my* life?" she asked, trembling at his touch.

"I would not be the only one."

"And I believe that only the worst of my kind would harm a human child." She pulled her arm from his light hold and strode back to the ruins.

"Artemis," he called after her.

She stopped without turning. "I do not wish to quarrel," she said.

"Neither do I," he said. His moon-cast shadow fell over her, and she felt his breath stir her hair. "We obviously don't understand each other very well yet."

"Perhaps it would be better if we did not."

"Our survival might depend on it."

She swung around to face him. "What is it that you do not understand?"

"I heard you tell Pericles that you believe it isn't in your people's true nature to kill each other over humans, or take human lives just because you can."

"Why is that a surprise to you?" she asked.

"Are you really concerned about saving humans, or only about Freebloods killing each other?"

Without answering, she broke into a fast walk back to camp, where she began to gather up her things. Garret did the same, though he moved more slowly. Artemis thought she sensed regret in his mind. He checked again to make certain the fire was out, and that the rabbit carcasses and entrails were well buried, not that an Opir hunter couldn't have smelled them if he'd been searching.

But there was still no sign of intruders, so Garret withdrew a folded sheet of paper from his pack, and carefully smoothed it across the cracked and overgrown floor of the building, right where a shaft of moonlight illuminated the ground. Artemis recognized a precise drawing of the western half of the former state of Oregon.

"If I judge correctly," he said, pressing his fingertip to a spot on old Highway 99E, "we're right about here, roughly twenty miles south of Albany." He glanced up at her for confirmation.

"Yes," she said, grateful for the need to focus on practicalities. "That is also my estimate."

"And ten miles north of Albany is the southern border of Oceanus," he said, indicating a large black square on the eastern slope of the Coast Range. "We have only limited information about this area. Do you know how far inland their territory reaches?"

"Why do you think *I* can tell you?" she asked.

"You were exiled from Oceanus, weren't you?"

"How do you know?"

"Because we've learned that most exiles stick pretty close to their home territory. There are only a few small Opiri outposts between Oceanus and the northern California Citadel, Erebus. And I know you didn't come from Erebus."

"What of the rogues who stole your son? Were they not from Erebus, nearer to your colony?"

"As near as I can tell, they were from a Citadel some distance away. They were acting out of character. It's all a mystery." He withdrew his hand and clenched his fist on his thigh. "From what the Freeblood—Pericles—told us, the rogues are taking Timon across the river into old Washington. God knows why. But if he was right, they'll probably have to cross the Columbia River near Portland, where one bridge is still supposed to be intact. They'll follow the path of least resistance, the I-5 corridor."

"But that will also be a more exposed route," Artemis said. "Oceanus itself may be situated in the foothills of the Coast Range, but its territory reaches across the valley to the western slope of the Cascades. The rogues will be summarily executed if they are caught." She tapped the map with her fingertip. "They might have gone farther into the Cascade foothills to avoid any chance of meeting a patrol."

"And that's much rougher terrain," Garret said. "If we can find a more direct route across the territory, we may catch up with them, or even get to the Columbia before them."

"Or we may be captured," she said. "I am of no use to them, so they will kill me quickly. But they will either take you as a serf or, if they think you are dangerous enough, execute you as an example to other humans."

"No surprises there," Garret said, carefully folding the map. "But I don't expect you to take unnecessary risks on my behalf."

"You always knew I would be taking such risks."

"Yes," he said, meeting her gaze. "But I'm prepared to release you from our pact."

"Because we quarreled?"

"I was wrong to interfere between you and the Freeblood. And I have no excuse for saying what I did about your motives for helping your fellow Freebloods. But my son must come first."

"Then nothing has changed," Artemis said, feeling another jolt of his worry and pain. "The most logical route to Portland is also the shortest, but there is still no guarantee that the rogues have not chosen the same route."

"Agreed."

"So we continue to parallel Interstate 5 for the time being."

She shrugged into her pack and returned to the path, leaving the young Freeblood to the elements and the scavengers that would return him to the earth.

Three days' cautious travel brought them to Oceanus's southern boundary. They crossed the Willamette River at

Albany and continued north, roughly paralleling Interstate
5, to the rural city of Salem—which, like most other pre-
War human cities, was a mishmash of half-fallen buildings and bare foundations, overgrown parking lots, cracked
streets and patches of woodland that filled every available
space in between. The river and a long line of hills stood
between them and the western half of the valley and the
Coast Range.

Patrols of Opiri and Daysiders from Oceanus would have
to cross those hills to find them, Garret thought, and the
presence of such a patrol on their side of the Willamette
would be a matter of very bad luck.

At the moment, he and Artemis were observing from the
edge of what had been a wide street bordered by parking
lots and the remains of large, warehouse-style buildings.
The woods ended here, replaced by scattered, smaller trees
and shrubs, and resumed a thousand feet to the northeast.

Artemis rose from a crouch, shaking her head. "Nothing new," she said.

Garret concealed his frustration. Artemis had been vig-
ilant; as they'd traveled, varying the hours between night
and day, she had found numerous indications that Freeblood
packs had passed this way. The "when" was more difficult
to pin down, and there had been no clear signs of the presence of a human child.

He's still alive, Garret told himself. *He's a fighter. And
they must have a reason for taking him so far.*

"Garret." Artemis laid a gloved hand on his shoulder, her
dark eyes catching reflected light under the shelter of her
hood. It was the first time they'd had any physical contact
since they'd left Pericles, and suddenly he was immersed
in the warmth of her body and the indescribable scent of
her skin drifting out from beneath her heavy cloak. His
heart began to race as it had when she had taken his blood,

triggering the same startling current of desire and longing he had felt before and had struggled to ignore ever since.

Her fingers began to shake, and she withdrew her hand. "It's still early," she said. "We can be halfway across the territory before night falls."

"How long since you've taken blood?" he asked, breathing deeply to slow his heartbeat and suppress his arousal before it became too obvious. "You haven't hunted for yourself since you took mine, have you?"

She shook her head in a distracted way that worried him. He'd expected her to hunt at least once during the times they'd stopped to rest, but he'd begun to suspect that she'd neglected herself because of his eagerness to keep moving.

"Go now," he said, "I can wait as long as it takes."

"Later," Artemis said. With an abrupt, almost clumsy motion, she hitched up her pack and headed north toward the next patch of forest. Garret jogged to catch up, and then strode ahead of her. He could see far better in daylight than she could, and though the chances of ambush seemed small, he wasn't prepared to risk her walking into one. The Vampire Slayer, though still hidden in his pack, was close enough at hand that he could pull the segments out, assemble them and fire in less than a minute.

Sooner or later Artemis would find out about the weapon. He just hoped it wasn't because he had to kill a Nightsider right in front of her eyes.

They cleared the ruins of Salem by midday and began to travel in a more northeasterly direction, moving well away from the river and mountains to the west. Garret kept a constant eye on Artemis, watching for any sign of weakness that would indicate an urgent need for blood. But she continued to behave as if everything were normal, and he knew that forcing the issue wouldn't do anything to gain her cooperation.

At last they crossed the old six-lane freeway, passing

through former pastures, farmland and orchards that had given way to mixed conifer and deciduous forest. Several times Artemis detected the scent or tracks of Opiri moving in groups, but again there was no indication that they carried a human prisoner. They met no patrols from Oceanus. It seemed to be going almost too smoothly until, soon after sunset, Artemis began to weave and stumble again.

Garret was looking for shelter where she could safely rest when she jumped the thicket of wild roses that stood between them and barreled into him, dragging him to the ground. Her hood barely stayed over her head.

"Opiri!" She flung her body across his as if to prevent him from rising.

His pack—and the VS—were trapped beneath him. He lay still as her breath puffed against his cheek, the gentle curves of her body seeming to fit against his like a missing piece of a puzzle falling into place.

"How close?" he asked.

Artemis turned her head, her lips inches from his. "Close," she said. "It is fortunate that the wind is with us."

"Patrol? Or rogues?" he asked.

"I believe they are Freebloods. I think there is a human with them, but—"

"Timon!" Garret began to rise, but she held him back with all her obviously waning strength.

"Don't be a fool!" she said. "If they have him, it won't do us any good to rush right up to them and try to take him."

Closing his eyes, Garret worked to regain his composure. Artemis was right. God knew what the Freebloods might do with Timon if they felt threatened. If it even *was* Timon.

"Yes," he said. "I'm all right."

She stared into his eyes for a long moment and then rolled off. Keeping low, he got to his knees and looked over the top of the thicket.

"You won't see them," Artemis said, kneeling beside

him. "They are some distance ahead." She slid him a glance out of the corner of her eye. "You know I have a far better chance of getting near them without alerting them."

"Not when you haven't fed," he said.

"I am well," she said.

"You'll have to take my blood again."

"No."

"You're being irrational, Artemis."

"I will not do it."

"Then you'll have to stay here while I scout, or you could get both of us killed."

"I tell you I am well!" she said, her voice nearly rising from a whisper.

He took her face between his hands, though he knew what it might do to both of them. "Are you so disgusted by what happened between us that you'd ignore your own health and risk your life?"

The moment he finished speaking, he realized how desperately he wanted her to say no.

Chapter 6

Her breath caught, and so did Garret's. Fear and desire surged through his body, and it almost seemed as though they were her feelings as well as his. She was afraid of him, and of herself. Afraid she would take, and give, too much. She sensed that he was desperately afraid for her. Not because she could help him find Timon, but—

Artemis pulled away, her face paler than it had been a moment before. "When we know whether or not your son is with these Opiri," she said, "I will do whatever is necessary. For the moment, you must let me go ahead."

"No," he said. "We go together."

"So that you can protect me?"

He knew how she would react if he admitted the truth. Yes, he wanted to protect her, as much as he'd ever wanted to protect Roxana. And he'd been in a far less advantageous position to help Roxana in the Citadel where he'd been a serf and she his mistress.

"If you're not in your right mind, you'll need my protection," he said. He glanced up at the sky. "It's nearly sunset. In a few minutes you won't need your heavier clothes, and you'll be able to move faster. But don't make a move without me, Artemis. I mean it."

She gave him a scathing glance. "And to think I had thought you a human male without undue pride in his own abilities."

"It's *your* pride I'm worried about. Let's go."

Bent nearly double, they ran northeast, Artemis pausing twice to get her bearings. A quarter mile on, she stopped again and threw back her hood. Only a trace of pink light lingered over the hills to the west.

"The Opiri are somewhere beyond those trees," she said, pointing at a wide stretch of mixed woodland. As she began to move forward, Garret knelt to check the VS parts in his pack.

He rose again and trotted after Artemis as she slipped from tree to tree as lightly as a leopardess. She was nearly crawling when they reached the border of the woods. He dropped to his belly behind her. An area of nearly unbroken grassland stretched ahead as far as he could see.

"Do you see the rogues?" he said, squinting into the darkness.

"No, but I know where they are." Her voice held a new note, and the hair prickled at the back of Garret's neck. "They are camped less than two hundred yards from here. There are seven, perhaps eight, of them, and—"

"Timon?"

"I…sense that there is more than one human in the area."

He tensed to move again. "We have to get closer."

"Wait." Her nose wrinkled. "These Opiri are ready to fight. They are expecting to attack or be attacked."

"Attacked by whom?"

"The humans, perhaps," she murmured. "Whoever they may be, they are remarkably foolish to venture within the Citadel's borders."

"And my son could be caught in the middle of whatever's about to happen."

She turned to meet his gaze. "If the Freebloods have protected him so far, they will not let him be hurt. And if the humans should win…"

"We can't stand by and let this—"

"We must. If we die, who can save Timon?"

Clenching his teeth, Garret tried to weigh the options objectively. Artemis was right. Whoever the humans were, they would want to help a human child, and in a fight, the rogues would keep Timon out of the way. He and Artemis would probably have a better chance of grabbing Timon when the battle was decided one way or the other.

"I know this is against your every instinct," Artemis said. "I am sorry. I will go ahead, and see if—"

"No," he said, pulling her down when she attempted to move. "Can we get any closer without the Nightsiders sensing us?"

"No. In fact we have to go back to be safe," she said.

She retreated. Garret lingered a moment, listening, but his human senses were not acute enough to gather any additional information. Reluctantly, he followed Artemis to a point well within the shelter of the woods but close enough to the grassland that she could monitor what was happening there.

They waited as the long minutes went by, sitting a long arm's reach apart from each other. Garret was constantly, painfully aware that Artemis was very near but not quite close enough to touch, and that he badly wanted to touch her. Even in the midst of so much uncertainty, those feelings refused to go away.

An hour passed in silence, and then another. Artemis's head began to droop, and her breathing grew shallow. Garret moved closer to her. He noted a new transparency to her pale skin, a dullness in her hair and a deepening of the shadows under her cheekbones and closed eyes.

"Artemis," he said, carefully touching her shoulder.

She jerked awake, her body snapping into a defensive posture far more slowly than it should have. She blinked, recognized him and clambered to her feet.

"What has happened?" she demanded.

"Nothing, as far as I can tell," he said. "But you were falling asleep."

"I wasn't—" She broke off and strode away through

the trees. Garret waited ten minutes and then got up to follow her.

He found her at the edge of the woods. "Nothing has changed," she said as he crouched beside her.

"That's right," he said. "You still need what you need. We have to be ready to move quickly."

"You will become weak if I take too much."

"I trust you to take only as much as is safe for both of us."

They stared at each other, and Garret could see her struggling with arguments he knew she didn't want to make. Arguments that had nothing to do with her fear of his becoming weak. But she knew he was right, and she was the first to look away.

"Very well," she said. "But we should use the other wrist."

Garret hesitated, reexamining the decision he'd made. He couldn't pretend that there wasn't a risk in giving her much more intimate access to his blood.

But she would derive nourishment from his throat more efficiently than she would by taking blood from his wrist. And if he couldn't trust her now, he might as well let those Opiri in the field kill him themselves.

He led her back to their camp, removed the blanket from his pack and laid it down at the foot of a tall pine. Then he removed his coat and unbuttoned his shirt. Her gaze flew to his hands, watching his progress with apparent fascination, and he found himself suddenly self-conscious. He could sense her need as if it were his own.

"What are you doing?" she asked in a slightly strained voice.

"Just what we agreed," he said.

Removing his shirt, he folded it and laid it on the ground behind him. He rested his palms on his thighs and settled into the calm, detached state that had always served him well when he had worked with the human Underground in Erebus. He would need all that detachment to treat this feeding like any other.

He tilted his head back, took a deep breath. "I'm ready," he said.

"You are…" Artemis stammered. "You expect me to…"

"It's fast, and it's practical," he said, staring up into the green boughs overhead. "The sooner we're finished, the sooner we'll both be ready to take whatever action is necessary."

"How many times have you done this?" she asked.

"Often enough to know what I'm doing."

He waited, holding himself ready, until he felt the heat of her body close to his, her breath sighing over his skin, her lips brushing his throat.

"Are you certain?" she asked softly.

"Look at me, Artemis."

Whatever she saw in his eyes apparently frightened her, and she almost bolted. But he grabbed her hand, and she settled down again, panting and trembling. Her teeth penetrated his flesh. She moaned as his blood began to flow, and he felt desire take hold exactly as he had prayed it wouldn't. He reached out to clasp his hands around her waist. He found the hem of her tunic and slipped his fingers beneath, sliding his palms over the skin below her ribs.

Then he paused, because she hadn't asked for his touch, because he knew that she was not Roxana. But Artemis gripped his wrist and held his hand where it was.

She was too far gone to stop. And so was he.

The moment Artemis tasted his blood, she knew it was too late.

She felt his warm breath stirring her hair, heard the rapid drumming of his heart, smelled the surge of his lust and only drank the more deeply, caught up in an ecstasy more overwhelming than any she had known before.

Even the last time he had given his blood, it hadn't been like this. She'd underestimated the impact of taking it directly from his throat. An intimate act, she'd thought when she'd first met him, one he surely wouldn't share with her.

And yet here she was, and her body and mind were opening to Garret, abandoning all caution, renewing the intense emotional connection she had wanted so badly to extinguish. She had forgotten what it could be like, how quickly one could lose control with the right partner. And she had never taken blood during what humans called "making love."

But now, when Garret touched her bare skin, she felt his excitement as well as her own. She was being carried away by a current she couldn't stop, delirious with feelings and sensations that superseded mere arousal or the sensual stimulation that so often accompanied feeding.

She wanted him. She wanted to possess him, to be possessed by him, to join in complete physical union. What happened afterward…

No. The unraveling thread of her sanity begged her to remember what she could lose, what she could do to Garret. Once she stepped onto this path, she might never find her way back again. A single reckless act might finally shatter any hope she had of closing the gate against Garret Fox.

But sanity had no hope when Garret's fingertips discovered her nipples and teased them into firm, sensitive peaks. His blood soothed her tongue. Erotic images shaped in Garret's mind slipped into hers as his fingers slid down her belly and to the waistband of her pants. He unfastened the fly and dipped inside. Callous skin touched tender flesh. She shifted her body, urging him to explore as she continued to drink.

Garret stroked her with one hand while his other worked at the buttons of her shirt. Cool air washed over her breasts, and she straightened as his emotions told her what he wanted to do. Acting entirely on instinct, she sealed the bite and leaned back, giving him complete access to her breasts.

When he took her nipple into his mouth, she moaned at the incredible sensation of his reaction as well as her own, desire doubled and redoubled as he suckled her hungrily. His other hand found its way between her thighs and grazed the tight little bud where pleasure was almost like pain. She gasped, and he gasped with her.

Somehow her pants came off and she was straddling his thighs, rubbing against the taut bulge of his erection. She felt herself floating, guided to the ground by strong arms, lying on her back with her thighs parted.

The touch of his lips and tongue in her most sensitive place drew a muffled cry from her throat, quieted only by some distant sense of self-preservation. She seemed to re-call something like this happening long ago, but the past was as unreal as the future. Garret knew exactly where and how to use his tongue to tickle and tease, drawing out each caress with rapid flicks and long strokes.

She arched her back, begging him with her entire body. He turned his attention to her breasts and continued his ministrations while she felt for the waistband of his pants.

"Garret," she whispered, filling her mind with the emo-tional images of taking and being taken. His aura erupted around him, emitting tongues of flame that strained toward her. Her own aura flared for the first time, a blue-tinged amethyst radiance that opened to accept the thrust of his fire as her body was ready to accept his.

Garret was more than ready. Her hand found him, large and very hard. The intensity of his need—hers—multiplied a thousandfold.

For a moment there was nothing between them. Noth-ing at all—no boundaries, no barriers, no walls. He eased himself over her, gazing down at her with his weight braced on his hands and his hips between her thighs.

Again she saw herself through his eyes, less a distinc-tive shape than an aura enclosing the interwoven strands of her emotions. But the image began to take form, and she glimpsed her face: eyes closed, lips parted, hair wild and tangled about her shoulders.

And beautiful. Beautiful in a way she could never have imagined. It was the face she'd seen in mirrors before her exile and sometimes in the imperfect reflection of water, but bathed in a gentle light that softened the blue of her aura to a silky violet. Violet water, smooth and untroubled.

Garret caught her lips with his, exploring the terrain of her mouth, coaxing her to open for him. With a low moan of surrender, she parted her lips, and his tongue found its way inside. He curled it around hers, sucked, kissed her more deeply than she would have believed possible.

Violet transformed to deep, hot purple. She pushed her fingers into his hair and bit lightly into his lower lip, drawing blood. He adjusted his position so that a single thrust would make them one at last.

Something remarkable happened then. Feelings she barely recognized bloomed in her mind, so astonishing that, at first, she didn't know how to name them.

But not all the memories were dead. There were no times, no places…only the joy and happiness and exhilaration of the single thing she had sought and found and lost before the change. The thing she wanted again, here within her grasp.

Everything else vanished. There was no more need to struggle, to aspire to anything greater than this. Her emotions swelled to obliterate all other desires. She would float in this perfect world forever, in endless bliss and exultation.

She had found what the humans called heaven.

But there was a bubble of disturbance in the flawless pool of eternal rapture, a devil in this paradise. It picked and prodded at her, mocking her with warnings she could not quite shut out.

There is no heaven for Opiri.

"Artemis," Garret said. His voice was hoarse and urgent, his mind spinning on the edge of euphoria. She knew that all she had to do was speak a single word, and every other voice would be silenced.

So would her dreams and hopes for her people. She would no longer care about them, because she had what she wanted, all she would ever want.

Forget them, she thought. *You owe them nothing.*

But her past would not be silent. *They are your people*, it said. *How can you abandon them for a human?*

"No," she whispered.

All we fought for destroyed, because of you. Because of him.

Garret's face came into sharp focus, blazing with ela-tion. *He* could destroy nothing, but he could give her—

"Roxana?" he murmured.

She saw her own face again...saw it change, felt Garret's bewilderment and her own turmoil as that other face slipped over hers like a mask. Eyes too dark, hair too long, features too...

"No," Garret said hoarsely. The stranger vanished, but the sheer weight of his emotions—regret, grief, confusion—bore down on her with such force that she thought they would crush her. Illusion shattered. Shock worked as no careful discipline could have done.

She pushed him out—out of her heart, her mind, her very being—and slammed the wall down between them, sever-ing all emotional ties, all the feelings that had tempted her into relinquishing the new way she had sought to win for her own kind.

The feelings that had nearly made her surrender to a human who saw another face even as he prepared to possess her.

Chapter 7

Artemis scrambled to her feet, snatching up her pants as she bolted away from him. Garret's face was drained of color, and though she could no longer sense his emotions, she saw the stark pain in his eyes.

For her, or for himself?

Roxana.

Somehow Artemis dressed, gathered her weapons and fled without looking at him again. She ran recklessly toward the border of the woods, as if by simply putting physical distance between herself and Garret she might undo the past hour and forget.

But she knew it was not possible to regain that safe sense of living in a fortress that could never be breached. There was no undoing *this*. The gate had closed, but she knew that she could never take Garret's blood again. It wasn't simply a matter of becoming dependent. Death would be preferable to losing herself, losing all she believed had made her what she was.

Garret had asked her if she remembered what love was. She hadn't been honest then. She remembered the physical and emotional closeness that accompanied complete faith in another: a lover, life partner, the one she could not live without. Garret had made her experience some of those feelings again. His blood, his touch, had engulfed her in passions she had left behind for a greater, nobler purpose.

But there was no reality behind those passions, no foundation. Garret's invocation of that other name was proof enough of that.

Had that other woman been so different from her,

though? Ivory hair, eyes the color of rich, purple wine—the distinctive traits of any Opir save for the newest converts.

Artemis filled her lungs with pine-scented air, and then expelled her agitation along with her breath. The only purpose in analyzing her emotions was to rid herself of them. If she could not be an impartial, dispassionate teacher, she could not help her own people break the chains of savagery that bound them to lives of degradation and self-destruction.

She slowed as she approached the field, focusing her attention on her surroundings. There was no sound, no movement in the sea of grass, but she knew the Freebloods and humans were still there.

Stretching out on her belly, Artemis rested her cheek against the cool earth. This was a test. If she truly considered the fate of her kind more important than anything else, she could leave this place and let Garret find his own way to his son, facing the dangers of capture and death alone.

But she could no more leave him than she could erase her empathic "gift." The test did not ask her to choose which commitment was more important. It asked for proof that she could remain by Garret's side and not lose herself again. If she succeeded, then she might be capable and worthy of carrying out her mentor Kronos's great dream. The one he had died for.

She was preparing to return to Garret when a flock of birds exploded from the tall grass, followed by the report of many guns firing in unison. She froze as cries of pain and terror and rage rent the night, and the thump of flesh meeting flesh accompanied the rising scent of blood.

"Timon!"

Garret staggered up behind her, his pack dangling from his shoulder by one strap. His face was pale, his breathing shallow. Artemis trapped her concern in a cage of logic, grateful that she could not feel what he felt, trying not to imagine what he had thought when she left him without explanation.

"I am certain that Timon is well," she said calmly. "You have lost a great deal of blood, and you have been running. You must rest."

He looked at her as if she had lost her sanity, let the pack drop to the ground and knelt beside it. He fumbled inside with shaking hands, withdrawing a handgun.

"You cannot go out there," Artemis said. "Certainly not with that."

There was another scream, but Garret never so much as glanced up. He set the gun aside and withdrew several components of a weapon Artemis didn't remember ever having seen before. He pushed the pieces together, pausing several times when his clumsy fingers lost their grip. When he was finished and raised the weapon to check his work, she knew what it was: the only projectile weapon the humans had produced that could kill an Opir with a single shot to almost any spot on the body.

"No," she said. "You will be killed before you can ever use that thing."

"There's no other choice." He met her gaze as he got to his feet. "Don't try to stop me."

"I said the same thing to *you* once," she reminded him. "I believe I managed to make it ten feet before I collapsed."

Jaw set, Garret stepped out into the darkness. He had gone perhaps three yards when one of his legs gave out from under him and he fell to his knee. Another spatter of gunshots blotted out whatever sound he might have made, and then a deep hush fell, even more absolute than the silence that had come before.

Garret clambered to his feet, swinging the rifle back into position. Artemis joined him. She sniffed the air, and it was as if she could *see* what had happened as surely as if she had been in the middle of it.

"Let me go ahead," she said. "If there are any survivors, I can move more quickly to do whatever must be done."

"Together," he said grimly.

Artemis knew that trying to stop him would be pointless. He was already moving again, ready to shoot at anything with pale skin and sharp incisors. All she could do was hope that she was right about his son.

Before them lay a scene of utter carnage. Bodies were scattered across the field, mostly Opiri, seven or eight of them lying in pools of dark red. There were several humans, dressed in the mottled clothing of militiamen. Their annihilation had left abstract, scarlet patterns on the grass and shrubs around them, attesting to the violence of their deaths.

Timon was not with them.

He squeezed his eyes shut, waiting for his heart to resume its normal speed. After a few moments he opened his eyes again and examined the battlefield. He'd seen such violence before, but somehow this seemed worse, as if he might have prevented the killing with a few well-chosen words in the same way he'd once rallied and encouraged members of the human Underground in Erebus.

He glanced at Artemis. Her face was expressionless. She, too, must regret the killings, but he had no way of knowing what else she thought.

And she wasn't going to tell him. Now he knew that she had been correct to hesitate before taking his blood again. If it had only been a matter of physical attraction, he might have been able to hold himself aloof. He had deceived himself into thinking he could donate without being affected by her the way he'd been the first time—wanting her, wanting to be inside her, to claim her for his own in a way he had no right to do.

But it wasn't just her beauty and his desire for her that

had created the danger. It wasn't even a matter of his admiration for her courage and determination, and for the compassion he had once believed no Freeblood was capable of feeling.

There was more to it, much more. It had been as if they'd joined in some profound meeting of minds and hearts, a union of a kind he'd never imagined was possible, a bond stronger than any he could remember experiencing in his life.

Except with Roxana.

He had seen Roxana's face, serene and untroubled, at the very moment when his inexplicable joy was at its highest. There had been no recriminations in that face, no censure of his need for Artemis, but the grief had come anyway.

And he'd spoken his wife's name.

The strange connection between him and Artemis had shattered, and she'd run as if the mere sight of him disgusted her.

He'd wondered then if she'd abandoned him. He wouldn't have been shocked if she had. He'd betrayed her. They had both wanted comfort in the midst of fear and savagery, and he had denied her even that small relief.

But she was still the same Artemis. Apparently they would go on as if nothing had happened. Go back to where they had begun.

"Something is moving," she said, cutting across his thoughts. She pointed west. "Over there, away from the others."

Lifting the rifle, Garret started forward, placing his feet carefully so that he wouldn't stumble again. A dozen yards on, he saw the grass quiver and heard the faint rustle of something still hidden from his view.

"Come out," he said, raising his voice.

The grass stilled.

Artemis glanced at him. "There are two," she said. "One is human."

"Get up—slowly," Garret said, breathing fast. "We won't hurt you."

A pair of hands rose above the grass, showing themselves empty of weapons, and then a head appeared—white hair, pale skin, dark eyes. A young face, little more than a blur in the darkness.

Garret aimed at the Freeblood's head, vaguely aware of Artemis's muffled protest.

"There is a human with you," he said. "Let me see him."

Another figure rose beside the Freeblood, much shorter and smaller, the head barely reaching the rogue's rib cage.

A child.

"Move away," Garret said to the Freeblood, gesturing with the barrel of the VS.

The rogue hesitated, biting his lip, and then edged sideways. The child made a low sound Garret couldn't quite make out.

"She is calling for him," Artemis said. "She's not afraid."

She. Tremors seized the muscles of Garret's arms, making the rifle shake. Not Timon, but given what had happened here…

Artemis walked ahead of him. "It's all right," she said in a voice perfectly pitched to soothe and reassure. "You can come out. No one will hurt you or Pericles."

Pericles. Garret stifled his surprise. "Send the girl ahead," he said.

"Her name is Beth," Pericles said, his hands still high above his head.

"Beth," Artemis repeated. Garret caught up with her and lowered the rifle. Slowly the girl emerged from the grass, her steps uncertain as she glanced back at the Freeblood.

But not in fear, Garret thought. He shifted the strap of the VS, pushing it behind him. "It's okay," he said to the girl, beckoning cautiously. Once she was within reach, he swept her up and retreated several yards. Artemis went with him.

"Pericles," the girl protested in a thready voice. She felt as light as an infant in Garret's arms, ragged and filthy, and with a face so dirty that he never would have known her gender if Artemis hadn't told him. Aside from her apparent concern for the Freeblood, she hardly seemed aware of her surroundings. He pressed her head gently against his shoulder.

"Artemis," Garret said, "you take Beth back to camp. I'll watch the rogue until we can figure out what to do about him."

"'Do about him'?" she echoed, meeting his gaze. "Apparently we saved his life. He has shown no hostility, then or now."

"Or maybe he let us think he was dying. And now he has a human child with him. How do you think that happened?" Garret heard the anger in his own voice and made an effort to moderate his tone. "I won't kill him," he said. "Not until we know what he has to do with this massacre."

"The child," Artemis said sharply. "She can hear you."

"I doubt she understands," Garret said, stroking the little girl's hair. "Beth, will you go with this lady?"

Beth blinked and met his gaze with bewildered brown eyes. "I'm lost," she said.

"We'll take care of you now. I promise."

The girl's unfocused stare shifted to Artemis's face. "Okay," she said, holding out her arms.

With uncharacteristic awkwardness, Artemis took the child and cradled her against her chest. Beth sighed and snuggled closer, tucking her head under Artemis's chin.

Garret turned to look for Pericles, but the Freeblood had already slipped away. Garret cursed under his breath.

"Go back to camp," he said to Artemis. "I'll be right behind you."

Moving as carefully as if she were holding a delicate porcelain doll, Artemis made her way back into the woods. Garret held the VS ready until they had reached the camp. Artemis set Beth down on the blanket and arranged it around her, using one of Garret's spare shirts as a pillow. She turned on his small lantern, poured a little water out of his canteen, wet a scrap of cloth and began to bathe the girl's face.

Memory cut through Garret's mind like a blade through a barely healed wound. Roxana, leaning over Timon, smiling and whispering in his ear. Roxana, doting so tenderly on the child that had come of a forbidden yet enduring love.

Garret saw that same tenderness in Artemis's face.

He cleared his throat and tried to focus on the child. In the light, he could see that Beth appeared to be about five years old, small for her age, and far too thin.

"How is she?" he asked, propping the VS within easy reach against a nearby tree trunk.

"She does not seem to be injured," Artemis said without looking up. "Perhaps we can get her to drink a little water."

Garret knelt on the other side of the blanket. Beth opened her eyes and blinked several times.

"How are you feeling, Beth?" Garret asked, smoothing matted hair away from the girl's face. "Does anything hurt?"

"Pericles?" she said.

"He's...away," Garret said. He rummaged through his pack, pulled out the first aid kit and gave Beth a brief but thorough examination. Except for a few shallow scratches and a bruise or two, she seemed unharmed.

When he was finished, Artemis propped Beth's head up and coaxed her into drinking a little water. Garret removed his coat and laid it over the blanket for extra warmth. Within minutes, the girl was deeply asleep.

"She's exhausted," he said, gesturing for Artemis to

join him a little distance away. "She's probably in a state of shock."

"What else can we do for her?"

"Until we know what the rogues did to her…"

"We do not know that they did anything."

"She's in very poor condition."

"She cannot have been hurt if she has so little fear of Opiri."

Artemis was right, Garret thought. Beth was dirty and underfed, but the rogues hadn't harmed her. That was important.

That gave him hope for Timon.

"Garret?" Artemis reached out as if to touch him, dropping her arm only at the last minute. "They will both be all right. We will make sure of it."

We. He looked into her eyes, but all he could see was her usual honesty.

"You were very good with Beth," he said. "Thank you."

"You entrusted her to me, and yet you are surprised?"

Her voice was pinched, and he realized he'd hurt her again, even though she would never admit it.

"No," he said. "I'm not surprised. You've done this before, haven't you?"

"You must rest," she said, turning away. "I will look for Pericles. Try not to shoot me when I return."

If there had been any humor in her voice, Garret might have laughed.

Two hours later, Artemis found Garret sitting beside the girl, watching her quietly. He glanced up as she approached, shooting to his feet when he saw Pericles walking freely behind her. His gaze swept from her bow in its case to the rifle propped against the tree.

"It is all right," Artemis said quickly. "He means no harm."

"I want to help," Pericles said, moving to her side. "Is Beth all—"

"Stay back," Garret snapped as the young Freeblood took a hesitant step toward the little girl. He looked Pericles up and down. "How did you survive when we left you in the south?"

"I don't know." Pericles wet his lips. "You must have saved me with your blood."

"Where is my son?"

Artemis couldn't *feel* Garret's anger, but she knew him too well to mistake his mood. "There was a misunderstanding," she said calmly. "When we questioned Pericles before, he thought you were asking about Beth."

"So *she* was the one he stole," Garret said. "That makes it so much better." He took a step toward Pericles.

"What was he doing with her out there after the battle? How did he survive *that*?"

Pericles edged behind Artemis. "The Freebloods who died are the same ones who left me for dead. After you saved me, I tracked them here to make sure that Beth was all right."

"Then you saw the battle," Garret said. "Who were the humans?"

"Militiamen. They found the pack south of here and followed them until the Opiri turned to fight."

"But you weren't part of the fighting?"

"I was only in the area because of Beth."

"Pericles had the task of caring for Beth, until the pack leader turned on him," Artemis said.

"It's true," Pericles said meekly. "I tried to keep her clean, get her enough to eat. But when I tried to get her away they—"

"You were with a pack of rogue kidnappers, and you tried to help her escape?" Garret asked, disbelief in his voice.

"Is that so astonishing to you," Artemis asked, "when *I* was willing to help you find your son? Is it so impossible to believe that there might be more than one Opir capable of such concern?"

Garret looked at her as if her words genuinely surprised him. "What makes you believe him?" he asked.

"What made you believe *me* when I promised to go with you?" Artemis said.

"I'm sorry about your son," Pericles said, shuffling from foot to foot like a hare torn between lying still and leaping away from the fox lurking nearby.

"Sorry?" Garret said, clenching his fists. "It was a pack just like yours who took him." His eyes widened. "My God." He sank into a crouch beside Beth. "My son *and* Beth."

"Yes," Artemis said, her heart aching for him in spite of all her efforts to remain detached. "Pericles told me they are taking children, Garret. Not only Beth and Timon, but many others."

Garret dragged his hand across his face, and then fixed his stare on Pericles. "Why?" he asked. "Where are they taking them?"

"To the north, as he said before," Artemis said. "He knows nothing else."

"Pericles?" Beth whispered, beginning to sit up.

"I am here," he said, venturing out from behind Artemis. Garret didn't move.

"At least let me give her something to eat," Pericles said. He reached inside his torn shirt, and Garret tensed.

Artemis held out her hand. Pericles gave her a packet of waxed paper and a small pouch. "It isn't much," he said, "but it's all I could find."

"Nutrition bars," Artemis said, looking inside the packet. She opened the pouch. "Seeds, nuts and dried fruits."

"Can I see her now?" Pericles asked.

After a long hesitation, Garret stepped out of his way, and Pericles crouched beside the girl. She reached for his hand and clung to it tightly.

"I am sorry I wasn't here to help you earlier, Beth," Pericles said, squeezing her fingers very gently.

Freeblood and human child began to speak in low voices, though Beth's words were brief and strained. Garret stared at them, one contradictory emotion after another sliding across his face in rapid succession.

"She obviously trusts him," Artemis said, when she and Garret stepped aside to talk. "Are you prepared to trust me again?"

He looked from her to Pericles. "When we helped him, you called him 'brother.' I know you believe in a new future for your kind. How can *you* be objective?"

"Is it so difficult for you to imagine that what you see here is no more or less than the truth?" she asked. "Or will you deny that such relationships are possible?"

Chapter 8

Artemis had intended simply to make him see reason, but her question had the unexpected effect of forcing her to relive that moment when she had believed there *could* be more between an Opir and a human than blood and sexual desire.

Joy. Happiness.

And then she remembered that other face...

"Are you basing that question on *our* relationship?" Garret asked softly.

She couldn't bring herself to speak of what she suspected of Garret and Roxana. "Pericles believes as I do, Garret," she said. "He shares my hope for a better future."

Garret sighed. "I trust you," he said. "Where did the rogues find Beth?"

"A human colony on the coast. A place called Coos Bay."

Unsealing the outer pocket of his pack, Garret removed the map and spread it across his thigh. "That's over two hundred miles southwest of here," he said.

Artemis knew what he was thinking—how far a southward journey would put him behind in his search for Timon—but he didn't say it aloud. He folded the map and returned it carefully to the pack.

"Did you look at the bodies?" he asked, getting to his feet.

"I found Pericles before I had the opportunity," she said.

"I want to get a better idea of what happened," he said. "I'm going out there."

"You are nearly night-blind," she protested.

"There's still a little moonlight," he said, "and I've done

well enough so far. While I'm gone, try to find out everything Pericles knows about these children."

"I believe he has told me—"

"Artemis," he said, meeting her gaze, "if he knows anything he *hasn't* told you, we have to get it out of him—
everything he's seen and heard regarding these abductions."

Neither of them moved. They stood half in, half out of
the small circle of lantern light as if nothing else existed
beyond them.

"There was still no sign of Citadel patrols when I found
Pericles," Artemis said when the silence had stretched too
long. "Nevertheless, this battle may have attracted attention. Please, be careful."

"I will be." He smiled, and she was glad that he couldn't
feel her fear for him. As long as he didn't try to touch her…

He didn't, though his hand rose to the level of his waist
before he dropped it again. He stepped outside the light and
grabbed his rifle. Pericles's head snapped up in alarm. Garret ignored him and strode into the woods.

Pericles scrambled to his feet. "Where is he going?"
he asked.

"To examine the battle site," Artemis said. "Beth is
well?"

"Sleeping." He hunched his shoulders. "The human
hates me."

"He's afraid for his son," she said. "But the better I know
you, the easier it will be for him to understand."

"Understand what?" Pericles asked, a little shaky as he
sat down again. "That I wasn't lying when I said I cared
about Beth?"

"And that Freebloods are not all barbarians. You are
proof that my mentor's goals are possible."

"No one in my pack cared about what happened to the
others, or to the humans they met."

"Perhaps they were not as strong as you are, Pericles."

He laughed. "Strong?"

"There are different kinds of strength." She sat down beside him. "You have only been Opir for a few years. It is easier for the youngest, who still remember their old lives, to accept a new way."

Pericles brought his legs to his chest and draped his narrow wrists over his knees. "I'm still not used to this. Maybe I'll never be."

"You are not alone," she said. "Not as long as you are with me."

"I know." He gnawed on his lower lip. "What about Garret? Does he know about what you did in Oceanus?"

"He does not," she said. "I wish to explain it myself, when the time is right."

"I won't say anything," Pericles said quickly, eager to please. "If you trust the human, so do I."

And so, Artemis thought, two who might be enemies were relying entirely on her to keep the peace. It seemed ironic after what had happened in Oceanus, where she had failed so miserably. She got up to pace, listening intently for Garret's return.

"You're really afraid for him, aren't you?" Pericles asked.

"Garret can take care of himself."

"Even that weapon wouldn't be enough if he came up against a patrol."

She rounded on him. "Did you see one and neglect to tell me?"

"No!" he said hastily. "I haven't seen any patrols." His gaze tracked her as she strode back and forth. "Have you… taken his blood?"

"Yes," she said curtly. "But only out of necessity."

"You didn't…force him?"

"Does it seem to you that such a thing would have been necessary?"

Pericles shook his head. "Why did you decide to help him find his son?"

"Garret saved my life from humans in the south. I owe him a debt."

"Oh." Pericles hugged his knees. "What are we going to do now? I want to make sure Beth is okay."

"As do we," Artemis said. "But you have not explained the circumstances of her abduction, or how you know that other children are being taken to the north." She sat beside him again. "Why is this being done?"

"I don't know." He clasped his hands together. "I only heard—"

He broke off as the sound of Garret's quiet footsteps announced his return. Still gripping the rifle, he dropped into a crouch beside Pericles and Artemis. His face was calm, his expression flat.

He must have seen ugly things out in the field, Artemis thought, but he had left emotion behind and become all unwavering purpose again. He barely seemed to notice her.

But he was safe.

"Heard what?" he asked, staring at Pericles.

The young Freeblood leaned away from Garret. "Our leader—Chares—wanted to find more children to deliver, to prove that our pack was better than the others who were doing the same thing."

"Other packs," Garret said in a monotone. "To whom were you supposed to deliver the children?"

"To a Bloodlord. Maybe a Bloodmaster. But someone very powerful. I heard that he might be in Canada, in the mountains. British Columbia, I think."

"And you didn't think to mention this until now?" Garret said, his fingers tightening around the barrel of the rifle.

"I'm sorry," Pericles whispered, his gaze darting between Garret and Artemis. "I was afraid."

"What were *you* getting out of this, you and the other child-stealers?"

"Chares never said," Pericles said meekly. "He didn't know what this Bloodlord wanted with the children. But we were supposed to keep Beth well and untouched until we reached this place in the north. There must have been some kind of reward."

"What else?"

Pericles looked at Artemis as if for reassurance. "There's a reason why the pack took Beth, and didn't want any of the other children from that particular colony."

"What do you mean?"

"Your son…he isn't a full human, is he?"

Artemis cast Garret a startled glance. He swung the rifle around, butting the muzzle up against Pericles's chest. The young Freeblood stopped breathing.

"How did you know?" Garret asked in a soft and very dangerous voice.

"Because the pack wouldn't have taken him otherwise. The Bloodlord in the north doesn't seem to…want normal human children."

The scent of Garret's hostility grew stronger, laced with a tinge of fear. Artemis curled her fingers around the rifle's barrel and pulled it away from Pericles's chest.

"If they do not want human children," she said to the young exile, "what *do* they want?"

"Mixed-bloods, like Darketans."

"Daysiders?" Garret said, using the human word.

"But Darketans aren't of mixed blood," Artemis protested. "They're mutations of normal Opiri, which is why they can walk in daylight."

Garret cast her an indecipherable look. "Beth is Darketan?" he asked Pericles, lowering his rifle.

"That's what the colonists told Chares."

"But you said she came from a human colony!" Artemis said. "What would an Opir mutation be doing there? Was she a prisoner?"

"Not a prisoner," Pericles said, breathing steadily again. "She looks human, and Darketans don't require blood until they're older, but…" His voice dropped very low. "The pack didn't have to raid the colony to get her. Some humans there sold her to us."

Garret's face went pale. "My God," he said. "Humans selling children."

"Opir children," Artemis said, thinking aloud. "I do not understand. It is true that Darketans do not have all the privileges of full Opiri in the Citadels. But Beth is far too young to have escaped a Citadel and found her way to this colony by herself."

"There's a far more likely explanation," Garret said, "but it may not be easy for you to accept."

"What is that?" Artemis asked with a twinge of alarm.

"What you said about Darketans being mutations…it isn't true. They're as much mixed-blood as the dhampires who work for the human Enclaves."

"You are wrong," Artemis said, shocked by his suggestion.

"The rulers of the Citadels have led you to believe a lie. We in the colonies only recently learned the truth when a high-ranked Bloodlord from Erebus chose to join us. He told us that Darketans are taken early from their mothers, trained as soldiers and forced to serve as daytime spies for the Citadels. It's possible that Beth was sent out of the Citadel to avoid that fate. But it's far more likely that her mother and father escaped, and sought refuge in the colony."

"Opiri…seeking refuge in a human colony?"

"Only the mother would have been Opir. The father was human. It's the opposite with dhampires—their fathers are Opiri and their mothers are human."

"But this is impossible," Artemis whispered. "All humans

in the Citadels are serfs. No female Opir would permit…
Any such child would be destroyed by command of the High
Council!"

"They aren't," Garret said. "The Citadels don't dare
admit it, even to their own citizens."

Artemis jumped to her feet. "I do not concede that what
you say is true. We would know. Humans would sow dis-
sension in the Citadels by spreading such rumors."

"What bothers you most, Artemis?" Garret asked, his
expression grim and sad. "That this might be a lie created
to undermine Opir society, or that female Opiri might allow
themselves to be impregnated by male humans?"

Unable to answer, Artemis leaned heavily against the
nearest tree. Garret had no reason to lie to her. He must
know that she would find this information—

Timon, she thought. She remembered when she had first
seen the boy's photograph. She had never doubted that he
was human.

But if the rogues only wanted half-blood children…

"Why would the rogues think that Timon is a half-
blood?" she asked.

"Artemis," Garret said with a low sigh, "you know the
answer."

She slid down the trunk and sat with her back to the tree.
"You mated with an Opir female," she said.

Garret pressed his hand over the pocket where he carried Timon's picture, as if someone might snatch it away
from him. "Yes," he said.

"Roxana," she said, remembering her earlier guess.

"She was my wife," Garret said.

An Opir who had turned against her own kind to help
one of his people.

Irrational anger overwhelmed Artemis's shock. "You
said you lived alone," she said. "But I knew that could not

have been true. You were too easy with me." Her eyes felt hot and dry. "Why did you lie?"

"I'm sorry, Artemis," he said. "It wasn't the right time to tell you the truth."

"You mean that you feared I might not help you if you admitted your former relationship with a female Opir?"

"I never intended to hide it from you."

"But you did. What else have you not told me? Where did you come from?"

Garret looked at her, and she saw the pain in his eyes.

"In old California," he said, "there are colonies where humans and Nightsiders live together in peace. I came from one of those colonies. We named it Avalon."

"I have heard of such places," she said, finding her composure again. "I thought they were forbidden."

"And I'm sure the Citadels in the north plan to keep it that way," Garret said. "Erebus has only accepted them because their Council realized that the colonies were no threat to them."

"But humans are free in these colonies, are they not?"

"Opiri and humans live as equals."

"How do the Opiri get their blood?"

"Through cooperation."

"And that is why you found it so easy to give yours to me?"

"No one is compelled to donate, but everyone—humans *and* Nightsiders—contributes to the general welfare of the colony." His lips thinned. "Unless the Nightsiders happen to forget where they are."

The bitterness had returned to his voice, and Artemis sensed that he spoke from very personal experience. She tried to imagine what life would be like for Opiri in such a settlement. They would have to change their habits and customs completely, and the motivation for such a change could only be a philosophical commitment to equality.

She knew that Opiri with egalitarian beliefs did exist, even in the Citadels. They generally kept their opinions to themselves, but if they left their Citadels or were exiled, they might seek places where they could live their ideals.

But could they maintain those lofty ideals in the face of constant temptation?

Isn't that what you would demand of your fellow Free-bloods? she asked herself. *To discard what they have known and begin afresh?*

But she had never asked her people to live among humans. It was a recipe for disaster. As it had been when she and Garret had become too intimate. When he had called his wife's name.

A wife he had spoken of in the past tense.

She didn't ask him for more details. She couldn't bear to feel his sorrow, and the longer she remained with him, the more she had to struggle to keep her empathic barriers in place.

"The only human settlements in the north are the militia compounds," she said, trying to focus on more practical matters. She turned to Pericles. "They would never have permitted an Opir female among them."

"It wasn't like that," Pericles said with a quick, uneasy glance at Garret. "They didn't try to shoot us when we approached the gate. Their defenses weren't very strong. The men who sold Beth to us did it to keep us from attacking, but they didn't want anyone else in their compound to know what they were doing."

"And what of her parents?"

"They were never mentioned."

"But they could have been there," Garret said. "Maybe someone decided to start a mixed Nightsider-human colony in Oregon, in spite of the danger."

"That would be madness," Artemis protested.

"It takes a kind of madness to attempt something that's

never been done before," Garret said. He gazed at Beth thoughtfully. "We have to decide what to do with her. We can't bring her with us to find Timon, but if her parents and the rest of the colonists didn't know that she was being sold to Freebloods, they'll take her back."

"Two hundred miles in the wrong direction," Artemis said.

Cradling the rifle in his arms, Garret seemed to lock himself away, torn between two equally terrible choices. Return the child to her home and hope for the best, or carry her on a dangerous journey to the north, possibly right into the arms of those who wanted her so badly.

"I'll take her back," Pericles said in a small voice. "She knows me. I've cared for her this long, and if it's just the two of us…"

"You can't defend *yourself*, let alone Beth," Garret said harshly. He began to pace. "Covering two hundred miles each way will take at least three weeks, probably more, even if we push ourselves."

Three weeks, Artemis thought. Three weeks' lost time in Garret's search for his son, and an exhausting pace that would leave them all drained and weary by the time they returned to the borderlands of Oceanus.

"Let *me* go," Artemis said. "You know where to look for Timon. If you head toward British Columbia, you are certain to find—"

"Leave you alone?" Garret interrupted. "No. We still don't know anything about these colonists."

"It is my risk to take."

"No." Garret met her gaze, and her barriers slipped just enough to let her feel his agony. "There seem to be many Freebloods involved in this child-stealing, and whoever takes Beth to her home has to be ready to fight off several at once and protect her at the same time." He closed his eyes, and Artemis began to reach for him, no longer caring what effect the contact might have on her.

Her fingertips brushed his arm. He flinched and opened his eyes.

"We will take Beth back to her people," he said.

Chapter 9

Closing her hand around his, Artemis willed him to feel her sympathy. She had known that Garret couldn't sacrifice one child for another, even if one of them was his own son.

"He'll be all right," Garret said in a voice that suggested he was trying to convince himself. He squeezed her hand. "He'll be all right."

A long silence fell. Reluctantly, Artemis released Garret's hand. When Pericles finally spoke, his voice was little more than a whisper.

"Will you let me come?" he asked "We can take turns carrying Beth."

"Aren't you afraid of humans?" Garret asked coldly.

The young Freeblood lifted his chin. "I promised to protect Beth and failed. Now I have another chance."

Garret visibly weighed the boy's statement. "How long since you've fed?"

"I… I hunted before I found Beth."

"Humans?"

"No! I'm… I believe the same things Artemis does."

"That's good, because you won't be getting any more blood from me."

"I never expected—"

"We will hunt game along the way," Artemis interrupted. "You and Beth will require food, as well. The rations Pericles carried will not last long, and I doubt your dried meats will be proper nourishment for a child."

Garret nodded his thanks. "As Pericles suggested," he said, "we'll take turns carrying Beth and move as fast as we can without exhausting ourselves, or her. And when it comes to dealing with any humans we meet, you both keep out of sight unless I say otherwise."

"Understood. As long as *you* stay out of sight if we meet Opiri."

"We'd better hope we can avoid them completely," Garret said.

They packed up quickly. Garret broke his rifle apart and tucked it in his pack. He looked in on Beth, stroking her hair and checking her pulse and breathing. The little girl barely did more than murmur drowsily when Pericles lifted her from her blankets and neatly devised a sling to hold her on his back.

It almost hurt to watch them, though Artemis was very careful not to let a hint of emotion show in her face or voice. Neither Pericles nor Garret—especially Garret—would ever know what she had felt when she'd held a child in her arms again.

South, Artemis thought. *Think only of the goal, a promise kept and freedom afterward.*

The three of them crept out of the woods, on the alert for Opir patrols. Garret agreed that Artemis should take the lead, while he fell to the rear and Pericles trotted between them, Beth securely cradled on his back. Garret tried to focus his attention on their surroundings, but he couldn't get his mind off what Pericles had told him of the kidnapped children and the unknown Bloodlord's mysterious purpose for them.

Timon was strong and brave. But he was still a child. The thought of his fear and bewilderment tore at Garret, constantly threatening to gut his hard-won dispassion.

But he knew he couldn't indulge in worry that would slow him or make him careless. He had to be ready to turn back north as soon as Beth was safe.

In the meantime, he and Artemis would remain close

to each other, at least physically, for an extra few weeks. He'd told her only a part of his past with Roxana and the mixed colonies, and he knew he couldn't keep her in the dark forever.

But to reveal everything would open a Pandora's box of emotion he wasn't prepared to deal with so soon after the last fiasco. He knew he'd hurt Artemis when he'd called Roxana's name. She had tried to keep her distance ever since, but at times, as on many previous occasions, she had seemed strangely attuned to his emotions. When they'd discussed Beth's fate, Artemis had touched him in an act of comfort, though it must have taken real courage to make herself so vulnerable with him.

That they had come to care for each other was not an issue. But he couldn't read her mind. He wondered if she could understand that he had once lived with an intimacy built not only on sharing blood, desire and mutual respect, but also on love. The love of a man for a woman, regardless of race or kind.

Love he never expected to feel again. But as they traveled, he was constantly aware of Artemis moving quietly ahead of him, her body swaying with natural grace, as lithe and strong and beautiful as a white tigress. Like a lioness, she would fight to defend those she considered her family. And, like a lioness, she was untouchable, forever beyond his reach.

He was grateful when necessity forced him to push Artemis out of his thoughts and concentrate on keeping his footing in the dark.

They traveled by night and by day, Pericles swathed in heavy clothes and a cloak foraged from Beth's fallen captors. Though they switched off carrying Beth, the young Freeblood insisted on taking her two-thirds of the time. No one spoke of weariness or rest until it was clear they could go no farther, and often it was more for Beth's sake than for their own.

They cut south for a day, and then traveled west along Highway 20 toward the ocean. That road wound through forested hills, and the trek took longer than Garret had hoped.

But their strength held. They met neither humans nor Opiri, and Artemis took Pericles hunting at regular intervals, returning with meat for Beth and Garret, while they apparently subsisted on animal blood.

When they reached the ocean, they made camp just off the beach in the fallen town of Newport. The sun was setting over the sea, a touch of nature's glory that not even the War and its aftermath could destroy.

"It is beautiful," Artemis said, as Garret readied the fire and Pericles rested a little distance away. "Though I lived in Oceanus, I never saw the sea."

"Our colony was—is—near the ocean," Garret said, "but you never get tired of something like this."

She smiled at him, and his heart turned over. In the peace of the moment he felt the absurd desire to take her hand and hold it in his. She must have guessed what he was thinking, because she clasped her hands in her lap and stared out across the beach.

"How are you feeling?" she asked abruptly. "Have you had enough rest?"

Garret fed more twigs to the tiny flame. "You don't have to worry about me," he said with a wry twist of his lips. "I know my limitations, *and* when I come too close to exceeding them."

"I did not mean to imply…" She cleared her throat. "Your endurance has never ceased to surprise me."

"I guess I should take that as a compliment."

Beth, lying on a pile of blankets a few feet away, began to whimper in her sleep. Without thinking, Garret gathered the girl into his arms and held her against his chest, humming under his breath.

"That is a pretty song," Artemis said, her voice wistful. "I used to—"

She broke off and looked away quickly. *Used to what?* Garret thought. Used to sing? It wasn't a common activity in the Citadels, though some took up music when they came to the colony.

Could she be speaking of her former human life?

"It's a lullaby Ro— I used to sing to Timon," Garret said. "Beth's asleep. Do you want to hold her while I finish with the fire?"

Hesitantly, Artemis reached for the little girl. She held Beth gently, her lips curving up in a tentative smile.

"She's so fragile," Artemis said. "Sometimes it amazes me that humans can survive in this world at all."

"Homo sapiens have gotten along well enough for over 150,000 years."

"Yet some adapted better than others. You were a leader in your colony, were you not?"

Maybe, Garret thought, it was time to tell Artemis the truth. Now, when they were at ease with each other.

Suddenly Artemis jerked up her head. "Someone is approaching," she said.

A moment later Pericles was sitting up on his bedroll, his nostrils flaring. "What is it?" he asked.

"Humans," Artemis said. She held Beth out to Garret. "I should go see."

"How many?" Garret asked.

"More than two, but less than ten," she said. "If they are militia…"

"I'll talk to them," Garret said. "The last thing we need is a firefight, and you know I can communicate with these people on their terms."

"Yes," Artemis said, "I know. But—"

"But you and Pericles stay here and look after Beth until I give the okay."

Artemis opened her mouth to protest, shook her head and subsided. She wouldn't look at him as he rose from the small fire, and her jaw was set.

Knowing that there was nothing he could do to satisfy her except return in one piece, Garret tucked his handgun under his coat and headed out in the direction she had indicated.

She'd been right in her estimate. Nine humans, ranging in age from early teens to late middle age, were huddled together under a stand of wind-beaten spruce a few hundred yards north of the camp. They were underdressed for the weather and the stiff ocean breezes, their clothing primarily made up of loose pants, long tunics and the occasional cloak. They had no weapons except for a couple of knives.

Serfs, Garret thought. Runaways, almost certainly from Oceanus.

The fact that they had escaped at all was a miracle. But that they'd come so far with so few resources was a testament to their fortitude and conviction.

Garret was doubly glad that he hadn't brought Artemis and Pericles.

"Hello," he called out, stepping into clear view and holding his arms out at his sides.

Immediately two men and a woman in their twenties or early thirties jumped up and confronted him, their faces creased in alarm. Garret walked toward them, his arms still well away from his weapon.

"Peace," he said. "My name is Garret Fox. I used to be a serf, just like you."

"They're heading to Coos Bay," Garret said.

Artemis stared at him. "Serfs?" she said. "Serfs who escaped from Oceanus?"

With a sigh, Garret sat down and poked at the embers that were all that remained of the fire. "They had a little help," he said.

"I do not understand," she said.

"From inside the Citadel," he said. "Is it so difficult for you to believe that there are humans willing to risk their lives for freedom, or Opiri who might help them?"

Artemis shook her head slowly. "I never heard of such a thing in Oceanus, though I—" She pushed her hair away from her face. "Are you suggesting that these are not the first?"

"They didn't discuss it in any detail, but there have probably been others."

"And surely the Council must know that there have been escapes." She met Garret's eyes. "They would kill any Opir who dared to break the Citadel's laws."

"If I was a serf, would you help *me*?"

She clenched her slender hands in her lap. "I would do everything in my power to see that you were not harmed."

"As a Freeblood, you'd have no control over my condition. And you were taught to believe that the keeping of serfs is part of the natural order of the world."

"What I was taught ceased to matter long ago," Artemis said.

"And you don't want to take human blood. You've never told me why."

Abruptly she looked up at him. "You asked me if I was more concerned about saving human lives or only about Freebloods killing each other," she said. "I do not believe that Opiri should be dependent upon human blood. It is a weakness in us, a source of corruption and violence that harms both my people and yours."

Garret sank down beside her. "Then you're opposed to the practice of serfdom primarily for the benefit of your own people."

She flinched as if she sensed his disappointment. But he knew he had no right to feel that way; the very fact that she was against human slavery for any reason put her far ahead of most Opiri. Even Roxana, in the beginning…

"I understand now," he said. "I'm a corrupting influence."

"No!" She shot to her feet. "You… You and I…it is different."

"Because I'm not actually a serf?"

Artemis began to tremble, and Garret cursed himself for his clumsiness. "I'm sorry," he said. "I've asked a lot of you. But I'm going to have to ask a little more."

Almost before he'd finished speaking, Pericles called from the beach. "They're coming," he said.

"We'll be traveling with the refugees," Garret said. "They're headed to the same colony, and it'll be easier for us to take Beth in with a group of serfs seeking a safe place away from the Citadels." He laid his hand on Artemis's shoulder. "Can you deal with that?"

"Will they not be frightened of me and Pericles?" she asked in a very soft voice.

"They've heard that Coos Bay might be a mixed colony," he said. "They're prepared to deal with peaceful Nightsiders. But I've given them certain assurances that you can be trusted."

"What assurances?"

Garret hesitated. "I didn't have time to consult with you," he said, "so you'll have to act a part until we've returned Beth to her caretakers."

Her shoulder tensed under his hand. "What have you done, Garret?"

"I've told them that you're my wife."

Artemis took the offered hand, careful not to grip the serf's fingers too firmly. The woman smiled with obvious unease and quickly dropped her hand, but not before she had unwittingly triggered Artemis's empathy.

After the long days of attempting to suppress her emotional connection to Garret, Artemis was surprised that merely touching another human could have such an effect. But the emotions of the former serfs were strong and unguarded, in spite of their reticence around her. They were afraid and uncertain, and yet brave and resolute...willing, as Garret had said, to risk everything for the mere possibility of freedom.

Artemis smiled at one of the male serfs and edged away as Garret began to speak with the group. Her anger with him had gradually subsided, but she was left to play a role she was ill prepared for—pretending to be his mate. In spite of his efforts to shield her from any real intimacy with the serfs, she still had little idea of how to behave as the Opir "wife" of a human.

The fact that the humans accepted her, she thought, was due more to Garret's efforts than her own playacting... efforts that included frequent brief touches, many smiles, and words of affection meant to prove his devotion to her. He was so good at it that, for moments at a time, she believed he really meant it.

"How are you doing?" he asked, drawing her aside. His hand on her arm made her breath catch, and something of his feelings transferred into her mind: relief, determination and pride—in *her*.

"You should tell *me*," she said, managing what she hoped was a persuasive smile. "Have I convinced them that I am your devoted mate?"

"You've even convinced *me*," he said lightly, though his gaze was anything but casual. "They've fully accepted our background story, and they're sure you've always believed that serfs should be free."

Artemis ducked her head. "Will we wait for daylight to travel again?"

"They're prepared to leave now, and if we stick to the highway we shouldn't have any difficulty. Pericles will carry Beth until he becomes tired."

"And what am I to do?"

"I hope you'll stay at my side," he said. His green eyes were like the sea itself, calm one moment, stormy the next. Now they were dark and mysterious, holding a world she imagined lay deep beneath the surface of the ocean.

And she could feel everything she had tried to shut out, a maelstrom of emotion that left her gasping and desperate to get away—or to fall into Garret's arms as if she truly were wife and lover and the chosen companion of his heart.

A *human* heart.

She broke free. "I will travel beside you," she said formally. "I will play my part for as long as it is necessary."

His eyes clouded. "I know you will," he said.

He walked away, and Artemis stared after him, wondering what she had done...and what she was becoming. As often as she resisted it, the empathy fought to return.

But that "gift" wasn't the source of her feelings now.

She put the thought out of her mind and retrieved her pack as Pericles secured Beth to his back with the sling and Garret finished speaking to the serfs. The group formed a loose column, and Garret nodded to Artemis, indicating that she should join him.

After a time, she took drag to watch for pursuit. A few of the serfs cast uneasy glances over their shoulders, but none of them faltered, and by dawn they had traveled over fifteen miles south on Highway 101, hugging the coastline.

Four days and nights later, they approached Coos Bay. Remarkably, the tall bridge crossing the eastern portion of the bay was still intact, and, except for its lack of inhabitants, the city beyond it seemed to have missed most of the War entirely.

Pericles, who knew the location of the colony, led them south and west across deserted suburbs and through a forest to a cluster of buildings that had obviously once been a public facility. An old, almost illegible sign identified it as a community college. The forest growing alongside the buildings provided the compound with a natural defense.

Closer to the buildings, the colonists had built a flimsy stockade around a section of the college, though not one that could hold off a concerted attack by Nightsiders who wanted to get in. Only a few humans were patrolling the stockade, and their weapons seemed to be in poor condition.

"They've been lucky," Garret said, stretched out beside Artemis in the small clearing among the trees and underbrush. "No one's been interested in going so far out of their way to bother them."

"Except for the rogue kidnappers."

"Yes," he said. "Artemis, I want you and Pericles to stay outside while I go in with the others. We still don't know the exact circumstances of how Beth came to be with the rogues. We need to find her parents first. If only a few of the colonists were involved in selling her, we'll be exposing them when we return Beth, and that could get tricky. I want you to be safe."

"Surely these people can be no threat to me."

"Believe me, Artemis," he said, "you don't have the experience to judge. Will you stay here?"

Reluctantly, she agreed. But as Garret went to join the other serfs, she couldn't shake the feeling that matters were not going to turn out quite as they hoped.

Chapter 10

"Beth's mother isn't here."

Garret crouched beside Artemis, gazing at the humans with whom he'd been speaking moments before. They stared in his direction, heads together in conversation, and then returned to the compound through the door in the stockade. It closed with a finality that made her very glad that Garret was with her again.

"What happened to her?" Pericles asked, quietly coming to join them.

"The colony is not what we hoped," Garret said. He turned back to Artemis. "We expected a mixed colony of humans and Opiri. Until fairly recently, it was."

The heaviness in his voice put Artemis on the alert. "Where are Beth's parents?" she asked.

"Her mother was a Freeblood from Oceanus," he said, "and the father was a serf she helped to escape. They came to this colony in search of a sanctuary where she could give birth." Garret grabbed a twig and snapped it in half. "Beth was born here, and soon afterward her mother died of an infection, one of those few that are fatal to Opiri."

"A sad fate for the child," Artemis said.

"And for her husband. He raised Beth with the help of his sister, who had come to the colony before him. There were six or seven other Opiri in the colony at the time."

"But they are not here now," Artemis said.

"Four years after the death of Beth's mother, her father left on a hunting trip. He never returned. Not long after that, the colony…" He sighed. "They didn't tell me this, not officially, but I was able to figure out the truth. I don't know why, but the human colonists gradually made the Nightsiders aware that they weren't welcome, and one by one the Opiri left the colony. In the end, Beth was the only colonist who had Nightsider blood."

Feeling a little ill, Artemis closed her eyes. "Who cared for her?" she asked.

"Her aunt. She has Beth now."

"She'll keep the child?" Pericles asked.

"She didn't know that certain members of the colony wanted Beth gone, as well, or that they intended to trade Beth to the rogues," Garret said, his lips thinning in disgust. "But she seems to have her suspicions."

"I don't know what they said to Chares," Pericles said, "but he decided not to risk attacking the colony once we had Beth."

"And the men who sold her are still in the colony?" Artemis asked, baring her teeth.

"If they are, they're keeping a very low profile. The leaders here didn't know what had happened to Beth, but they did know that the rogues who had approached the colony suddenly decided to leave and that was when her absence was noted. They sent out search parties, but gave up after two days."

"We should not leave her here, among such people," Artemis said. "How does her aunt expect to protect her?"

"She believes she has allies in the colony."

"But are they enough? The fact that the humans virtually drove the Opiri away suggests otherwise. You spoke of peace between Opiri and humans in colonies such as this, and yet here is proof that such a thing cannot last."

"It's only proof that these people couldn't handle living at close quarters with Nightsiders," Garret said. "Every one of the colonists here is a former serf, and none of them have forgotten their lives in the Citadels."

"And you find this easy to understand?" she demanded.

Garret gazed at her in silence, and a little of his emotion leaked through to her. She tried to shut off the connection, but not before she realized that he was considering whether or not to trust her.

After all the time they had spent together, she found it remarkably painful to sense his doubts. She was angry, yes, but it was more than that. Her chest ached, and her ribs seemed to contract into a tight, hard coil. She had agreed to all his plans, even playing the part of his—

"I was a serf in Erebus," he said, interrupting her thoughts. "So I do understand their resentment. Even their hate."

Astonished by his confession, Artemis scrambled to her feet. "*You* were a serf?" she asked.

"For many years. I saw how most humans were treated in the Citadel." He pushed his hair away from his face. "I was lucky. I was chosen by a Bloodmistress who treated her serfs well. But most serfs in Erebus were regarded as cattle, as they are by most of your people."

The ache in Artemis's chest spread throughout her body, twisting her stomach into knots and making her head throb. Garret seemed so superior to the serfs she had seen in Oceanus, or the men and women they had found in the town on the beach. He had courage and will equal to that of any Opir.

But she knew he could not be the only human like this.

"I'm not very different from those people in there," he said, as if he'd read her thoughts. "I was sent as tribute from the San Francisco Enclave because I'd committed the crime of trying to help other convicts. I was just like the other serfs, except that I learned to love my mistress. And she learned to love me."

Suddenly Artemis knew what he was about to say. "Roxana was your mistress," she said.

"Yes." He took a long, slow breath. "Roxana and I

cared deeply for each other almost from the beginning. She treated me as an equal in private. In public, we had to play a game. But when she became pregnant…"

"You had to hide her condition," Artemis said, forgetting her own anguish.

"They would have forced her to give up the child and raised it as Darketan. Roxana would have been punished, and of course I would have been executed as an example to the other serfs."

"So you escaped."

His gaze grew unfocused, looking into a past Artemis could scarcely imagine. "Yes. Because serfs and Opiri were prepared to risk their lives to help make it happen. We had an Underground in Erebus, humans and Nightsiders trying to make serfs' lives easier and sometimes help them escape brutal masters. I joined it before Roxana and I… Before we became lovers. When she found out, she became part of it and met with other Opiri who were willing to help. Eventually they were able to get us out of Erebus, along with dozens of other serfs." His voice thickened. "Timon was born in freedom."

"And then Freebloods stole him from you." Artemis sank back into a crouch. "If you had told me this earlier…"

"Would it have made a difference? I'm the same man either way."

"Yet you hesitated to reveal your past," she said. "Did you think I would refuse to help you if I knew?"

The slight rustle of undergrowth marked Pericles's sudden disappearance, and Artemis realized that the young Freeblood had felt like an intruder in a very intimate world. She wished she could run after him.

Coward, she thought. She was ashamed of having felt a twinge of disgust at the idea of a Bloodmistress bearing a human's child; she couldn't bear to acknowledge the possibility that she might have treated Garret far worse than he deserved if she had realized he was an escaped serf.

"You gave your blood to me, even though you knew so little of me," she said softly. "How is it that you could trust me at all?"

"If it hadn't been for Roxana and the other Nightsiders I knew in Erebus, I might not have," he said. "But as I said, I was fortunate. Many serfs have nothing to help them survive but hate, even after they escape."

"Then how could these serfs bear to come near me?"

"It wasn't easy for some of them, but they knew I would never have married a Freeblood if I didn't believe she could be trusted."

"And the colonists?"

"I don't know what they might have experienced that turned them against the Nightsiders here, but—"

"It makes them no better than Opiri in their prejudice. More evidence that expecting humans and Opiri to live together in harmony is a foolish dream."

"I've seen it work," he said. "I've learned that civilized, rational Nightsiders and humans are far more alike than they want to acknowledge." He looked into her eyes. "You and I, Artemis, are not so different."

His words filled her with a kind of nonsensical joy, as if they had somehow relieved her of the burden of this new and unexpected guilt. It wasn't quite so simple, of course, but she was grateful. Grateful and warmed by the acceptance in his eyes.

She had learned to value the judgment of a human. *This* human.

For a moment she dared to open her mind, to let the empathy awaken again. Garret's aura flared around his head, radiating heat like a fire. The heat was not merely sexual but inextricably intermingled with emotions that frightened her with their potency.

But she remembered how it had ended the last time, when Garret had spoken another name. She hesitated, torn between giving way and holding back. At last she leaned forward and kissed him. Then his arms were around her, and he was returning the kiss with a passion that filled her mind and redoubled her own need for him.

"Artemis," he murmured into her neck, tracing her ear with his lips and tongue. She could so easily have cast aside all her fears, stripped off her clothes and relieved him of his. But there was another need even more pressing. She felt him recognize and accept that need gladly, suppressing his own.

She had fought so rigorously to keep this from happening again, but now all her former worries seemed unimportant, of no greater interest than the way she cut her hair. Her defenses crumbled. She kissed his face from forehead to jaw, sucked on his neck without breaking the skin. She licked his shoulder and then grazed the base of his neck with her teeth. When she bit, he exhaled as if he had been holding his breath and whispered words she couldn't quite understand.

She drank lightly, because she didn't want to make him weak for the return journey to the north. But something happened she hadn't expected. She felt not only the vibrant blaze of his emotion—a pleasure as sensual as any joining of bodies—but also a slight but noticeable change in the taste of his blood, a change that made the sharing almost painful in its intensity. It was far more than mere nourishment; it rolled over her tongue like the sweetest ambrosia, unlike anything she had ever tasted before.

When Artemis realized what seemed to be happening, her heart stuttered to a stop. Surely it couldn't have occurred so quickly. Surely it was all in her mind. Blood-bonds didn't occur until an Opir had taken a human's blood for some time, and then only under extraordinary circumstances.

Even if it was only beginning to happen, she had to stop it.

She sealed Garret's wound, her hands trembling on his shoulders. He opened his eyes, and she thought they had never been so bright, so vibrant with life.

Did hers look the same? Could she ever expect to feel this euphoria again, this magical strength that came from something sweeter than any blood?

Not with Garret. Never again with him. She must hold true this time. She must not permit—

Someone loudly cleared his throat. Artemis and Garret broke apart, and Pericles crept into the tiny clearing, looking everywhere but at them.

"What is it?" Garret said, his voice gruff with frustration.

His face still averted, Pericles crouched at the edge of the clearing. "Beth's aunt is outside the stockade," he said. "She wants to speak to you."

Garret's expression turned grim. "Wait for me here," he said to Artemis.

"Something is wrong, isn't it?" she said, pushing aside her fear. "What haven't you told me?"

Hiding his gun under his coat, Garret met her gaze. "I don't know. But it's strange that Beth's aunt would want to speak to me now."

"I am coming," Artemis said. "Beth is as much my concern as yours, and now that it is dark you have no advantage over me."

"All right. But please, Artemis…trust my judgment. Stay behind me."

With a powerful sense of foreboding, Artemis followed Garret and Pericles toward the colony walls. A small human woman was standing just outside the gate, her arm around a little girl.

Beth.

The woman looked past Garret into the darkness, as if she could see Artemis in the shadows. "I am sorry," she said, tears in her voice. "I thought the colony would accept her back. But there has been something wrong here since Beth disappeared. Certain men of this colony…" She bit her lip and hugged Beth more tightly. "I can't trust them. I don't think Beth will be safe here."

As if she only half understood her aunt's words, Beth smiled at Garret and yawned. Garret looked back at Artemis. His anger was palpable.

"Please," the woman said, "take Beth away with you. You can find a better place for her, a place where she won't be the only one of her kind." Tears rolled down her cheeks. "I want her to be happy. Please help us."

"Why would she come with us?" Garret asked. "She'll want to stay with you."

"But I can't protect her," the woman said. She pulled a small packet out of her pants pocket. "I have something to…quiet her down. I've already given a little to her, and if you give her the rest, she'll be calm until you've taken her far from here."

"We're going on a dangerous journey," Garret said. "Do you understand what you're asking?"

"You took good care of her. You know how to deal with people who aren't… Who don't fit in. I would not entrust her with anyone else but the ones who saved her life."

Artemis stepped forward. "We will take her," she said, glancing up at Garret. "We will keep her safe."

Garret met her gaze and took her hand in his. "My wife is right," he said. "We'll do all we can to help her."

"Thank God," the woman said, clearly struggling to hold back her sobs. "Please, take her before I—"

Artemis stepped forward and held out her hand. Beth

took it, innocent trust on her face. Pericles joined them, draping a cloak over the little girl's jacket.

"Is anyone apt to follow us?" Garret asked.

"They only want the problem gone," the woman said bitterly.

"Then we'll leave within the hour," Garret said. "We have a few preparations to make."

"Thank you," the woman said. She pushed a sack into his hands. "These are some of Beth's things." Abruptly she rushed to Beth and planted a kiss on the girl's forehead. "Be good, Bethy."

She rushed back inside the wall and closed the gate behind her. Beth stared after her in bewilderment, and Garret looked down at the small packet in his hand.

"I hope we won't have to use this," he said.

Artemis lifted the girl into her arms. "Let us make sure we do not," she said. She carried Beth back to the clearing. Beth stirred restlessly and called her aunt's name once, then dropped into a light sleep.

Laying the girl down on a blanket, Artemis waited for Pericles and Garret to join her. Garret's expression was dark, as if he had a bad taste in his mouth. Pericles was very quiet.

"They would harm a child?" Artemis demanded. "Even though she is half human?"

"They wouldn't harm her," Garret said, "but her life wouldn't be a happy one."

"In other words, this is another case in which humans and Opiri cannot live together in harmony."

He sidestepped her statement. "The important thing is that we must find a safe place to take her."

"Your own colony," Pericles said hesitantly.

Garret closed his eyes. "Another two hundred miles to the south," he said. "Timon—"

He didn't finish, but his despair was a living thing in the air between them.

"There must be a place to the north," she said. "What of the human Enclave of SeaTac? I have never been so far north, but perhaps they would take her in."

"A long and difficult journey," Garret said. "And there's no guarantee that they would accept her."

"There's another place," Pericles said. "It's still in the north. But it's on your way to the river crossing into Canada."

"What is this place?" Garret asked.

"A compound on the Willamette River in the old city of Portland."

"Portland?" Artemis said. "I heard that the last human settlement there was destroyed ten years ago."

"They built a new one. Chares talked about it. It's guarded by strong walls, nothing like this place. The people there are very well armed."

"A militia compound?" Garret asked. "But Beth is half Opir."

"Chares said the Portland compound uses mixed Opiri and human patrols. They coexist peacefully." Pericles hesitated. "There's only one problem. They hate Freebloods. Chares said they've been under siege by rogues working for the Bloodlord in the north, so *he* wouldn't go anywhere near them."

"Beth is not a Freeblood," Artemis said.

Garret's expression softened as he looked down at Beth. "I don't want to leave her in a place where such prejudice exists," he said, "but you may be wrong, and I can't put off finding Timon any longer." He met Artemis's gaze. "I won't let either one of you fall into their hands. If you're still willing to come with me."

"How do we get to this place, Pericles?" Artemis asked.

"I don't know exactly where it is," Pericles said, "but I

know it's on the river in the old city, close to a bridge they can guard easily."

A little of the tension went out of Garret's body. He pulled the map from his pack. "So we return to our previous route and continue past Salem along the Willamette until we reach Portland. Once we've seen to Beth, we'll continue northeast to the bridge over the Columbia at Government Island." He folded the map. "We'll still have to pass Oceanus, but our luck held the last time. It's our only option."

Pericles nodded. Artemis stared at the map. It would be a long walk to this other colony, but at least they would be going in the right direction. Garret needed that goal now, the belief that he would finally find his son.

But she would have to fight doubly hard against feeding from Garret now that she understood the consequences of what had happened between them at the last blood-taking. It would be painful and unpleasant, but there was still a chance to break the cord before it became too strong to sever.

"If we're ready...?" Garret said.

Lifting Beth into the sling on his back, Pericles nodded. Artemis donned her own pack.

None of them looked back when they left the walls of the colony behind.

Chapter 11

Garret's hopes were fulfilled, and twelve days later, foot-sore and weary, they reached Oceanus's northern border without incident. Their road had taken them back to the winding Willamette, and they had agreed to keep to the east side of the river as they approached Portland.

For most of the journey Beth had been quiet and coop-erative, seemingly content to be with her rescuers and only occasionally calling out for her aunt. Between them, Gar-ret, Artemis and Pericles kept her clean, comfortable and well fed with meat and any edible plants they could find. Pericles remembered several games from his human life, and Garret told her stories he'd once told Timon. Artemis made it her business to hold Beth as often as possible, as committed to Beth's welfare as any mother would be.

As Roxana would have been.

But it was not Beth who Garret was worried about. As each day passed, he had noticed changes in Artemis's ap-pearance and energy. After a few days' travel, her face began to look drawn. Halfway to Salem, she began to stumble occasionally, and by the time they reached their camp south of Portland, her eyes were clouded and her lips pinched with discomfort.

Garret knew the signs. She obviously wasn't getting enough blood from animal sources, but she refused to ask him for what she needed. He'd thought she was over that particular inhibition after Coos Bay. Instead, it seemed to have gotten worse.

Still, he kept his thoughts to himself as they forded the Clackamas River and found a sheltered area where the remains of a bridge disappeared into the forest on its way to the ruins of a string of towns, suburbs and small cities stretching in an almost continuous line toward the Columbia River. Pericles set Beth down under a tree, and Garret removed the girl's food from his pack.

"We have somewhere between ten and twelve miles to go," he said, giving Beth a carefully harvested handful of late blackberries.

"We should hunt," Artemis said. She gathered her bow and checked her arrows.

"Let Pericles go ahead," Garret said. "I'd like to speak to you."

Her face took on the stubborn look he knew all too well. "It is better if we hunt while it is still dark."

"I'll scout for game," Pericles said, slipping into the trees.

Garret held Artemis's gaze. "I know what's wrong with you," he said bluntly. "You're starving yourself again. Why?"

"I don't know what you—" She broke off and jumped to her feet. A second later Garret's more limited human senses alerted him to movement in the trees. He dropped his pack and scrambled for the pieces of the partially assembled VS.

The muzzle of an automatic rifle pressed into his skull from behind.

"Stand down," a soft, cultured voice said.

Garret released the VS. He knew the rifle's wielder was Opir and that his chances of bringing the Nightsider down were slim. He looked for Artemis. Even as he watched, a woman—clearly dhampir, dark-haired and stocky, with the typical "cat eyes"—and a male Nightsider of indeterminate rank dragged Artemis out of the woods. All three of them bore the marks of a vicious scuffle.

And they were not alone. Garret's Opir guard grabbed the sections of the VS and tossed them to someone out of the range of Garret's sight.

"There's a kid here," another voice, rough and human, said from Beth's direction. Garret pulled his hunting knife from its sheath and twisted to sink it into the Nightsiders leg. The Opir kicked the knife away, grabbed Garret by the throat and slammed him against the tree.

"Back off, Varus," the human said. "Don't hurt him."

Without argument, Varus let Garret go. A whip-thin human with a short wiry beard and several scars appeared in front of Garret, and others closed in around him: a mix of humans, Opiri and dhampires, all armed and clearly working together. Garret managed to catch a glimpse of Beth, who was sitting up and staring at the human woman kneeling close to her.

"Leave her alone," Garret said, calculating the best angle of attack. "Who are you?" he asked the thin man. "What do you want?"

"My name's Cody," the man said.

"Why did you attack us?" Artemis asked, the dhampir's pistol poking into her ribs.

"We don't plan to hurt you," Cody said, meeting his stare. "But if you try to attack one of us again, we might have to."

Unwilling to risk Beth's or Artemis's safety, Garret raised his hands above his head. The human woman bent to pick Beth up, but the little girl jerked away and ran toward Artemis.

"Where's Pericles?" she cried, grabbing Artemis around the legs.

"Are there other people with you?" the leader demanded.

Thank God, Garret thought, that Pericles had taken his small pack with him. "Pericles's her stuffed toy," he said, cautiously meeting Artemis's gaze. "She lost it."

Artemis stroked Beth's hair. "If you touch her—" she began.

"Let the girl go to Rachel," the thin human said, indicating the woman who had been talking to Beth earlier.

"What do you want with her?"

"The question is what *you're* doing with her."

Garret forced himself to relax. "My name is Garret Fox. We're trying to take this child to safety. If you're what I think you are, you'll either let us go or help me."

"Take her to safety?" the dhampir asked. "From what?"

"We found her amid the bodies of Freebloods and humans who'd slaughtered each other. She was the only survivor. We were looking for a settlement willing to take her in and care for her."

"And where would that be?" the thin human said.

"We heard that there was one in old Portland, on the Willamette River," Artemis said.

"Where did *you* come from?"

"Far south of here, from a colony where humans and Opiri live together in peace," Garret said.

"Why didn't you take the girl back to your own colony?" the dhampir asked Garret.

"We were much closer to Portland," Garret said. "And we're looking for another child, taken from our colony by rogue Freebloods." He glanced at the dhampir. "I have no reason to lie."

"You would if you're one of the humans selling children to the packs," Cody said.

Given what had happened to Beth, Garret was far less shocked than he might have been. Still, he felt bile rise in his throat at the idea that other humans might do the same thing…and that he was being accused of it.

"He hasn't sold any children," Artemis said with a scornful laugh.

"You're a Freeblood, are you not?" Varus asked.

"Aresia is a Bloodlady from Oceanus who has found a new life in our colony," Garret said, giving Artemis a quick and meaningful glance urging her to play along. He didn't want anyone recognizing her as a Freeblood now. "She has nothing to do with those rogues."

Hard, unblinking eyes examined him as if he were one of the ubiquitous and immense yellow slugs that lived beneath the leaf mold. Garret looked from one suspicious face to another. There was no chance that he and Artemis could fight their way out of this one.

But if these people were concerned about kidnapped children, they wouldn't hurt Beth, whatever they might think of him and Artemis.

"If you are who I think you are," he said, "you're what we've been looking for. Will you help Beth?"

"He asks if we'll *help* her," the dhampir woman said with a twist of her mouth.

"Can it, Sonja," Cody said. "You," he said to Artemis, "let the girl go, or we'll have to hurt your friend."

"I have good things to eat," Rachel said, holding out a crisp, firm apple to Beth. "I'll bet you're hungry."

Artemis knelt and held Beth gently by the shoulders. "These people are going to help us," she said. "You go on to that lady there. She'll take care of you for a while." She looked up and fixed Varus with a severe gaze. "Don't be afraid of these Nightsiders. They aren't like the ones who took you."

"I'm not afraid." Beth thrust out her lower lip. "Where's Pericles?"

"I'll find him for you. I promise." She released Beth to Rachel, who gave Beth the apple.

"Both of you," Cody said to Garret and Artemis, "turn toward me."

With a quick shared glance, Garret and Artemis did as they were told. Rough hands wrenched Garret's arms behind his back. Artemis's body was coiled and ready to spring, but she knew as well as he did that they had to go along until fighting, however doomed, became their only option.

"Good," Cody said. "Keep cooperating and we won't have any problems."

"The child we're looking for is still out there," Garret said. "The longer you hold us, the longer he'll be alone with those monsters."

"You'll get to speak your piece when we get to the compound."

"How far?"

"You should be able to figure it out, if you really were looking for our colony." Cody turned away, and the muzzle of a gun prodded Garret in the back. Sonja gathered up Garret's supplies and stuffed them into his pack, while Artemis's Nightsider guard threw her hooded daycoat over her. The other full-blooded Opiri put on their own. Keeping Garret and Artemis apart, the patrol spaced themselves out to cover all possible angles of attack and keep an eye on their prisoners at the same time.

As they moved northeast through the overgrown suburbs and low, forested hills, the Willamette River always to the west, Garret watched and listened for Pericles. He would find out soon enough what had happened, if he didn't already know.

Garret hoped for the boy's sake that he would stay well away from them and their captors. He managed to catch Artemis's eye from time to time when their guards moved slightly out of formation. He knew that she was looking for Beth. He was, too, occasionally catching glimpses of the girl's dark hair.

Cody called for frequent stops to allow Beth to rest, so the going was slow. But Artemis still looked wan and pale, and Garret knew that if she got much worse he would have to beg these people to give her blood. She would certainly never ask for herself.

The group crossed the Willamette over a barely intact bridge at a place called Ross Island, and then continued west to the hills framing the southern portion of old Portland before continuing north again.

By the time the sun was at its apex, they had paused on a ridge overlooking the river, which glittered like a silver ribbon in the sun. Cody consulted with Sonja and several of his other compatriots, pointing toward the sprawling ruins in the valley below. Varus, Beth, Rachel and two others split off and descended at a fast pace. Artemis moved to follow, but her guard had already anticipated the attempt and jammed the muzzle of his gun into her neck. Garret's guard did the same to him.

"Don't worry about her," Cody said, addressing both of them. "If you pass muster, you'll see her again soon."

Garret followed Cody's gaze, squinting against the glare of sunlight on water. The four men and women with Beth were only specks against the slope of asphalt, concrete and faded autumn grass.

Cody held a pair of binoculars up to Garret's eyes, giving him his first glimpse of their destination: the high walls of a fortress on the river shore, built almost on top of a bridge that connected the western half of the fallen city with the east.

"Delos," Cody said, a note of pride in his voice. He glanced at the others. "Let's go."

Like almost every settlement, mixed colony or militia compound Garret had ever seen, Delos was a garrison designed to hold off an army of enemies if the need arose. But it seemed even more martial than most: the battlements were bristling with weapons, including what looked like a cannon and an array of machine guns. The eastern wall of the fortress literally butted up against the riverbank, with the bridge accessed by heavily guarded rear gates.

If Avalon had been protected this well, he thought, he might never have lost Roxana or Timon. But once the front gates swung open, he could see that the interior was not so different from Avalon's, with rows of barracks, a wide central commons for colony meetings, social gatherings and entertainment, an extensive garden, storage units, and a handful of smaller buildings that served as administrative offices.

"Is this what we were looking for?" Artemis asked Garret, twisting to see around the guards.

"I hope so," he said. "Are you—"

She held up her hand and looked across the commons, her eyes narrowed under her hood. Garret followed her gaze. Halfway across the central plaza, Rachel held Beth in her arms as she consulted with a tall woman in a much-mended lab coat.

"The doctor," Cody said, coming to join Garret. "She'll put Beth to rights."

"One of us should go with her," Garret said. "She'll be frightened without us."

"No can do. We'll have to confine you until the boss can talk to you." He narrowed his eyes. "You sure you don't have anything to tell me? Something you might have forgotten before we left your camp?"

"Let us speak to your leader," Artemis said.

"In time," Cody said, his attention already focused on something else.

"I think we have the same enemies," Garret said. "The child I'm looking for is—"

Cody turned and walked away before Garret could finish. Sonja took his place and grabbed Garret's elbow.

"Do yourself a favor," she said, "and don't try lying to the boss."

"Garret!" Artemis called as her guards escorted her across the commons.

"Where are you taking her?" Garret demanded.

Sonja didn't answer. She and Garret's other guards waited until Artemis was out of sight, and then dragged him in the same general direction. People at work—humans, dhampires and presumably Daysiders, who could tolerate the sun—paused in their building, repairing, harvesting and sweeping to watch Garret and his escort pass, but he was clearly not much of a novelty. If Delos was anything like Avalon, they would have seen many people come to them in hopes of finding refuge.

Or maybe, Garret thought grimly, *arriving as prisoners*.

"Where have you taken Aresia?" he asked again, deliberately slowing his pace.

"You don't need to know that right now, though I'm sure she appreciates your concern," Sonja said. "Just remember that her treatment depends on your good behavior. And vice versa."

Muscles knotted with the compulsion to search for Artemis, Garret barely maintained his composure. The guards half dragged him past the rows of barracks to a windowless building near the eastern wall of the fortress. An armed sentinel unlocked the door and stepped aside as Garret was pushed into one of several small, dark rooms with a tiny barred aperture set in the door. He stumbled into a cot set against the wall, and the cell door slammed shut before he could straighten and turn back.

"Wait!" he called, pressing his face against the bars. "If you're worried about the children, I can tell you where they're taking them!"

No one answered. The outer door closed. Garret knew perfectly well that it would be futile to bang on the cell door, so he walked the perimeter of the tiny room, looking for a means of escape. He wasn't surprised to find that there wasn't one. This place had obviously been built to hold Opiri, who were stronger than any human.

Garret sat on the cot and assessed his situation. Unless his captors were as bad as the militias and intended to try to sweat the "truth" out of him by confining him in a cold room without food or water for a few days, he doubted that he would be left alone too long.

But if Artemis was left without blood…

Garret lay back, closed his eyes and quieted his mind. He woke to the sound of metal scraping metal as someone unlocked the outer door. He rolled off the cot and jumped to his feet.

The cell door swung open. Cody and Varus stood just outside, rifles aimed at his chest.

"The boss will see you now," Cody said, jerking his gun toward the door.

Garret moved past them out of the jail. The sun was on the decline, and he realized that he'd slept far longer than he'd planned. His mouth was dry and his head ached, but he was already planning what to say to the "boss." He knew how to be very diplomatic when he had to be.

And if diplomacy didn't work, he would find something that did.

His guards' destination was another of the freestanding smaller buildings near the front of the colony, but Cody stopped midway to stare at a commotion near the colony's front gate. Garret swore under his breath as several Opiri dragged a cloaked and hooded Nightsider inside the stockade. Pericles hung limp between the arms of his guards, but he seemed unharmed and in one piece.

Garret knew better than to acknowledge him now. First, he had to find out what the hell was going on. He ignored the activity near the gate and didn't stop until they reached the building. Cody held the door open and pushed Garret in front of a plain pine desk, a battered chair and a wall covered with detailed maps of the area, each one marked with notations and pins.

While they waited Garret listened to the raised voices outside and clenched his teeth against his anger and worry. "Keep me informed," a masculine voice said somewhere behind the door at the back of the room. Then the door opened, and a man walked in to stand behind the desk. He looked at Cody expectantly, barely sparing a glance for Garret.

"We have something of a crisis, Cody," he said. "You'll have to—"

"Daniel?" Garret said.

Chapter 12

The man stared at Garret, clearly as startled as *he* was. Daniel moved around the desk to clasp Garret's shoulders. "What in hell are you doing here?" he asked.

"I could ask you the same question," Garret said, relief replacing his astonishment.

"Sir, you know this man?" Cody asked.

Daniel shot him a weary, impatient look. "You're usually a keen observer, Cody. Perhaps you need more time to rest between patrols."

"No, sir," Cody said, flinching at Daniel's sarcasm.

"*This* is the man you reported as being a potential child-stealer?"

"There seems to have been a misunderstanding," Garret said.

"Apparently," Daniel said. "Uncuff him, Cody."

Clumsy in his haste, Cody released Garret's hands. Garret rubbed his wrists, thinking about Artemis and Beth.

Hold on, he urged Artemis in his mind. *This won't take much longer.*

"You're far from your home ground," Daniel said, stepping back.

"So are you," Garret said. "It's been a long time."

"A strange time," Daniel said. He gestured toward a chair behind Garret. "Tell me what happened."

Garret perched on the edge of the chair and studied Daniel's face. It was clear that the past few years hadn't been easy on the man who had been a fellow serf in Erebus. Born into slavery, Daniel had been treated brutally for much of his early life in the Citadel and had learned to behave like any good human: quiet, obedient and controlled. He had only revealed the extent of his rebellious side when he had learned that his master, the Bloodmaster Ares, was actually his father, and that in spite of his appearance, he wasn't human. He'd risked his life to save Ares from his enemies, and had helped Roxana and Garret get dozens of captive humans out of the Citadel.

He had escaped with them, only to be overwhelmed at first by the vast world outside the Citadel's high walls. He'd adapted quickly, but the man who stood before Garret now had clearly done far more than merely adjust to a strange and hostile environment. He'd become like the soldiers who followed him: battle-tested, wary and tempered by hard experience.

Garret knew he was fortunate that Daniel wasn't his enemy. "I assume Cody told you most of it already," he said. "Your people found us traveling with a little girl about twelve miles southeast of here and apparently assumed we'd kidnapped her."

"My soldiers have reason to be suspicious," Daniel said, taking his own seat behind the desk. "Other humans in the area have been seen working with the rogues."

"Working as in side by side? You can't believe that they'd be traveling together."

"But you were with an Opir," Daniel said. "If I had been there, I never would have suspected you, of course." He steepled his fingers on the desk. "You were trying to get the child to safety?"

"We heard there was a mixed settlement somewhere near the river in Portland. If I'd known you were here—"

"Fortunately," Daniel said, "I was elected commander three years ago." He glanced at a paper on his desk. "I assure you that Beth will be well looked after. Who is the woman?"

Garret took a long, careful breath. "Aresia is a fellow

colonist from Avalon, a former Bloodlady from Oceanus. She's no threat to anyone."

"Cody tells me that you are searching for another child."

"My son, Timon. He was taken from Avalon by rogue Freebloods nine weeks ago."

"I'm sorry. Aresia volunteered to help you find him?"

"She did."

"Then she is welcome here." Daniel tapped his fingers on the desk. "We knew the rogues have been stealing children wherever they can find them, but they must be ranging far if they've reached Avalon."

"Yes," Garret said tightly. "Have they stolen any of yours?"

"No, but only because we've taken steps to make sure they don't get the chance. We send out regular patrols to look for packs that might have children with them."

"And the humans who are helping them."

Daniel's eyes turned cold. "I was told that you know where the rogues are taking the children."

"North, over the border to Canada. Some kind of stronghold in the mountains."

"Yes. There are rumors that this stronghold is a Freeblood encampment, but we don't have any details." Daniel's fists clenched. "Even if we can't provide you with much additional information, we may be able to spare a few fighters to help you after we've dealt with the current problem."

"The Nightsider you just brought in?"

"You saw him?"

And I told Pericles that I wouldn't let him fall into their hands, Garret thought. "Not clearly," he said. "What has he done?"

"There's a good chance that he's one of the rogue scouts who look for vulnerable settlements to raid."

"We didn't encounter any rogues on the way here."

"They come in waves, and we're in a lull at the moment."

Daniel frowned. "We have reason to believe that the prisoner has been a spotter for the child-stealers. He locates settlements and colonies where the others can break in."

It seemed, Garret thought, that this was a day for nasty surprises. "You've seen him before?"

"He's been described to us in considerable detail."

Garret almost spoke up then, but something in Daniel's manner convinced him to wait. "What do you do with prisoners?" he asked.

"Question them about our enemy's intentions. I don't expect them to tell the truth."

"And then?"

"We can't afford to keep them here for long."

A chill settled at the base of Garret's spine. This was definitely not the old Daniel. "It seems almost personal with you," he said.

"Opiri like my father and our people here can be trusted. Most Freebloods can't." Daniel cocked his head. "You don't hate them for what they did to your son?"

"Yes," Garret said, "and for what they did to Roxana. Raiders killed her four years ago."

"I'm sorry. I don't have to tell you how highly I thought of her. Does Ares know?"

Garret tried to remember the last time he'd seen Daniel's father and Ares's mate, Trinity, who like Garret had come from the Enclave of San Francisco. "Ares left Avalon not long after you did," he said. "I don't know where he is now."

"I understand." Daniel rose abruptly. "For the time being, you'll be assigned quarters and everything you'll need until our patrols report that it's safe for you to leave."

"And Aresia?"

"We'll release her on your recognizance." Daniel ran his hand over his face. "But this isn't like Avalon. We have strict rules here and tend to be suspicious of strangers. I'll make sure everyone knows you're guests, so feel free to talk to anyone in the colony if you have questions." He cocked his head. "Do you prefer shared accommodations with your companion or a separate room?"

"Shared will be fine," Daniel said. "I...should have told you that she is my wife."

"I see," Daniel said in a neutral voice. "I'll arrange it."

Garret nodded his thanks. "After you've released Aresia," he said, "I'd like to speak to the prisoner. He may know something about Timon."

"We know how to get that kind of information very quickly," Daniel said. "There's no need to dirty your hands."

"We're talking about my *son*."

With an unreadable glance at Cody, Daniel nodded. "Find me or Cody when you're ready."

"Thank you." Garret offered his hand.

Daniel took it, gripping hard. "Good luck," he said.

Concealing his deep disquiet, Garret followed Cody back outside. Daniel might be a little too eager to find guilt in Pericles, but it wasn't as if Garret or Artemis had known the boy for more than a few weeks. If he was what Daniel had claimed...

"I'll take you on a short tour of the camp, and then to the Bloodlady's holding cell," Cody said, interrupting Garret's thoughts. "Your quarters should be ready within the hour."

"You seem to trust Daniel's judgment without question," Garret said.

"He's kept us alive," Cody said. "That's good enough for me."

Artemis knew that Garret was coming before he set foot in the prison. She breathed in his scent and closed her eyes. Though she hadn't been mistreated in any way and didn't expect that the soldiers would seriously harm Garret, she'd had grave doubts about the nature of this colony. Though it did appear to be one of those in which Opiri and humans lived and worked together, the soldiers' behavior suggested that it was little better than a typical militia compound—run with military precision, bound by almost rigid order and tainted by overt hostility toward outsiders.

"Where is she?" Garret's voice demanded from outside the building.

She inhaled sharply. Garret wasn't alone, but his words were clear and strong.

Perhaps there wouldn't need to be any violence, after all.

The key turned in the lock, and the door to her cell swung open. Garret stood framed in the light seeping in from the outer door, straight and still. Footsteps receded, and in an instant Garret's arms were around her, and he was pressing his lips to her neck as if he were the Opir and she the human donor. He released her quickly and closed the cell door behind him.

"They set you free," she breathed, pulling him down on the cot beside her.

"They've set us both free," Garret said. "We have the run of the colony."

She took his hand. "How did you manage that?"

"I know the man who runs this place."

"You *know* him?"

"I knew Daniel in the south. And I know why we were brought here as prisoners. Apparently there are humans helping to steal children for the rogues."

"Humans?" she asked. "Like the ones in the other colony who sold Beth?"

"I don't know if they're connected in any way," he said, "but the soldiers who found us thought I might be one of them. They've seen more than one kidnapped child pass through this area, and have been intervening whenever they can."

"And they thought a human would work so closely with a Freeblood?" she asked.

"You're not a Freeblood, remember?" he said, touching her face with his fingertips. "You're the Bloodlady Aresia. And I'd like to keep pretending that you're my wife."

Her heart thumped heavily in her chest, but not with fear. "You think I would be in danger if they knew who I really was?" she asked.

"They've been under nearly constant attack by Freebloods," he said. "They've seen citizens killed by rogues who have no regard for human life." His hand slipped down to her wrist, and he lifted her hand as if to expose the cuff marks that had already disappeared. "If they'd hurt you—"

He broke off, but he didn't need to finish. Artemis knew what he'd wanted to do, because she would have done the same thing herself.

Too many feelings, she thought. His very nearness made her entire body vibrate with desire—and hunger. The barriers in her mind were holding, but barely. In such a crisis, it would be all too easy to let go.

Stop, she told herself. *Think.*

"Was your colony like this?" she asked.

"No. Avalon's leaders didn't take the necessary steps to protect its citizens, including my son. Daniel has corrected that problem here."

"By assuming guilt in any Freeblood they bring in?"

"I told you that Delos has been continuously attacked. Their suspicions are not unjustified." He hesitated. "There are no Freeblood colonists here."

"Your friend's decision?"

"The colonists'."

"Human colonists?"

"Opiri as well." He cleared his throat. "I'm sorry, Artemis. There's one more thing. They've taken Pericles."

"He must have been following us," she said. "You told your friend that he was with us?"

"No. Daniel seems to think Pericles is a spy for the child-stealers. They say he's a scout who looks for vulnerable settlements with half-blood children."

"Surely you do not believe this?" she asked.

"We've taken Pericles's word about everything that happened to him and Beth. The part about her colony was true, but we've only assumed that the rest of what he told us is also the truth."

Artemis lowered her voice with an effort. "Before we came here, you believed that Pericles was like me. Yet now you would accept the judgment of those who assumed *you* to be a criminal?"

Garret got to his feet and paced across the cell. "You're convinced Pericles has been telling the truth."

She gripped the edge of the cot until her fingers ached. "Did you wonder if *I* might also have been lying to you?" she asked. "If perhaps I knew about Pericles's true purpose and was protecting him from you?"

"No. Never." He returned to the cot and looked down at her, deep creases between his brows. "I *do* think even you might have been deceived."

Could he be right? Artemis thought. If Pericles had fooled her, how could she ever be certain that any of her fellow Freebloods could learn a new way of life, completely separate from the influence of the Citadels and the old customs?

"Will you tell them how he helped Beth?" she asked. "Or will you stand by and let them punish him for crimes he may not have committed?"

"I'll do what I can for Pericles," Garret said. "But if we can't get him released, we still have to go on with our search."

"And what if I should choose to admit that I am a Freeblood like him?"

"To punish me?" He took her by the shoulders, squeezing just enough so that she knew how serious he was. "If you do, I won't be able to leave you. And I can't stay here, Artemis. I've delayed far too long already, and Timon…"

He had pushed his worry for his son so far back in his mind that Artemis had been mercifully spared from sharing his fear. Now it flooded over her again, freezing her blood and filling her mind with the terror of unbearable loss.

Close your mind, she told herself. But even when she tried to block him out, the echo of his emotion was still within her. The effort left her breathless and dizzy.

I won't be able to leave you, he'd said. And he'd meant it.

Her knees gave way.

"Artemis!" Garret said, easing her back down on the cot.

"I'm fine," she said, scraping her hair away from her face. "Garret, promise me one thing. Ask the commander to let Pericles and me speak to him with Beth present. Let him *see* Pericles's compassion for her, and her feelings for him."

The expression in Garret's eyes shifted from worry to one of deep consideration. "That's a reasonable request," he said. "I'll tell Daniel everything we know about Pericles, and ask him to give Pericles a chance to speak for himself. That's all I can promise."

"That is all I ask."

For a time, neither of them spoke.

"You know I didn't intend to cause you pain," Garret said at last.

"I know."

He expelled his breath. "It's time to get you out of this cell. You and I have been given our own quarters, if you have no objection to staying with me."

"You know I have not."

"Good. I think you need rest." He pulled her up. "You need blood, too."

She tried to pull away from him, but he put his arm around her shoulders and didn't let go. "Come," he said gently.

The compound looked very different by night. Torches and lanterns atop high poles had been lit to accommodate the few humans moving about, and Artemis could identify far more Opiri, as well as a few dhampires. Some of the colonists glanced her way, but none showed any overt signs of suspicion or hostility.

It was almost as if the entire tenor of the place had changed now that the humans had retreated into their barracks. To an Opir, Artemis thought, darkness smoothed away the rough edges and lent an air of civilization absent in the presence of daylight.

But she knew that was her own prejudice speaking. The Opiri who had taken her and Garret had been no more sympathetic than the human patrollers. As far as she was concerned, that was only more proof that mixed colonies created a poisonous atmosphere for both humans and Opiri alike, a place where ordinary suspicions only festered and increased with proximity.

Garret seemed blind to such possibilities. He took her elbow and led her to a cluster of small, cabin-like buildings branching off from a path near a sandy area that Artemis assumed to be some kind of training ground. He stopped before the smallest cabin, opened the unlocked door and stood aside to let her precede him.

The single room was furnished with a cot, a desk and a chair. The wall behind the desk was covered with pinned maps, a few handwritten lists and what looked like a child's drawings, scribbled in charcoal. Artemis's pack lay on the cot, along with her knife and bow.

She stopped just inside the door and leaned against the wall, trying not to stare at the bed. She hadn't slept in one for many years.

But she wasn't thinking of sleep just now.

The room suddenly seemed very small. Too small to contain her and Garret at the same time. She tried not to look at him again, though she would have felt his presence even if he had been halfway across the settlement.

"I asked if you could bathe," he said. "I can escort you to the women's bathhouse. And Daniel has arranged for us to have clean clothes while ours are washed."

"Very hospitable of him," she said. "But then I am a Bloodlady, not a monstrous Freeblood."

"Artemis—" Garret began.

Someone rapped on the door. "Fox?" a man's voice called.

"Daniel must be ready to see us earlier than I expected," Garret said. "Are we all right, Aresia?"

He was asking again if she agreed to his deception, Artemis thought. But what choice did she have, if she wanted her words to be acknowledged and accepted by Delos's tyrannical human commander?

She followed Garret outside, where Cody was waiting for them. He turned away without comment and set out along the torch-lit path toward the commons.

Their destination was one of the separate buildings near the barracks. Inside it stood a large table and a dozen chairs—a conference room, Artemis guessed, currently unoccupied except for a single light-haired human.

The colony's leader rose from his chair, looked Artemis over with a frank, assessing stare, and gestured for her and Garret to be seated.

"Lady Aresia," he said tersely. "I won't waste your time with trivialities. I assume Garret informed you of the situation here. I apologize for our error."

"I understand the reason for it," she said, drawing upon the gracious manners of a Bloodlady. "But we have certain concerns about your other prisoner."

"The Freeblood, Pericles," Garret said. "I should have told you before that we've been traveling with him, and have every reason to believe that he has severed any ties with the rogues who are taking the children."

"In fact," Artemis said, "he had been caring for the little girl, Beth, even before we met him. He is no criminal."

Daniel tilted his head in acknowledgment. "I am sorry to disappoint you," he said. "We interviewed him in depth and called witnesses who had seen him with other children, delivering them to packs headed north. This testimony upheld our original assessment of his guilt."

Chapter 13

"You mean that you have already tried and sentenced him," Artemis said.

"I intended to ask you to let him talk to Beth in your presence," Garret said. "You'd see that he never harmed her. He protected her from other Freebloods and saved her life."

"Even if he was sincere in his feelings for the girl," Daniel said, "his behavior with her does not mitigate his previous bad acts." He met Artemis's gaze with a probing stare. "I admit to wondering why a Bloodlady is so intent on defending a mere Freeblood rogue. The elite of the Citadels regard them as hardly better than animals."

"You're speaking to my wife, Daniel," Garret said, half rising.

Artemis held up her hand. "I am no longer of the Citadel," she said, "and I clearly have greater hope for *all* my people than you do."

"Pericles could have betrayed us at any time on our way here," Garret said, "but he didn't."

"He ran from our patrol," Daniel said.

"Given the circumstances here, he would have had reason regardless of his guilt or innocence."

Daniel's face was grave, but there was no regret in his light blue eyes. "We have too many enemies outside our gates, and no margin for error. I'm sorry, but we cannot set him free."

Artemis began to rise, but Garret stopped her with a firm hand on her arm. "What do you plan to do with him?" he asked.

"Keep him confined, for the time being. When I return, we will make the final decision."

"Return?" Garret asked, speaking again before Artemis could protest.

"I'll be going with you to find Timon."

Some wordless, very private communication passed between the two men, a reflection of a shared past that Artemis knew she could never fully understand. She felt strangely bereft.

At that moment, she hated Daniel for more than his ruthlessness.

"With so many enemies at the gates, as you said, won't you be needed here?" Garret asked.

"There are many competent men and women who can take my place," he said. "As a dhampir, I can be of use to both of you."

"A dhampir?" Artemis said, startled out of her anger. "But your eyes...your teeth..."

"There are a few dhampires who don't have the usual features, and Daniel's father wasn't the usual kind of Opir," Garret said, sliding his hand down her arm to clasp her hand. "His father was a Bloodmaster in Erebus."

"Erebus?" Artemis echoed. "How is that possible?"

"We were serfs together," Garret said. "But Daniel was born in the Citadel."

"And you were permitted to live?" Artemis asked Daniel.

"My father, Lord Ares, didn't know who I was until shortly before Garret and I escaped from Erebus. Only his greatest rival knew of my true parentage, and he kept me alive to spite Ares."

"Then you have good reason to despise my people."

"I don't, Lady Aresia. My father and his Opir allies helped save my life, and the lives of many other serfs." He glanced at Garret with a slight frown. "You didn't tell her everything."

"Evidently he did not," Artemis said, freeing her hand from Garret's. "But I wonder, Daniel, if your experiences have not made it easier for you to pass overhasty judgment on the least-powerful Opiri who fall into your hands."

"Aresia," Garret said, "you have no idea what he suffered in Erebus, and what it took for him to get to where he is now."

"Garret overstates his case," Daniel said to Artemis. "I am sorry that your traveling companion is not who you believed him to be."

Garret stared at the tabletop, his fist clenching and unclenching on the chair. "Daniel, what if Pericles could help us track down some of these other packs? Would you reconsider?"

"He would require constant watching," Daniel said. "We can't do that and concentrate on finding your son."

"Let me speak to him," Artemis said, beginning to rise. "There must be a way for him to prove that he has changed."

"That will not be possible," Daniel said.

"What do you think she'll do?" Garret asked, leaning over the table. "Help him escape?"

"Would you?" Daniel asked her.

"Either you trust my judgment or you don't," Garret said to Daniel.

"Stop," Artemis said. "I am not a child to be argued over." She pushed away from the table, nearly upsetting her chair, and strode out of the room.

Walking blindly, she started across the commons. She avoided contact with the colonists she passed, including the Opiri. Pericles was being held in some detention facility, and she knew she could find it easily enough by scent, if not by simply looking for it.

But it would surely be guarded, and she wasn't prepared for another confrontation. She walked once around the camp, observing silently, and then returned to the cabin. She threw open the door and walked inside.

Garret was already there, one of the child's drawings in his hands. He didn't seem to hear her come in. She knew he was thinking of Timon, and her anger drained away.

"I did not intend for the conversation with your friend to end as it did," she said.

He looked up slowly. "I should not have spoken to you as I did, especially in front of Daniel." His gaze focused on her face. "You look even worse than before," he said, setting the drawing on the desk.

"What is it you humans say?" she asked. "You are like a hen with one chick."

"I would never mistake you for a chick, Artemis," he said with a wry smile. "Not even an eaglet. I'd say you're fully grown."

She felt her tension give way to the soothing warmth of his voice. She sat on the cot. "I know you did what you could for Pericles," she said. "I thank you for that."

He knelt beside the cot. "I'm sorry I couldn't do more." He took her hand, turned it over and kissed her palm. The brush of his lips startled her as much as if he had never touched her with his mouth, though she remembered every caress with excruciating clarity.

Apparently his memory was equally keen, for he quickly let her go, rose and stepped back. "I know how you feel about Delos, and Daniel's judgment," he said. "You have doubts about humans and Opiri living together. There are times I've had the same doubts. I told you that Avalon made mistakes. So did Beth's colony. Daniel has managed to avoid those mistakes." He moved to the door. "There's something I'd like you to see."

Reluctantly, she went with him. They followed one of the paths between the individual cabins back to the commons, passing a dozen dhampires and Opiri engaged in hand-to-hand fighting. Lights flickered behind the small windows of the barracks, suggesting that their human occupants were engaged in their own evening activities.

"This is the mess hall," Garret said, indicating a building about half the size of the smallest barracks. "Many of the human citizens are eating their evening meal."

Artemis balked. "If it is a human place…"

"Everyone is welcome." Tugging gently on her hand, he led her to the mess hall and opened the door. Immediately Artemis was struck by a blast of scent and sound—humans of every age gathered around long tables, eating with obvious pleasure, engaged in dozens of conversations, laughing and clearly enjoying themselves. In addition to the tables, there were clusters of mismatched, much-mended chairs scattered around an open area at the far side of the single room, also occupied with people lost in discussion or playing unfamiliar games on smaller tables.

The contrast to what Artemis had seen outside was great, but most surprising was the presence of children. Children with adult kin, or playing with balls, cloth dolls and wooden horses.

And not all of the children were human. Artemis saw that several had the distinctive eyes of dhampires, and once she had noticed them, she also realized that there were a number of full-blooded Opiri among the humans. One male Opir was at the table opposite a human female, gazing at her with rapt attention, while a dhampir child sat beside him, scribbling on rough paper with a piece of charcoal and kicking his legs vigorously under the bench. In the open area, a female Opir was holding an infant on her knee while a male human looked on with obvious pride, as if the child were his own.

Garret followed her gaze. "That's what Daniel is trying to save," he said. "He's doing what my former colony failed to accomplish—protecting children like these, providing the only kind of settlement where civilized Opir and humans can live in peace without the constant fear of attack."

He took her hand again and led her to the couple with the infant. The female Opir glanced up with a smile of such open welcome that Artemis was astonished all over again.

"You must be Garret," she said, "and Aresia."

"Welcome," the human father said, standing to greet them. "I'm Johan, and this is my wife, Deineira."

"And this," Deineira said, lifting her squirming baby, "is Sophia Johanna."

"Quite a mouthful," Johan said with a grin. He offered his hand to Artemis. She took it gingerly. A flush of heat raced up her arm, carrying the human's emotions into her mind: pride, contentment…and love, powerful enough to breach her empathic barriers.

While she was recovering from the intensity of Johan's feelings, Deineira abruptly pushed Sophia Johanna into Artemis's arms. Artemis had no choice but to hold the squirming, blanket-wrapped bundle, cradling the round head and swaddled bottom against her chest.

She looked down into the chubby, wide-eyed face, and the memories she had fought so hard to contain came rushing back. Holding her own infant in her arms, only days before the first Opir she had ever met had nearly killed her. The infant she had lost because Kronos had saved her life by converting her, forcing her to leave her human life behind. Her life, and everything she had loved.

With the greatest of care, Artemis bent to return Sophia Johanna to Deineira's arms. "Your daughter is beautiful," she murmured.

The Bloodlady beamed, no trace of Opir reserve in her eyes. "She is, isn't she? She will grow up to walk in daylight, like her father."

Artemis's vision blurred, though there was no physical

reason for it. She looked for Garret, who was eating what humans called a "sandwich" and talking to Johan between ravenous bites. Artemis realized, with a twinge of guilt, that she hadn't given enough thought to Garret's physical needs. Now, at least, he had decent food and a real chance to rest.

He couldn't have known what seeing Deineira's family and holding the infant would do to her. He'd asked her about children once, and she'd evaded his question, as she'd evaded so many others.

Garret had wanted to make a point, and he had succeeded.

"Lady Aresia," Johan said, briefly touching her arm. "You are ill."

"No," she said, overwhelmed by his genuine concern for her. "I'm only a little—"

"Hungry," Johan said. "I know the signs. You have not been feeding."

Artemis knew that she couldn't lie to Johan. There was a quiet wisdom in him that defied any attempt to deceive him.

"You need not tell me why you have not taken your husband's blood," he said. "It is none of my business. But let me help you. I have not made a donation in three days and will not suffer for it."

Startled, she stared into Johan's eyes. "You would give me your blood?"

He lifted a brow. "It cannot be so different in the colony you came from, surely?"

"No," she said quickly. "No, not at all."

"Then, please." He gestured to three doors in the back of the hall.

"But your wife…"

"She suggested it."

Artemis felt faint. There was clearly nothing sexual in the invitation, and it was possible that taking blood from another human would solve the problem she had been facing since Coos Bay. If it did, she could honestly tell Garret that she was well and did not need *his* blood. There would be no need for dodging his questions again and again.

She looked around for Garret. He was nowhere to be seen. What would he think if he knew what she had done? Would he consider it a betrayal?

"Come, now," Johan said. He nodded to Deineira, who smiled at Artemis, and started toward the back of the hall. Half in a daze, Artemis followed him into one of the small rooms, comfortably furnished with a couch and a pair of chairs.

The entire procedure was almost clinical, and she felt not the slightest arousal or any sense of real intimacy, in body or mind. Johan's mind seemed focused on pleasant thoughts that matched his mellow personality, and all Artemis felt was profound relief.

When it was over and Johan was rolling down his sleeve, she thanked him and hesitated at the door.

"I envy you and Deineira," she said softly.

"Our Sophia?" he asked. "I have no doubt that you will have a child of your own when the time is right for you."

Unable to bear his sympathy, Artemis fled the room. She still saw no sign of Garret. She returned to the cabin and lay on the cot with her arm over her eyes. The door opened, and Garret's boots crossed the floor. Wood scraped on wood as he drew the desk chair close to the bed and sat down.

"What is it, Artemis?" he asked. "If I'd known seeing the children would upset you so much…"

"I'm not upset," she said.

"Sometimes you're very good at hiding your feelings," he said, "but this isn't one of those times."

"I know why you took me to see them," she said. "You wanted me to understand what it was like with you and Roxana. And Timon."

She felt the movement of air as he reached toward her

and then dropped his hand before he made contact. A profound ache filled her body.

"It was like that, for a while," he said. "But not at the beginning. It wasn't until we escaped Erebus that we could live as equals and try to give Timon a good life."

Artemis swallowed. "What happened to Roxana, Garret?" she asked.

"She died fighting rogue Freebloods, defending our colony. Timon never got a chance to know his mother."

Remembering how she had berated Garret for not telling her about Roxana in the beginning, Artemis felt a terrible remorse. She swung her legs over the side of the cot and brushed his hand with her fingertips. Emotion overwhelmed her, and sensory images flooded her mind: two kindred spirits bound together, bright lights in a great darkness, gathering other lights to themselves, projecting warmth and hope and joy.

And then the sundering, the unbearable loss, one of the bright lights extinguished in pain and fear. And the other soul…crippling bereavement that altered everything—more devastating than slavery or any other ordeal, save one: the disappearance of the child he and his mate had created.

Shuddering violently, Artemis fell back on the cot. "I see why you would despise us, those of my rank. I, too, would hate."

Garret knelt beside the cot. "I blame myself for what happened to Roxana and Timon," he said. "When we founded Avalon, we were too idealistic, too invested in the philosophy of peace to take the necessary precautions. We accepted nearly everyone who came to us from the Citadel and Enclave, human or Nightsider. That was a mistake." He laced his hands together, gripping with such force that his fingers turned red and his knuckles white. "Some of the bad ones, the humans, were only troublemakers, antisocial. But others, especially the Freebloods, assumed that they could simply take what they wanted without giving what was required of them in return. Still, we believed they could be taught to discard their old ways. Roxana was the biggest idealist of all of us, and she had the courage to stand by her convictions. She had faith. But she was wrong."

Barely able to endure the bitterness of his grief, Artemis covered his rigid hands with hers. "The Freebloods betrayed you," she said.

"They betrayed all of us. They opened the gates to rogues. We killed nearly all of them. But even afterward, the council didn't do enough to make certain it never happened again. When the raiders broke through to steal Timon, they got away with it because too many of the colonists wouldn't compromise their *principles*." He laughed hoarsely. "I should have taken Timon away from that place long ago, before…"

"But you still want what *they* did," she said, "or you would not have protected me from the militia in the south, or taken me to see Deineira and Johan tonight."

"I believe in a philosophy that doesn't destroy itself," he said, his jaw so tight that the words seemed barely able to escape.

Daniel's philosophy, she thought. No wonder Garret admired this colony for protecting its citizens as his old one had not.

How could she blame Garret for doubting Pericles…or for expecting her to abandon him after he'd saved her from the militiamen?

Slowly and carefully, she withdrew her hands. "Perhaps you would like to be by yourself now," she said. "I can—"

"No," he said. "I wanted to tell you all this because there's no more need for secrets between us. It's all in the past."

But it is not, she thought. The distress was still there,

raw and throbbing. She could give him comfort with words, but beyond that…

She was afraid of where such comforting might lead. Afraid to let down her guard, lower the gate, cross the moat she had dug around herself. Now that there was so much more between them than the empathy and their mutual desire…

But she was well fed now. There was no danger that she would slip. If she didn't reinforce the bond again, surely it would continue to fade.

Stripping her mind of all thought beyond the moment, she put her arms around his shoulders. He stiffened, sighed and buried his face against the curve of her neck. His anguish flowed into her like blood, and her body seemed to absorb it, striving to heal the wound that refused to close. Garret held her as if he believed she was the key to his mortal salvation, and she pulled him down onto the cot, the wish to heal and the need to feel flesh against flesh blending to become one overwhelming compulsion.

"Are you sure, Artemis?" he murmured. "You don't have to do this, just because I—"

In answer, she kissed him. After a moment he yielded, slipping his tongue inside her mouth. She took it gladly, hungrily. He eased himself over her, resting his weight on his hands, grazing her breast with his chest. Even that slight contact brought her nipples to aching peaks. Everything they had done in the woods returned to her in a burst of light and lust.

His lips left hers, brushing her cheeks and teasing the lobe of her ear. He suckled ever so gently, tugging, awakening a sympathetic response in her nipples.

"Garret," she whispered.

He withdrew. His face was flushed, his eyes unfocused.

"Touch me," she said. "*Touch* me."

He rolled onto his side, watching her face as he rested

his palm just above her breasts. Her heart felt as if it would leap right into his hand. He teased loose the uppermost button of her sturdy, shapeless shirt and parted the plackets. His fingers slid into the gap and traced tiny circles, sending wild shivers along the length of her spine. Garret was not so hesitant after that. He undid one button and then another, discovering that she wore no bra. He grazed one nipple with his fingertip. She arched and gasped. He lifted her and slipped the shirt back over her shoulders. Then he eased her back down and began to stroke her breasts, the calluses on his fingertips only heightening the erotic sensation. She bit her lip and closed her eyes.

"Am I too rough?" he asked.

She took his wrist and pressed his palm over her right breast. He bent over her and flicked his tongue over the peak of her nipple. Pleasure radiated outward to every point of her body, and a rush of heat blossomed between her thighs. She tilted her head back, breathing deeply as he drew her nipple into his mouth and suckled more vigorously, moving from one breast to the other until both were thoroughly tender and the smallest touch set her gasping. She was so lost in sensation that she moved more by instinct than thought when he reached down and unzipped her pants. He slipped them down over her hips, leaving her underpants the only physical barrier between him and her naked flesh.

Her emotional barriers, too, were giving way. His sorrow was beginning to ease. Giving herself, letting him give, was a balm to his grief. And to her own.

Thought gave way to pure sensation as his fingers slipped inside her underpants and found the slick wetness beneath. She moaned, and he stroked the swollen lips at her entrance, running his fingers up and down the cleft without probing deeper. It was the sweetest torment, unbearable excitement.

Her pleasure heightened his and echoed back to her. She whimpered as his thumb slid over the nub that could bring so much ecstasy. He pinched and released, stroked and withdrew. Artemis began to shudder.

It was coming too soon. She didn't want it, not this way, not with him still outside her. Even when he found her entrance and slid his finger into it, she kept enough of her sense to remember how much she needed to know that he had become a part of her.

"You're tight," he said. "So tight."

"Garret, I… I want…"

He kissed her lips and forehead, and began the caresses all over again. Then he was removing the last of her clothing, and his warm breath was where his fingers had been. His mouth pressed against her, and then his tongue glided over the same moist, plump flesh his fingers had explored. She couldn't stop the cries of pleasure as he flicked his tongue up and down, licking up the wetness with relish, thrusting his tongue inside until she could think only of feeling his hardness filling her to the brim.

She didn't have to find the words. His desire and tenderness filled her mind. When he paused, it was only to remove his clothing and lie naked beside her.

Almost shyly, she reached down to touch him. He inhaled sharply, raised himself onto his arms and crouched over her, his hips above the cradle of her spread thighs.

Let go.

She let him feel everything she had withheld from him since their last sexual encounter. His eyes widened, a look of wonder crossing his face. His aura awakened, shimmering over his head and shoulders. With infinite care he eased down, the head of his cock, hot and full, just grazing her. When he entered, it was like a homecoming, a fulfillment of dreams she had never held long enough to discard.

The rhythm was gentle at first, testing her readiness. He leaned down to kiss the corner of her mouth. "Artemis…"

Then he said no more. He tilted back his head and moved more quickly, gliding in and out more forcefully but never so strongly as to cause her anything but the utmost pleasure. She found herself moving with him, arching into his thrusts, joining a dance whose steps she had almost forgotten. Their emotions intertwined, strengthened each other, built toward a pinnacle of joy just as before. The ecstatic tension expanded as Garret's motions grew more urgent.

Artemis knew it was nearly over, and she didn't want it to be. She tried to hold him inside. He paused, breathing fast, and then thrust again, shuddering as he reached his completion. She experienced it as if it were her own. Her hips lifted, and she cried out, waves of indescribable sensation pulsing outward from her core.

Garret withdrew and rolled onto his side, one arm draped possessively over her waist.

"My God," he breathed. "What's happening to us?"

Chapter 14

It wouldn't be so difficult to tell him now, Artemis thought, gradually settling back into her own body. She ached, inside and out, but the joy was there, pushing the pain and sorrow out of her mind—and his.

But she couldn't spoil this moment with explanations that might make him consider the implications of what she—they—had done. If she told him of her empathic abilities and the new bond between them, this peace would come to an end. Even if he accepted, there would be questions. Too many questions.

So she remained silent. His arm lay heavy on her ribs, and his breathing slowed into the cadence of sleep. She turned her head to look at his face. So peaceful now, the harsh lines of experience and adversity softened with contentment. He didn't hear her as she collected her clothes, put them on and left the cabin.

She was fortunate. There were still Opiri and a few humans about, but they only glanced at her and went about their business.

After a brief search, she found Pericles in a small building similar to the one in which she had been imprisoned. If there had been a guard, he had abandoned his post. No one saw her break the lock and enter.

"Artemis?" Pericles said from behind the cell door.

"Yes," she said. "Are you well?"

"They haven't hurt me." The door creaked as he leaned against it. "They questioned me. They believe I've been involved in stealing other children."

"Have you?"

"No! They have me confused with someone else."

She laid her palms flat on the wood as if she could draw his innermost thoughts through the door and feel the truth of his words.

"We tried to make the commander understand how you saved Beth and helped us take care of her," she said.

"It didn't do any good, did it?"

He sounded so small and sad that Artemis was racked by a fresh pang of guilt. "Many of the colonists have spoken against you," she said.

"I'm not who they think I am," he said, his voice rising. "Why would I have come anywhere near this place if I thought they would accuse me?" He gulped in a breath. "Artemis, tell them that if they let me go, I can help them. I can make myself useful to some other pack and try to learn more about why they want the children. If I can get to this place in the north, maybe I can report back to you before you arrive."

Artemis closed her eyes. "Pericles—"

"They'll have to kill me, Artemis," he said. "They won't let me go, and they can't keep me in this cell forever."

Daniel had said that Pericles's fate wouldn't be determined until he returned from helping Garret find Timon, but Artemis had never doubted what he meant. Pericles would die.

Unless she set him free.

She backed away from the door and leaned against the opposite wall. A mistake now would not only betray Garret but possibly put other half-blood children in danger.

Even if she tried to use her empathy now, it had never worked as a simple lie detector. She had to rely on her own judgment. If she surrendered all belief in that judgment and assumed that Pericles was the villain Daniel believed him to be, she would lose the dream she had refused to abandon for so long.

"There's something else," Pericles said, his voice dropping to a whisper. "Did you know that they've got other Freeblood prisoners here, in another building?"

Artemis started. "What?"

"I think it's a secret from everyone but a few of their leaders. There are five of them, and I was in a cell next to them for a little while, before the humans took me out to question me."

"They must have been captured during one of the rogues' attacks on Delos."

"The prisoners say they weren't part of any attack and were taken because they were mistaken for the ones who are trying to break in. They say that the rogues outside want to kill them, because they're opposed to what the child-stealers are doing."

The story sounded utterly implausible to Artemis. "Opposed? In what way?"

"The same way we are. Why should we be the only ones?" He took a breath. "Listen to me, Artemis. They're like these colonists, working against the thieves, but from a different direction. Isn't that important?"

A bud of hope formed somewhere beneath Artemis's ribs. "Have you ever met these Freebloods before?" she asked.

"I didn't see their faces," Pericles said. "Their voices weren't familiar."

"Then why did they confide in you?"

"I don't know," Pericles admitted.

"What did you tell them about yourself?"

"Just that I was being held for things I didn't do."

"Did they know how you came to be here and think that you could help them?"

"I don't know!" Pericles said, frustration rising in his voice. "They said that when they tried to explain why they were in the area, the leaders here didn't believe them, just like they don't believe me. Or you."

"Garret's wife, a Bloodlady, was killed by Freeblood raiders."

There was a thump from behind the door as Pericles sat heavily on his cot. "He had an Opir mate?" he asked. "I didn't know."

"I did not know, either, until a very short time ago," she said. "You can see that he has reasons for mistrusting Freebloods."

"But he still helped us," Pericles said. The cot creaked as he got up again. "Why are the leaders here keeping these prisoners a secret? What if they *know* these Opiri really are working against the rogues but can't admit that there are Freebloods who aren't their enemies?"

"You are suggesting some kind of conspiracy," Artemis said. "Daniel, the leader of the colony, has no love for Freebloods, either, but I see no reason to believe that he would deliberately hide evidence that some might be allies."

"Then why did you tell him that you're a Bloodlady? You must not have believed he'd treat you fairly if you told him the truth."

She wondered how Pericles had learned what Garret had done. "It was Garret's decision," she said. "He did not consult me in advance."

"But you aren't a prisoner, are you?" Pericles asked with uncharacteristic bitterness.

"You assume too much," she said. "You still know only what other Freebloods have told you, without objective evidence of any kind."

"You want to believe that we can live differently than we always have," Pericles said. "You're looking for Freebloods who can see something beyond their own ability to obtain serfs and rise to become Bloodlords. Maybe these prisoners are what you've been looking for.

"Talk to them," Pericles urged. "Just listen to what they have to say."

"I doubt I would be permitted to see them if they are being held in secret," Artemis said. "But I will do what I can."

"Thank you," he said.

His relief was so obvious that Artemis was glad that she could give him some measure of peace at such a terrible time. But now she had to determine how to gain access to the other prisoners.

Asking Daniel directly was out of the question, and she wouldn't expect Garret to intercede for her, which would undoubtedly arouse suspicion.

Keeping low, she peered out the jail door. The guard, if there had been one, hadn't returned, but there was a change in the air, an electric tension that didn't make sense to her until she saw a woman running from one of the barracks, a rifle clutched in her hands.

Alarm. Fear. The rise of adrenaline in bloodstreams, the instincts of fight or flight.

She shrank back inside the door until the woman was out of sight and then slipped out. As she worked to hide the damage to the lock, raised voices echoed across the compound, and other figures—male and female, human and Opir—began to spill out into the commons from the surrounding buildings.

Something was wrong, and Artemis suspected she knew what it was. She was just turning back toward the cabin when Garret walked into view, obviously looking for her. As she raised her hand to catch his attention, a bell began to ring from somewhere along the walls. Colonists armed with rifles and compound bows dashed toward the front gate and ramparts.

Garret saw Artemis and jogged toward her. "Where have you been?" he asked, gripping her arms. His concern swept over her, possessive and a little afraid. "When I woke up, and you weren't there…"

"I wanted to walk a little," she said, her body responding almost instantly to his touch and his scent and the vivid memory of their lovemaking. "I didn't mean to worry you."

"I know you can take care of yourself," he said. "But I don't like to think I did something to scare you away."

"What you did," she said, "was anything but frightening. But I…" She hesitated, faced by an unpalatable decision. "I was too inclined to continue, and I knew you needed your rest."

"You thought I wasn't up to it?" he asked, drawing his fingers over her cheeks and lips. "You look much better. I hope I had something to do with that."

A part of her reveled in the desire in his voice and mind, the slightly rough texture of his fingertips, the way his body so clearly reacted to her presence. She wanted to run back to the cabin and begin all over again.

But the bell was still ringing, and neither one of them could ignore what it must portend. She covered his hand with hers and clasped his fingers.

"What has happened?" she asked.

A little of the brightness left Garret's eyes, and his emotions darkened. "A Freeblood attack," he said. "Daniel knew another one would be coming soon. There's not much chance that the rogues can break in, but everyone who can fight is taking up defensive positions."

"Does Daniel know why these rogues continue to attack when they have so little chance of succeeding?" she asked, thinking of what Pericles had told her.

"We didn't discuss it," Garret said with a frown. "But whatever they want, they have to be reminded that they're the ones who suffer most in these attacks. If enough of them die, they may give up."

Artemis looked away. "I'm sorry," Garret said, clearly

meaning it, "But they're as much a threat to you as to anyone else here." He cupped her chin. "You're not expected to fight, but I have to help the colonists. If you want to do something, you can stay with the children and the noncombatants who are looking after them. I'll be on the stockade."

He kissed her, hard and fast, and then was gone. Artemis felt cold inside, as if his kiss had pulled all the warmth out of her body. Letting him fight alone felt utterly wrong to her, and she knew it wasn't impossible that he could be hurt.

But the odds were small, and the colony didn't appear to be in any serious danger.

There was still another way she might make a difference.

Coming to a decision, she began to search. Pericles had said that the prisoners were hidden, so it didn't seem likely that they would be in the obvious place.

In the chaos of the colonists' response to the rogues' attack, no one seemed to notice that she was heading away from the battle. Nevertheless, she walked briskly and with a show of purpose until she was among the storage buildings and more extensive gardens close to the northern wall, where the compound abutted the river and the fortified bridge. A handful of soldiers were patrolling the parapet there, but their attention was focused outward.

Artemis moved among the buildings, listening and scenting the air. If Daniel meant to hide the prisoners from the Opiri colonists, he would have needed to muffle smell as well as sound.

In the end, she found that only one of the buildings was guarded. A single apparently human soldier paced back and forth in front of the door, his attention clearly focused on the sounds of the battle he hadn't been permitted to join.

Unless the structure contained some treasure of greater worth than the children of Delos, Artemis thought, it must hold the secret prisoners.

Now she had another choice to make, and a dangerous one. Under the circumstances, she couldn't imagine that the guard would simply let a stranger in to see captives she should not even know existed. But if she forced her way in…

Artemis almost turned back. But a powerful feeling of something very like compulsion sent her running between the doused torches, creeping in the shadows and using all her survival skills to reach the side of the building, just out of the guard's sight. She waited until her breathing was steady again and then inched forward until she was only a few feet away from the soldier.

She struck the human with carefully measured strength, caught him as he began to fall and laid him out on the ground. A set of keys hung on his belt. She found the right one, opened the lock and carried the guard inside the building, laying him down gently.

She knew at once that Pericles had been correct: there were five Opiri here, each one in a separate cell.

"Who are you?" a male voice asked. The others shifted and murmured.

Of course they would know by her scent that she was not their usual guard, Artemis thought. She hesitated again, wondering how to begin.

"You are one of us," the voice said. It held a vibrant, commanding note that suggested an Opir of age and experience, reminiscent of a Bloodlord or Bloodmaster rather than a typical Freeblood.

It was also eerily familiar.

"I spoke to Pericles," she said, bypassing unnecessary explanations. "He conveyed to me what you had claimed about your opposition to the rogues who are stealing halfblood children."

There was a measure of silence as the speaker absorbed her words. "What Pericles told you is correct," he said. "But who are *you*?"

"Someone who also opposes the rogues," she said.

"But you are not human."

"I am Opir," she said.

"Not from this colony."

Artemis approached the speaker's cell. "How do you know?" she asked.

"You are the Opir who arrived with the human, are you not?"

Realizing she had already revealed too much, Artemis saw no reason to lie. "Yes," she said.

"And you trust Pericles?"

"I did not know that he was an accused child-stealer."

"So the humans claim," the speaker said. "What is your relationship to the human who came with you?"

Naturally the Freeblood would detect Garret's scent on her body. "We are searching for a child taken by the rogues," she said, dodging his question.

"Then that is why the half-blood commander came to question us."

"Did you tell him what you told Pericles?" she asked.

"We told him and were not believed." Artemis heard fabric rustle as he moved behind the door. "They will not believe we could be working for a common cause."

"And how are you doing this?" she asked. "Are you fighting those who steal innocents? Are you freeing children?"

"We are still gathering others who share our beliefs," he said, "convincing them that this wholesale abduction will only lead to another war that may destroy us all."

"And that is your sole purpose? To prevent another war?"

"No. That is, not all of it. We believe that Freebloods need not be rogues, killing each other over humans and accepting either a short, brutish life or a constant struggle to maintain status in the stagnant world of the Citadels. We believe there is another—"

"Another way," Artemis interrupted. "You sound very much like someone I used to know."

"I *do* know you," he said. "I know why you were exiled from Oceanus."

"Then everything you say is merely tailored to win my sympathy," she said. "I cannot help you." She spun on her heel and headed for the door.

"Wait!" he called after her. Fingers scraped at the hatch over the aperture cut into his door. "I know you have a gift. Touch my hand."

She froze, her heartbeat slamming to a halt. Almost as if drawn by some ancient sorcery, she drifted back to the cell door and opened the hatch.

The face she saw through the opening was not one she recognized. But when he pushed long, slender fingers through the gap and she touched them, she knew.

"Kron—" she began.

"My real name is not known here," he said. "I go by the name Nomos. The world believes that Kronos is dead, and now I am known as a Freeblood. But if you still believe as I do, you realize that the words I speak are true."

Artemis didn't bother saying it wasn't possible. It clearly was. Kronos had not died in challenge. He had left Oceanus alive. He had changed his face—with genetic manipulation, or with surgery—and his name. He was in hiding.

And he was…he *must* be doing the work he claimed, the same work she had tried to take up in his absence.

What if they know these Opiri really are working against the rogues but can't admit that there are Freebloods who aren't their enemies? Pericles had asked. She'd scoffed at the idea of such a conspiracy. But now?

"Can you get us out, Artemis?" Kronos asked. "I fear that if you do not, our fate will be the same as that of every other Freeblood prisoner Daniel and his soldiers have ever taken alive."

She closed her eyes. The question was no surprise to her. What came as a shock was the depth of feeling she still had for her former master, the sense of obligation and loyalty even his supposed death had not erased. Kronos had been family to her when all her old human connections had vanished along with her humanity.

"I know you must feel I abandoned you," he said. "I escaped, leaving you to do the work in Oceanus. I only learned much later that you had been exiled. I spoke to many Freebloods, and heard that you were in the south. I was hoping to find you, Artemis. To have you at my side again."

"You were looking for me when you were captured?" she whispered.

"It was one of my goals," he said. "As the humans say, 'in the wrong place at the wrong time.' But now we can work together to end this madness and lead the most oppressed Opiri from the path of ruination." He pressed his face close to the aperture. "You are our only hope."

Backing away from the door, she wrapped her arms around her chest. Old loyalties and new. They were in direct conflict, and she knew she had no hope of convincing Daniel that these Opiri were speaking the truth. Though she might make Garret believe her, she would only force him to turn against his friend.

"It is the human, isn't it?" Kronos asked, sympathy in his voice. "You have some affection for him. Pericles said that he saved your life."

"He did."

"And yet it is more than that. You were never like my other vassals, Artemis. In so many ways."

She banged her fist against the wall. "Rogues are attacking the colony as we speak," she said. "There is no time—"

"No time," he repeated softly. "Help me, Artemis."

"And if I do? What will *you* do?"

"Go north. Try to discover a way to organize a resistance to this Bloodlord who takes children. I have developed contacts over a wide region, and you know that I can make other Opiri listen to me. That is why they tried to kill me in Oceanus. Let me try, Artemis."

He was right, she thought. If anyone could persuade other exiles to turn against the child-stealers, it would be Kronos. He could be instrumental in saving Timon and every other child who had been taken. He could unite Freebloods as she never could, even with her abilities. And in any case, her empathy had proven to be far more a burden than a gift.

"I will," she said. She glanced at the guard who, to her great relief, was beginning to move slightly. "This may be your only chance to escape. But you must swear to me, Kronos, that you will not harm any of the people in this colony as you leave it."

"If we must fight," he said, "we will take great care not to do lasting harm to anyone here."

Artemis knew she couldn't ask for more. And since she would be with him and his disciples, she would do everything within her power to make sure that such fighting wouldn't be necessary.

Stepping carefully over the guard, she looked out the door. The battle outside clearly hadn't ended, and there was still no sign of colonists in this part of the compound. Backed by the river as it was, the eastern wall had been left untouched by the attacking Freebloods. But the sky had taken on the faintest tint of light, and soon the rogues outside would be compelled to retreat.

She unlocked the door to Kronos's cell. She didn't waste any time dwelling on his changed appearance or their strange reunion, but quickly released the other four Freebloods. The two females and two males were clearly ready to move as soon as Kronos gave the command.

"There will be no room for mistakes," she said to them, hoping that Kronos had chosen his allies well. "We must get to the woods before daylight. We will go straight over the wall and into the water."

"We?" Kronos asked.

"I am coming with you."

Chapter 15

"You will abandon your human friend?" Kronos asked.

"The guard didn't see me," she said, "but Daniel will certainly realize that I am the one who released you. If I allow Garret to defend me, I will put him in an untenable position."

Kronos nodded gravely. "And Pericles?"

"We have no time to save him," she said, fighting desperately against paralyzing grief, anger and guilt.

"It is unfortunate," Kronos said, "but I believe that he will gladly make the sacrifice."

Artemis grabbed one of the daycoats hung outside the cell and tossed it to Kronos, while his disciples claimed the others. There wasn't one left for her, but she trusted in her well-honed ability to get to cover before the sun rose.

"I will go first," she said, "and try to distract the guards on the wall. Stay behind me until I give the signal."

She left the building as she had approached it, crouching low as she ran, and made straight for the eastern wall.

"You!" she called, waving at the nearest of the four guards. Once she'd caught his attention, she said, "I was sent to tell you that rogues have gotten into the compound, and that all soldiers must report immediately to the front gate!"

The dhampir hesitated, eyes narrowed as he studied her face. "Lady Aresia?" he asked. "Why did they send you with this message?"

"No one else could be spared. Daniel says that you must come!"

Someone behind Artemis darted forward, passed her in a blur and launched himself up the stairway close to where the dhampir stood. The guard never saw him coming. The dhampir fell onto the parapet walk, and the Freeblood crouched beside the still body, his expression tense with excitement and fear.

Furious that the exile had acted without her signal, Artemis started forward. But the other three guards were charging the Freeblood, and Kronos's disciples leaped up the steps to confront them. Artemis joined them in time to watch the brief struggle, prepared to interfere the instant one of the exiles acted too forcefully.

But they were skilled, and kept Kronos's promise. They took the soldiers down with carefully calibrated blows that rendered them temporarily unconscious, as she'd done with the guard at the storage building. She quickly checked the dhampir's pulse, and found it strong and even. He would wake within minutes.

"We must jump," she said as Kronos came to stand beside her. He nodded and signaled to the others. Together, the six of them leaped over the wall. Shouts of anger rang from the stockade.

Artemis rolled as she struck the ground and plunged over the riverbank into the water. The bridge loomed over her to the right. Kronos splashed down beside her, and she heard the others nearby. They turned left, wading parallel to the bank as bullets cut the surface of the river directly behind them.

Then, suddenly, the barrage stopped. Artemis could no longer hear raised voices or the chatter of weapons. The sky was growing lighter. Trees bunched thickly along the riverside beyond the area the colonists had cleared around the walls, the only real shelter in sight.

She and Kronos clambered onto the bank and ran toward the hills to the west, his followers on their heels. She began to feel ill halfway across the clearing, and by the time they made it to the trees she knew that her body was rejecting the blood she had taken from Johan.

It isn't the blood, she thought. It simply wasn't the *right* blood.

She kept running alongside the others as they weaved their way through the remains of a once-thriving city. Dawn brightened the sky behind them. At last they found an old warehouse with three walls, a back door and part of its roof intact, and settled deep in the shadows. Artemis found herself panting and sweating, her stomach struggling to empty its contents.

"Have you not fed?" Kronos asked, crouching beside her.

"How did they feed *you*?"

"Animals," Kronos said. "But of course that is how we have been getting our nourishment for some time now."

Artemis knew him too well to miss the slight curl of his lip when he spoke the words, but she was deeply relieved. Of course they had agreed on the need to end Opir dependence on human blood, but that had been a matter of philosophy rather than practice within the Citadel, where there were no other sources available. She could not have accepted his hunting humans outside it.

"I am well," she insisted. "But you must keep moving. It would be best for you to continue into the hills and wait for nightfall to cross the Willamette. The colonists will soon be after you, and they have the advantage of daylight."

He frowned. "Why do you say 'you'?" he asked.

Artemis realized that she didn't know exactly when she'd changed her mind. It wasn't the sudden illness, but she was just as certain now that she had to go back as, less than an hour ago, she had been about leaving.

"I can't go," she said. "I should have stayed and tried to explain."

"They will never believe you." Kronos cupped her cheek as Garret had done, but his touch seemed icy on her flushed skin. "You say this only because you believe you will slow us down, but I will not lose you again."

"I'm sorry." She got up, swayed and straightened with a hand braced against the crumbling wall. "I must go back."

"No." He rose and stood in her way as she moved toward the remains of the fallen wall. "Whatever you feel for this human is not worth your life."

"There is shade enough in the forest," she said, "at least for a time. If I cannot stand by my convictions—"

Kronos jerked up his head, silencing her with a raised hand. The sharp rustling of leaves outside the warehouse walls brought the other Freebloods to their feet.

"Human," Kronos said. "He is not making much effort to conceal his approach."

He. She took a breath and shivered. "Go," she said. "I will meet him."

"Artemis—"

"Go!"

With a slow shake of his head, Kronos gestured for the others, who still wore their daycoats, to follow him out the back doorway. Artemis emptied her stomach, cleaned her face and waited tensely.

Garret stepped across the rubble of the fourth wall, his silhouette framed against sunlit trees. He wore heavy clothing, his pack, and her bow and quiver. The VS was slung over his shoulder.

She caught a flash of relief on his face, and then his expression hardened. He looked toward the rear door. "Where are the others?" he asked.

"Gone." She shivered again. "I take full responsibility for their escape."

"Why did they leave you behind?"

"I stayed of my own accord. I had hoped—"

"Don't hope," he said. "And don't try to explain. The attack on the colony is over, and there are already two patrols out searching for you and the prisoners. Since they believe you're my wife, I said I'd look for you."

"How did you explain…?"

"I didn't."

"I will not resist," she said, starting toward him.

"I'm not taking you back."

"If we return, I can try to explain, and you will not become a traitor to your friend and his people."

"I won't let them treat you like a criminal."

"Did I not betray *you*?" she asked.

"You must have had a reason for what you did."

"And if you cannot accept my reason?"

"I've made my choice."

He held her gaze for an uncomfortable length of time. She stared down at her feet, utterly vulnerable to the emotions he unconsciously projected so powerfully.

He knew what he was doing, and what it meant for his own future.

And still he chose *her*.

"We're getting away from here as fast as we can," he said into her silence. "We can't cross the Willamette at Delos, and if we go west to one of the closer bridges we could run right into the patrols. We'll have to try the northwest St. John's Bridge." He unslung the rifle, removed the pack and her weapons, and then pulled off the heavy, hooded coat and tossed it to her, revealing his usual heavy jacket. "We have about six miles to go. Don't let that slip." He nodded at her bow and quiver. "Get your weapons."

Breaking into a jog, he headed northwest parallel to the river. Artemis pulled on the coat, retrieved her weapons and fell in behind him.

"I cannot let you do this," she said.

"You can't stop me," he said, "unless you plan to leave me here half-conscious, like those guards."

"Are they all right?"

"Yes. I'm guessing you did your best to make sure of that."

She felt light-headed. "I am glad," she said.

He stared straight ahead. "I think we'd better pick up the pace. Can you keep up?"

"I was not injured."

Garret began to run, choosing the clearest path between the trees and dodging the thick patches of undergrowth. Artemis listened for pursuit and heard movement some distance behind. She had no idea if the followers were rogue Freebloods or colony soldiers, and she didn't want to find out.

What had become of Kronos?

"We're coming to the end of the woods," Garret said, slowing down as he spoke. "Put your hood up."

She did as he asked. The woods ended abruptly at the edge of a vast expanse of fallen buildings, disintegrated asphalt and cracked concrete, through which smaller trees had forced their way. Sunlight beat down on the broken surface like a hammer.

Garret grabbed her arm and roughly pulled a pair of oversize gloves over her hands. "With luck," he said, "the rogues will stay well away from here, and Daniel's patrols won't expect us to cross open ground. We may get a little farther ahead of them."

"Garret—" she began.

"Let's go." He took her hand, and then they were flying across the urban plain, Garret pulling her along as if he were some unstoppable machine. She nearly fell several times, and only his desperate strength kept her on her feet. They paused once or twice in the shade of structures that hadn't completely crumbled, but he kept them moving with relentless determination.

When they reached the wooded area on the other side of the tract, Artemis was only slightly burned where the coat and hood had slipped once or twice, but she was weak from her reaction to the blood, and the world rushing by began to tilt and spin. Garret slowed, swept her up in his arms and continued to run until it was obvious that he had exhausted his own strength.

They collapsed near a thicket of densely interwoven brambles. She could smell the river nearby, but the scent only made her empty stomach heave again. Garret drew his hunting knife and hacked at the branches, making a shallow hollow into which he could push her. She resisted, realized it was futile and let him tuck her into the cramped space. Breathing hard, he laid the rifle on the ground beside him and pulled off his pack.

"Drink," he said, pushing a canteen into her hands.

She held the canteen and stared at it blankly. "You should go back," she said. "Daniel said he would help you find Timon."

He turned his head just enough so that she could see his strong profile against the dim light filtering through the trees. "We can't stay here long," he said. "It would be better if you rest."

"Did he blame you for my escape?" she asked.

"It doesn't matter."

"But I want you to understand. One of the prisoners was the Bloodlord who saved my life over two centuries ago, when I was human, after the Opir who nearly drained my blood left me for dead."

"It sounds like a long story," he said. His voice was heavy, and she realized how fantastic the explanation must sound.

"I know it seems to be an amazing coincidence," she said earnestly. "But I had thought him dead for years. I was not only his vassal for decades…he gave me reason to live when I had lost everything." She leaned toward Garret. "You have always wondered why I maintained such faith in my fellow Freebloods. Kro—" She paused, remembering that Kronos was using an alias. She felt she had to respect his wishes, even with Garret. "Nomos wanted to alter the inequitable structure of Opir society. The work he and I carried out together was based upon the idea that Freebloods might be taught a better way than they know in the Citadels, and that such a way might lead to peace with humanity and true freedom for all."

"A way that didn't involve dependence on human blood."

"Yes."

Garret ran a hand through his stiff hair. "I knew he couldn't have been a Freeblood himself."

"He had his own Household in Oceanus, but he was compelled to leave the Citadel because of his teachings. He has been posing as a Freeblood to evade his enemies. Believe me, Garret, he was the last Opir I ever expected to meet."

The emotions she sensed from Garret were so contradictory that she couldn't begin to untangle them. Fresh queasiness settled in the pit of her stomach.

"Did he tell you that I questioned him?" he asked.

"Yes. He said he tried to convince you and Daniel that he was opposed to the stealing of half-blood children."

"We had no reason to accept his story."

Her throat felt as if invisible hands had slipped a rope around it and were tightening it bit by bit. "Nomos is a good Opir, Garret."

"He wants to prevent another war...or so he said."

"That has always been his goal," Artemis said. "And mine."

For the first time since they had made love again, Garret's aura flickered to life, dancing wildly around his body. "I was sure you felt you had a good reason for helping them escape." He looked up through the tattered leaves at a patch of bright morning sky. "Do you know where Nomos has gone?"

Just for a moment, she doubted him. She considered the possibility that he wanted her to tell him so that he and Daniel could track Kronos down, recapture him…

Garret's aura contracted like a wounded animal seeking shelter. He looked at her, a peculiar expression on his face.

Then his emotions hit her all at once, and she knew how badly she had wounded him with her unfounded, unforgivable doubts. Doubts *he* had felt as clearly as she felt his pain. The queasy sensation in her belly turned to full-blown nausea.

He had not only sensed her feelings the way he sometimes seemed to do when they were closest, she had *projected*, pushing her emotions outward without conscious effort. He could not have defended himself from them without learning to build mental barriers of his own.

The emotional bond made it so simple to forget that she could do such things as easily as she might brush his skin with her fingertips. Their link was by no means growing weaker, in spite of her efforts.

And now she knew that accepting other human blood was not the solution. The blood-bond had already taken hold, in spite of her best efforts. The empathy had made it all the more powerful.

But she didn't dare tell Garret. Not yet. It would be possible to subsist on animal blood for the time being, though it would not be pleasant.

She crawled out of her shelter, determined to face her fears, and projected her regret, hoping that he would absorb and accept it as easily as he had her ugly distrust. "I only know that he also intends to travel to the north," she said.

The tension eased from Garret's face, but his aura remained flat and inert. "If you trust this man so much," he said, "then maybe you'd be better off rejoining him. I don't hold you to your agreement to help me find Timon."

The words seemed angry, but she sensed no blame. He

was not trying to punish her. Still, she nearly doubled over with sickness.

"You *want* me to leave you?" she asked.

Denial sent Garret's aura into another turbulent dance. "I want you to understand that I know I've been hard on you," he said. "I had no right to expect you to be other than what you are."

"I *did* fail you," she whispered, "but not because you expected too much."

"I put you in an impossible position," he said. "I won't do it again."

Artemis turned her head aside and retched again. At once Garret was with her, his arm around her, supporting her head with a gentle hand.

"What's wrong?" he asked, nearly smothering her with his self-recrimination.

Weak and shaking, she tried to push him away. "The sun," she said.

"No." He stroked her hair away from her face. "Artemis, I know you took blood in Delos, but clearly something went wrong. You're not keeping it down."

She wondered how he had learned about Johan's donation. She sensed no anger or jealousy from him, only deep concern.

"There was no need to go elsewhere for blood," he said. "You could have come to me anytime."

"I…didn't want to impair you before we left Delos," she said, scrambling for an explanation. She met his gaze. "Garret, no matter what I have done up to this moment, my loyalty has not altered since the day I promised to come with you. As long as you want me by your side, I will never leave you again."

She felt something inside him let go. His aura flowed over and around her, soft and fierce at the same time. He wiped her mouth with a cloth and cradled her head in the curve of his shoulder.

Against all reason, Garret had believed her. *Did* believe her. And he still wanted her.

"There is something more I must tell you," she said, burrowing more deeply into the protective curve of his body. "Pericles was the one who urged me to speak to the prisoners. He was persuaded by my mentor's story before I knew who Nomos was. Or who he pretended to be. I am no longer certain of Pericles's motives."

"It's a little late to worry about that now. I let him go."

She wriggled out of his arms. "What?"

"I think it was all a setup," he said, his humor evaporating. "I think Daniel still believed you were an enemy, and that you'd tricked me into trusting you. He left Pericles unguarded and only one soldier to watch the other prisoners, expecting you to try to communicate with them. He just didn't anticipate that the rogues outside would cause so much of a distraction, and that you'd be so efficient in helping the other Freebloods." He cleared his throat. "I don't know if he actually believed that Pericles was a child-stealer, but I can't accept anything he told me without wondering how much of it was true."

Real anguish radiated from his mind. If his speculation about Daniel was correct, then his friend had never trusted *him*.

"Perhaps he meant only to protect you," she said.

"Or you were right when you said his experiences made it easier for him to pass judgment on Opiri enemies who fall into his hands."

"Will Beth be safe there?"

"Daniel will protect her with his life. I'm sure someone in the colony will adopt her."

Artemis closed her eyes. "Where is Pericles now?" she asked.

"I told him to run. I don't know where he went." He glanced up at the sky again. "We should move. Do you need blood?"

The idea of telling Garret the truth about the blood-bond still terrified her. *Soon*, she told herself. *Soon*.

"No. I...only had a slight reaction to the other... To Johan's blood. I took enough nourishment."

To her vast relief, he didn't pursue the matter. They gathered their things, and continued west and north through tracts of woodland, decaying city blocks and open areas where buildings had collapsed like fatally wounded soldiers. The shattered road they followed passed through an increasingly narrow neck between the hills and the river. Artemis warned Garret when she heard sounds of pursuit, but those who followed them never seemed to gain much ground. Artemis began to wonder if Daniel was letting them escape.

The thought did not comfort her.

The sun was beginning its westward arc when they reached the bridge Garret had identified as the St. John's. Except there was no bridge at all—nothing but a few pylons still standing on either side of the river.

"We're out of luck," Garret said. "There aren't any other bridges farther west than this one."

She looked up at him. "Can you swim?"

"It must be a good eight hundred feet across here, and I don't know how strong the current is."

"Yes, but can you swim?"

He met her gaze. "In the Enclave, we used to go to Ocean Beach. It was cold, and the currents were dangerous, but we used to dare each other to swim as far out as we could. I usually won."

"I happen to be a very good swimmer. I believe I can beat you," she said, pretending her body hadn't just decided to declare war against her.

Chapter 16

Garret's approval rode on waves of warmth and admiration. Artemis basked in it the way a human might bask in the sun, forgetting the hollow feeling in her body and the hunger that had returned with such a vengeance.

"We'll need to wait until nightfall," he said, "or you'll be too exposed. But I accept that challenge."

She smiled. Moving as quickly as an Opir, he grabbed her and captured her mouth with his. Her knees nearly buckled with the force of her desire and relief and happiness. And *his*, pouring into her through their kiss. Hard muscle—and more—pressed against her, raising an exquisite ache in her nipples and between her thighs.

When they separated at last, she could still feel him all through her body. And it wasn't enough. She wanted to find the nearest shelter, fall with him to the ground—soft or hard, wet or dry—and join with him, with no thought to the consequences.

But Garret had more sense than she did. He led her away from the river in search of a safe place to wait out the rest of the day. The hours passed with no sign of their pursuers, and at sunset they returned to the riverbank.

It was a hard swim. Artemis was most concerned about Garret's exposure to the frigid waters of the river, but he swam strongly and reached the other side without faltering, beating her by two yards. She insisted that they build a small, sheltered fire while their clothing dried. He slept the sleep of exhaustion while she watched, and by dawn they were ready to move again.

Before the detour to Delos, they had originally planned

to cross the Columbia River at Government Island. But they agreed to take a chance on the shorter route to the bridge at Hayden Island, some five miles to the northeast. They cut across a neighborhood that had been old and worn even before the War, then waded through a slough and a soggy wetland onto the abandoned marina beside the Columbia River.

The bridge itself was impassable. A large portion of the first span had tumbled into the river, leaving half a mile of unbroken water from the buckled road on which they stood to the bank of Hayden Island.

"The damage seems recent," Artemis said. "Could the colonists have destroyed it in order to prevent the child-stealers from traveling north by this route?"

"It's possible," Garret said, a grim set to his mouth. "We have to assume that the bridge is down on the other side, as well. It'll be much too wide to swim across there, even if the currents aren't too powerful and we make it to the island. We'll have to head for the bridge at Government Island and hope it's still standing."

"If the colonists know of this," Artemis said, "they may be waiting there."

"It's a chance we'll have to take." He squinted at the sun. "It's only about ten miles to the southeast as the crow flies, but we don't want to push too hard, or we'll be useless if it comes to another fight." He eyed her critically. "Artemis…"

"I am well," she said. *But not for much longer.* "Let us continue as long as we can."

He nodded, accepting her word, and gestured for her to precede him.

The Glenn L. Jackson Memorial Bridge was empty.

Not, Garret suspected, that it had been that way for long. Though portions of the span had fallen away and the rest was badly rusted, the buckled road rising onto it was guarded by a small, fortified brick building, barely large enough to house a dozen people but strategically placed so that no one could pass without coming under fire.

"Do you sense anything?" he asked Artemis, who crouched beside him in the thick brush encroaching on the old freeway.

"No," she said. She wrinkled her nose. "There were humans here not long ago. Opiri and half-bloods, as well. But they have been gone for some time, perhaps as much as half a day."

"If Daniel got word to them to stop us," he said, "they wouldn't have deserted their post."

She gazed at him, a trace of anxiety lingering in her eyes. He guessed what she was thinking. Sometimes it felt as if he knew every single thing she was feeling.

Including what she felt for *him*. He wasn't sure when it had happened, just as he wasn't sure when he'd realized how much he cared for her. The way she'd looked after Beth and Pericles, her courage, her capacity for compassion, the way it felt when he and Artemis made love—with all the closeness and joy that came so easily to them when they touched—had convinced him that his ability to care for another woman hadn't died with Roxana.

Still, though he couldn't conceive of feeling this way about any other living woman, there was a hole in his heart that had scarred over, impenetrable and hard as stone. Inside that hole were words he couldn't speak, that he never expected to speak again.

But that didn't change his need for Artemis, even though he feared that this ugly conflict might finally come between them.

Not if she keeps her word never to leave me, he thought. If they survived all this, if he got Timon back and found some way to make Artemis happy…

"I do not smell blood," she said, relieving him of

thoughts he didn't want to examine too closely. "At least not…" She hesitated, biting her lip. "At least not in quantities that would suggest death."

"No bodies, and no killing," Garret said. It should have been good news, but he knew—as Artemis clearly did—that something was very wrong.

"Did Nomos pass this way?" he asked.

"I think—" Artemis released her breath in a sharp puff. "There *are* Opiri nearby," she said.

"Where?" he asked, scanning the area intently.

"Behind us."

They rose and turned as one, facing south toward the labyrinth of intersecting freeways and ramps that ended at the riverbank.

"We can try to cross before they get to us," Garret said.

"There are several of them," she said. "If they are hunting us, they will not stop."

"And if they catch us on the bridge or the island, we'll be at a disadvantage."

Artemis picked up her bow and nocked an arrow. Garret checked over the VS and held it muzzle down, but he could see Artemis stiffen.

"I won't use it unless I have to," he said. "If they're rogues, I may not have a choice."

"And if they are from the colony?"

"I won't let them take you."

"Garret—" she began. She broke off, lifting her head. "They are not enemies."

He knew what she was about to say. "Nomos," he said.

"Yes." She lowered the bow. "They are no danger to either one of us."

But how the hell did they get here after us? Garret thought.

Releasing his grip on the rifle, he tried to relax. He'd chosen to suppress his doubts and accept Artemis's faith in this Opir. Now he had to put his commitment to the test.

"I will meet him," she said, starting forward.

He put out his arm to stop her. "Wait."

The Opiri emerged from the woods rising around the freeway—nine, not the five who had been imprisoned in the colony. There wasn't enough light left for Garret to make out faces, but he didn't doubt that the one in the lead was Nomos.

"It is all right," Artemis said. Her voice was breathy with excitement. Before Garret could stop her again, she began to run toward the Opiri. They stopped when Artemis reached them, and she gestured toward Garret with an expressive wave of her arm.

The leader inclined his head, and the Opiri continued toward Garret, Artemis speaking to her former sire with great animation as she walked beside him. It was obvious to Garret that the two Nightsiders had been very close. He could see the rapport between them even though he couldn't hear their conversation.

No wonder she had set him free.

His body chose that moment to ignore the advice of his mind and he tensed up again, instinctively preparing for a fight. Or a challenge to a rival. A challenge any Nightsider would sense within a dozen yards of him.

He let the rifle swing back on its strap and held himself still as Artemis and Nomos approached. Now that he was no longer in a cell, the Opir—with his handsome, ageless face and long white hair drawn back in a queue—seemed more like the elite Bloodmasters Garret had known in Erebus. He exuded authority and the natural arrogance of his kind.

And when he looked at Garret, there was no particular friendliness in his eyes, even when he smiled with his teeth carefully hidden.

"Garret Fox," he said, extending his hand in the human way. "Artemis has spoken of you in the most glowing terms.

It's fortunate that we have been given the opportunity to meet again under more favorable circumstances."

"I assume you weren't lying about stealing children."

"Garret," Artemis said, casting him a reproachful glance.

Nomos laughed. "You have courage, even when you aren't on the other side of a cell door," he said. He nodded at the VS. "Or is it the weapon that gives you such confidence?"

Artemis stepped between them and glared at Nomos. "If it is your intention to bait Garret…"

"I apologize," Nomos said, brushing his fingers across Artemis's cheek. "My experiences in Delos have somewhat soured my mood." He nodded regally to Garret. "You saved her life. That alone earns my gratitude."

Shove your gratitude, Garret thought. But he knew he was being irrational. The sight of Nomos touching Artemis fed his visceral dislike, but he couldn't trust his emotions where she was concerned.

Belatedly Garret remembered the outpost and looked over his shoulder. No sound, no movement. If there had been a single living soul left in the place, they would have reacted by now. And Nomos would know that, just as Artemis had.

"You needn't be concerned with those who kept watch here," Nomos said, following his gaze. "We convinced them that retreat was the better part of valor."

"You were here before?" Artemis asked, taking a step away from Nomos. "You attacked them?"

Garret touched the barrel of the VS, and Nomos's eyes snapped down to Garret's hand.

"There is no need to be alarmed," the Nightsider said. "I believe they meant to prevent you from crossing. We told them to abandon their station and they would not be harmed." He met Garret's stare. "We even escorted them part of the way back to Delos, so that there would be less chance of their being attacked by rogues fleeing the failed attack on the colony."

"You went back," Artemis said, "even though you said those same rogues wanted to kill you for opposing them?"

"Now that we are free, we are capable of protecting ourselves," Nomos said. "And as we wish to stop our fellow Opiri from provoking another war, it would hardly do to drive the sentinels from shelter and leave them vulnerable." His gaze returned to Artemis. "Have you forgotten the rest of what I said? You can still help me end this threat and save the misguided, desperate Freebloods who have fallen under the power of this madman in the north."

Garret stiffened. "Artemis is with *me*," he said.

"Garret," Artemis said, turning to face him, "Nomos has offered to help us find Timon."

"Has he?" Garret asked, making no attempt to hide his suspicion.

"Of course I would not attempt to interfere with your plans in any way," Nomos said with another smile. "I merely thought that I could be of assistance, and you have proven yourself unlike those humans who, like the leader of Delos, hate all Opiri because of the actions of the worst of us."

"Daniel isn't human," Garret said. "And he doesn't hate all Opiri, but he's had plenty of experience with 'the worst of you.'"

"Garret," Artemis said. She laid her hand on his arm and looked at her mentor. "Nomos, you do not know—"

"It's no matter," Nomos said, speaking to Garret over her head. "I am aware that you and Daniel were serfs, and that you have reasons for your opinions."

"You must have had a longer conversation with him than I realized," Garret said to Artemis.

"I said nothing of that," Artemis protested.

"Do not blame her," Nomos said. "I had already heard of Daniel and determined his motives."

"And what have you determined about *me*?" Garret asked him. "That I don't have a chance of getting my son back without your help?"

Nomos shook his head. "I am not here to bicker with you. I have offered my assistance, and you may accept or not as you choose. But I would suggest that you cross the river quickly, in case Delos sends a larger party to deal with us."

"He's right, Garret," Artemis said. "We should cross while we can."

"And we must hunt," Nomos said. "It would be better if we did so on the other side, if you can tolerate our company for a brief while."

Artemis looked at Garret steadily, watching to see if he would accept her reassurances. He knew he couldn't disappoint her.

"I have no objection," he said. "Artemis said you saved her life when she became an Opir. I'll be very interested to hear the rest of that story, if she's willing to tell it."

"Then let us be on our way," Nomos said. "Oh, and I should correct a misapprehension. My name is Kronos. Nomos was a name I used to conceal my identity from those who wished to kill me. But I am out of their reach— for the present."

He walked past Garret and Artemis, his men and women behind him, and continued onto the bridge until he and the others were lost in darkness.

"I am sorry," Artemis said, reaching for Garret's hand. "I should have told you more about him on our way here. You were not prepared, and neither was he."

"You didn't know we'd meet him again. I didn't exactly make things easier for you."

"And he…" She hesitated, and then rushed on. "He

knows of my connection to you, and he does not completely approve."

"I gathered as much. The feeling is mutual."

She released his hand. "Garret, I will not be fought over as if I were a—"

"Serf?" he said, injecting a little humor into his voice for her sake. "Does he think I'll hurt you, or just that I'm not good enough for you?"

"I do not know what experiences he has had since he escaped Oceanus. He never mistreated humans there, but now he knows what it is like to be hunted by them."

"Why didn't he try to contact you once he escaped?"

"He did not exactly escape. They believed that he had been killed, as I did. I was exiled only after he was declared dead, because of my attempts to carry on our work."

"I'd like to hear about your work," he said, "when we have time for a longer conversation."

Her lips curved in a smile, and he knew he'd said the right thing. "I am glad," she said. "I can tell you that I believe without doubt that Kronos means to resist the Bloodlord in the north and help us find your son, if you permit it."

"And you think he was telling the truth about the people at this post?" he asked.

"Kronos is not a killer." She took his hand again. "But if you choose to go on alone, just the two of us, I will support your decision."

Garret cursed silently. Of course she would. But he would be crazy to reject any advantage that could help him get to Timon, first impressions be damned.

"No," he said. "As long as you think it's safe, we'll take him up on his offer to travel together."

He bent quickly to kiss her, irrationally driven to remind her—and himself—that they had an alliance Kronos could try to break only at his own peril.

They stepped onto the bridge, passing by the post and

continuing over the water. It was black as oil to Garret's eyes, and he could just make out the bulk of the island ahead. They walked through the dense woods and reached the other side of the island without meeting Kronos and his followers.

The second span had been repaired many times, and one fallen section had been rebuilt with wood that had begun to rot. Garret wondered if the Bloodmaster in the north would see to its continued repair to ensure that the flow of children wasn't cut off.

The thought made his stomach churn with rage. As always, Artemis caught his mood. She took his arm.

"We're almost to the other side," she said. "They're waiting for us."

"They must have decided that you'd persuade me to take Kronos up on his offer," Garret said drily.

"He said they had to hunt. Perhaps their need is urgent."

"I suspect that your needs are getting urgent, too," he said as they stepped off the road. "I don't care where you get the blood, as long as it does the job. Why don't you join them?"

"I can't leave you alone."

"If I set up camp close to the bridge, I can watch for anyone coming from the south."

"You will need to sleep."

"I can do that when you get back."

"I will bring you food. I'll speak to Kronos and let him know what we have decided."

They kept going, Garret behind Artemis as they followed the road. As she had predicted, Kronos and his band had stopped not far ahead.

Kronos didn't comment on Garret and Artemis's arrival except to smile at his former vassal and favor Garret with a brief but amiable nod. Artemis spoke to Kronos briefly and returned to Garret.

"He was about to go after the Freebloods he sent to scout for game," she said. "I am welcome to join them."

"Good," Garret said. "Tell him that I'm heading back to the bridge to keep watch."

"He will probably wish to send one of his Opiri to watch with you."

"Tell him that this human can take care of himself. And that it would be better if none of his people suddenly show up when I'm not expecting them."

Her gaze fell to the VS. "I will."

With obvious reluctance, she returned to Kronos. The Bloodlord looked at Garret, gave a very human shrug and beckoned her to accompany him.

The sight of them together triggered irrational jealousy in Garret, and he quickly walked away. Once he'd chosen a place from which to watch the bridge, he made himself as comfortable as possible with his blanket over his shoulders and his back against a tree trunk.

Tired as he was, he didn't intend to be taken by surprise the next time someone approached, friend or enemy. Without the constant distraction of immediate danger—or of Artemis's engaging, alluring and often frustrating company—he had plenty of time to think of what had happened, and what was yet to come.

There had been too many delays in his search for Timon, and he blamed himself for that. If he'd been more alert, he and Artemis would never have been taken by Delos's patrol. There would have been no questions from Daniel and no trap set for Artemis.

But she also wouldn't have seen, with her own eyes, what it could mean when Nightsiders and humans lived in harmony and produced children together…wanted children, raised with love.

He rose abruptly, peering into the darkness toward the bridge, and swung the VS into firing position. Two figures came into view—a male and a female—their eyes catching the moon's faint light like those of night-prowling cats.

Freebloods, Garret thought, but coming from the north. Kronos's followers. They continued to approach until they were a dozen yards away.

"You watch well, human," the male said. "Better than most of your breed."

"What do you want?" Garret asked, holding the rifle steady.

"Why, only to more closely observe the human with whom Artemis seems so enamored," the female said. "Kronos has many questions."

"You weren't with him in Delos," Garret said.

The Nightsiders exchanged glances. "We were not taken prisoner with the others," the male said.

"Well, you'll have plenty of time to satisfy your curiosity," Garret said. "Artemis and I will be traveling with you." He smiled. "Assuming you have no objections."

"Why should we?" The male's gaze fell to the vicinity of Garret's throat. "Are you not from one of the colonies where humans willingly donate their blood to their Opir allies?"

Garret knew that look, and the intent behind the words. "Originally," he said, "but we had a slight difference of opinion."

"Perhaps you would feel safer with company," the female said, flashing her teeth. "The night holds many dangers for your breed."

"I'm fine. And I'm sure Kronos will appreciate your help in the hunt."

Nodding curtly, the male Freeblood made to pass by Garret. Garret turned to keep him in sight, but all at once the female came at him, attacking with superhuman strength and speed.

Chapter 17

Acting even before he could think, Garret reversed the rifle and swung at her. The butt struck her a glancing blow across the forehead, and she staggered. But the male was almost on him, and he had just enough time to turn the VS and jam the rifle's muzzle into the Nightsider's stomach.

The male snarled at him, and the female bared her fangs as she recovered and lunged toward him again. All he had to do was pull the trigger.

Kronos walked up behind the female and casually struck her across the neck. She gagged and fell, alive but disabled.

"You disappoint me, Flavia," Kronos said. He cast the male an icy glare. "Are you all right, Garret?"

"In perfect health," Garret said. "I assume you don't want me to shoot this one?"

"Xenophon has broken my law," Kronos said. "It is your right to kill him, if you wish."

"Step back," Garret said, pushing Xenophon with the rifle. The Nightsider backed away, glanced at Kronos and then ran.

Garret let him go.

"Your mercy does you credit," Kronos said. He glanced down at the female. "I doubt that Flavia will give us any further trouble now that her companion is gone."

Garret lowered the rifle. "They meant to take my blood," he said.

"Yes. As I said, in attacking you they disregarded the rules I have laid down for my followers." He nudged Flavia with the toe of his boot. "Get up," he told her, "and join the others."

She scrambled to her feet and sprinted away.

"Where's Artemis?" Garret asked.

"I had hoped that you and I might speak in private."

"About her?" Garret asked, tensing up again.

Kronos strolled away, his hands clasped behind his back. "About what she and I have worked for and still hope to achieve." He stopped to gaze at the bridge. "She told you of our relationship and my feigned death in Oceanus?"

"She thought you were dead, but instead you abandoned her."

"Yes," Kronos said, regret in his voice. "I did not learn she had been exiled for some time, and I was unable to search for her until recently."

"Recently? As in before you were captured by the colony patrol?"

"Yes." Kronos faced him again. "She had been a close companion for two centuries, devoted to our cause. She spoke of that, as well?"

"She mentioned it."

"Ah." Kronos's eyes crinkled. "I confess that I do not fully understand the nature of your relationship with her. It does surprise me, however."

"That she could think well of a human?" Garret rested the VS against the tree and squatted beside it. "I picked up on your skepticism."

"She can be very loyal to those to whom she feels she owes a debt."

"Like the debt she owed you?"

Kronos brushed a fallen leaf from his shoulder. "I like your directness, Mr. Fox," he said, the formal address a kind of mockery. "I confess that I didn't learn to view humans as much more than chattel until I left Oceanus and experienced more of the world as it is now."

"You were involved in the War, weren't you?"

"On the sidelines, like most of my rank."

"Was Artemis forced to fight?"

"She didn't tell you?"

"I never asked."

"You *do* surprise me." Kronos ran a long-fingered, almost delicate hand over his loose hair. "We were fighting for what we perceived as our very survival, but all we desire now is peace." He nodded toward the rifle. "*You* do not seem so committed to peace, Mr. Fox. Neither did your fellow humans in Delos."

"You had something to say about Artemis?"

Smiling ruefully, Kronos bent to pick up a branch fallen from a nearby tree. "She told you that I saved her life. The Bloodlord who attacked her in the early nineteenth century had no interest in converting her."

"Neither one of you went into hibernation in ancient times with the rest of the Opiri?"

"No. And for most of the centuries until the Awakening of our kind, those of us who had remained active during the Long Sleep kept few servants and moved frequently. The Bloodlord had nearly drained her dry when I found her, healed her and converted her."

"Did she have children?"

Kronos's gaze was far away. "I believe she had a single child, and that it was given to a relative to raise."

"And you gave no more thought to it, or how she felt about it."

"As an Opiri, she could not have kept the child with her, nor remain with it." He focused on Garret. "Why? Has she spoken of it?"

"No," Garret said, concealing both his anger and his pity.

"Her old life came to an end, and I took her with me on my travels," Kronos said. "I came to see how remarkable and intelligent she was. She was my constant, loyal companion."

"But you didn't free her from vassalage."

"She would have been at far greater risk as a Freeblood. So many vassals and Freebloods died during the beginning of the War that Bloodlords and Bloodmasters began converting large numbers of humans to replenish our ranks of fighters. After the Citadels were founded, it was soon apparent that there were insufficient resources to accommodate all the Freebloods who *did* survive."

"Not enough serfs, you mean," Garret said.

"Even when the Armistice called for the human Enclaves to send their lawbreakers to serve in the Citadels, the majority was claimed by the elite. The number of public serfs available to provide blood to the lower-ranked diminished, as well. I saw that the life awaiting Artemis—a life of constant conflict, fighting her way to the position of a Bloodlady of property or dying in battle—was not worthy of her."

"And why would you, one of the elite yourself, feel concern for Opiri your kind consider little better than serfs?"

"I came to realize that our treatment of Freebloods was a rot within the Citadels, a barbarity that had to be changed if we were to survive as a race. That was when I freed Artemis and we began to work together to encourage those changes."

"It obviously didn't work out quite as you expected."

The stick in Kronos's hands snapped with a loud crack. "Change requires sacrifice, Mr. Fox, and can only be accomplished in small steps if it is to last. I spoke out on behalf of the Freebloods. I suggested that it would soon become necessary to redistribute our resources more equitably. I was blamed for fomenting rebellion among them."

"So the leaders of Oceanus arranged your death?"

"I was challenged again and again in rapid succession, as my enemies attempted to wear me down and eventually kill me. Fortunately, I had allies who were able to help me feign my death and get me out of Oceanus. I had hoped that Artemis, with her bravery and skill, could carry on with my work."

"Even though you must have known her life would be in constant danger."

"You underestimate her strength."

"That's the last thing I would do."

"Has she taken your blood?"

The question was both unexpected and intrusive, as if Kronos were asking for the intimate details of his and Artemis's lovemaking. "How is that any of your business?"

"Because she was fully committed to ending the traditional consumption of human blood."

"She never expected that to work in the Citadels," Garret said.

"We had been discussing that very problem when I was challenged," Kronos said. "I know that she wished to set an example for her people. Now that she is outside the Citadel, any violation of her principles would arouse great conflict within her."

That, Garret knew all too well. "She's not taking my blood now," he said shortly.

"I am glad to hear it. We would not want further misunderstandings between you, Artemis and my disciples if we are to travel together. They are forbidden from taking human blood as long as they follow me, but Flavia and Xenophon were provoked by the belief that Artemis had sole access to you."

"You can tell them they're wrong."

"Yet my followers will continue to see you and Artemis in close contact."

"They'll have to get used to it."

"You seem to be losing your temper, Mr. Fox. Is it possible that you have something to prove, not only to Artemis or to me, but to yourself? Do you wish to possess her, perhaps to display your ability to control one of my kind? Or can it be possible that you actually believe you love her?"

"I'm damned sure that *you* don't feel anything like that for her."

"You are dodging the question. Of course you must realize that Artemis cannot return your feelings, but she is committed to standing by you for the time being, and she will constantly feel obligated to protect you from any of our people who express the slightest hostility toward you." Kronos plucked a dangling yellow leaf from a branch overhead. "You will be prepared to do the same for her, but though you have an abundance of courage, you lack our strength and speed."

"She'll let me know if it becomes a problem. I trust her judgment, or we wouldn't be here now."

"Perhaps that is true, Mr. Fox. You are not totally lacking in experience with Opiri females."

Garret felt for the rifle and stopped, clenching his fist. "What are you talking about?"

"Believe me when I tell you that I do regret the loss of your wife."

"Artemis told you?"

"There are other ways of learning such things, especially when you have my connections."

Making certain that the VS remained within easy reach, Garret got to his feet. "Do you know who killed my wife?"

"Not at all. But her work to aid human serfs was known even outside Erebus, and with so many rogues running wild, rumors spread. It is no small matter to take the life of a Bloodlady of her status."

Garret began to shake. "If I ever find out that you know anything about this…"

"Your threats do not impress me, Mr. Fox. But I assure you that I will inform you if I hear anything at all." Kronos looked to the north. "I only ask you to remember that

such relationships between Opiri and humans are by nature both complex and dangerous. And where Artemis is
concerned, you have not faced the final test. Her true devotion is to her people. Will you stand in her way when she
does what she must?"

Before Garret could answer, Artemis arrived, a brace
of rabbits slung over her shoulder. She looked from Garret
to the Bloodlord with an arch of her brow that conveyed
worry more eloquently than any direct inquiry.

"I have brought you dinner, Garret," she said. "I hope I
am not interrupting."

"We have had a most illuminating discussion," Kronos
said. "But now I will leave you to your meal."

He strode away.

Artemis studied Garret's face. "You quarreled," she said.

"I'm sure that doesn't surprise you," he said, well aware
that he wasn't able to hide his anger.

"Will you tell me why?" she asked.

Garret couldn't trust himself to speak. He slung the VS
over his arm and took the rabbits from her. "Thanks for
these. Did you get enough for yourself?"

"Did Kronos threaten you?" she demanded.

"He's very protective of you."

"You are not telling me everything."

"If I'm going to cook those rabbits," he said, "we'd better return to the others."

They fell into step and headed back to the place where
Kronos had set up his temporary camp. Garret told her
briefly about the Freeblood attack and what Kronos had
told him about the reason behind it.

She stopped. "I am sorry, Garret," she said, her lip
twitching above her upper teeth. "It will not happen again."

He took her arm and led her forward. "I don't want you
fighting them, Artemis. It won't advance your cause. Kro-

nos explained more about what you and he were hoping to accomplish in Oceanus."

She stopped again and wrapped her arms around him, pressing her cheek to his chest. Holding the rabbits awkwardly in one hand, he returned the embrace and closed his eyes.

"Garret," Artemis said, her voice muffled against his shirt. "I don't want you to hate Kronos."

He dropped the rabbits on the ground and put both arms around her. "I don't hate him," he said.

Her lips brushed the base of his neck, sending almost violent tremors through his body. "Whatever I am as an Opir," she said, "he is responsible for it."

"No one is responsible for what you are but you." He set her back so that he could see her face. "And that's something pretty damned remarkable."

She gazed at him, her eyes bright and expressive. Her feelings seemed as real and solid as her lithe body and the tender lips so eager for his touch.

"Garret," she murmured, "have I told you that I—"

"Garret? Artemis?"

Garret started at the sound of the familiar voice and let her go. Pericles stood behind her, grinning, and as flush with health and happiness as any Nightsider could be.

"Pericles!" Artemis said. "How did you find us?"

"I'm sorry I didn't come earlier," Pericles said, looking from her to Garret, "but I was scouting for Kronos." He beamed at Garret. "After you set me free, I searched for him." His gaze darted back to Artemis. "He's amazing. He welcomed me, and I've been—" He broke off, like a child unable to keep his mind on one subject at a time. "You saved my life, Garret. I know you had to leave Delos because of that." He sobered. "I'm sorry."

"I knew what I was doing," Garret said, hoping he was

right. "Did you see Daniel or any of the patrols who were hunting us?"

"I managed to evade them," Pericles said. "But as far as I know, no one else has seen them since we got close to the river."

"I am glad you are safe," Artemis said.

"Now nothing can stop us from finding Timon," Garret said.

And nothing, Garret thought—not paranoid humans, hungry Freebloods, or even his own doubt—was going to slow him down again.

But it wasn't quite that simple.

Garret had taken precautions to prevent another incident like the one with Flavia and Xenophon. He and Artemis had agreed that they should travel a little apart from Kronos's band and maintain some physical distance from one another, but it was obvious from the second night how much of a challenge it would be to stay apart. Garret was hyperaware of Artemis's presence as they crossed the border into old Washington State, and made their way through fallen cities, dense forest, and over hill and mountain. His body seemed attuned to hers to a degree he hadn't experienced with anyone else, including Roxana, and he always knew where she was relative to his own position at any given moment.

She seemed equally aware of him, and they would find themselves staring at each other across the small fires he made to cook game or to warm himself as the nights grew increasingly cold. He was haunted by vivid images of her supple figure, arms and legs wrapped around him, nipples peaked and tight against his chest as she took him inside her. There were times when he knew she was seeing the same images; her lips would part and her eyes become dazed with memory and hunger.

By unspoken agreement, they never discussed her taking his blood again. Even if she hadn't already inexplicably chosen to avoid it since Coos Bay, she had excellent reason to reject it now.

Sometimes, when she returned from a hunt with the other Opiri, Garret would see her locked deep in conversation with Kronos. Each time he swallowed his envy, and each time she returned to him, even if all they did together was sit quietly and companionably while the Nightsiders rested after their feeding.

Pericles spent nearly all his time trailing in Kronos's wake like an eager acolyte, accepting any attention with the kind of gratitude he'd once bestowed on Artemis. He seemed so focused on his new hero that he seldom spoke to her or Garret.

By night and by day they traveled, careful to stay hidden, always alert for other groups of Opiri. Their scouts observed more and more such packs the farther north they went.

And there were children. Stolen half-bloods, sometimes several with the larger packs. The first few times Garret and Artemis had argued in favor of saving the children, but Kronos had refused to help. There was nowhere to keep them safe, and there were far too many rogues to fight on equal terms.

But other Freebloods joined Kronos along the journey, most of them obviously acquainted with him and willing to follow his lead. They provided more information about the mysterious Bloodlord known as "the Master," and confirmed that he had gathered large numbers of Freebloods near a fortress, or possibly a castle, in the Canadian mountains, promising them some unknown reward for delivering the half-bloods.

Everything had been going smoothly—almost too

smoothly, Garret thought—when several of Kronos's Free-bloods returned with the human captives.

Garret was the first to see them and their captors hiding in the woods just outside the small clearing where the Opiri had made their temporary night camp. The three humans were dressed in camouflage uniforms, clearly soldiers or scouts of some kind. The Freebloods—Flavia among them—were arguing among themselves, and Garret listened from cover as they discussed taking blood from the humans right under Kronos's nose.

Knowing better than to confront them directly, Garret went looking for Kronos. He was speaking sternly to Artemis, whose face was unusually pale.

Garret interrupted the conversation. "You have Free-bloods flouting your laws," he said with a quick, probing glance at Artemis. "They've captured three humans, and plan to take their blood. I won't let that happen."

"Nor will I," Kronos said, getting to his feet. He and Artemis followed Garret to the hiding place, Garret automatically reaching out to steady Artemis when she stumbled several times along the way.

But he didn't get a chance to ask her what was wrong. The Freebloods had sensed their coming and were already arrayed in a defiant line, with the bound humans behind them.

"What is this?" Kronos demanded.

"We found these humans sniffing around the camp," Flavia said.

"And so you took them, against my express orders?" Kronos asked.

"They're spies, fair game," Flavia said. She sneered at Garret and Artemis. "We'll find out who sent them soon enough."

Garret positioned himself between Artemis and the Freebloods, cursing himself for having left the VS behind at his campsite. "I thought Kronos taught you a lesson," he said.

"He said that you were not to be touched," Flavia said. "But we know that *she* takes your blood even now."

"Why do you believe this?" Kronos asked.

"It is obvious," one of the male Freebloods said. "She barely touches the game we hunt. It repulses her. There is only one reason why an Opir will refuse animal blood. She must have a blood-bond with the human."

A current of shock raced through Garret's body. A blood-bond. It happened between some Opiri and their serfs in the Citadels, and among free Opiri-human couples. It was not rare, but it wasn't common, either. When it occurred, the body chemistry of both partners was altered, and all other sources of blood became unpalatable to the Nightsider.

But he'd never suspected that the growing closeness between Artemis and himself might be part of such a physical bond. Now her ongoing fatigue, in spite of regular hunts, made perfect sense.

Was she starving herself to set an example for Kronos's other followers, or because she rejected the bond itself?

Chapter 18

Artemis stared at Garret, her distress emanating from her body like a ragged halo. "It is not true," she said.

"Of course it is not," Kronos said. "Artemis abides by our compact."

The rustle of moving bodies followed his denial, and Garret became aware that they had attracted an audience. All but a few of Kronos's disciples were now listening intently, waiting to hear how the drama would play out.

If it went wrong, Garret thought, Artemis would face a crowd of angry Freebloods—and continue to starve until she died.

"Your feelings for the human are clear," Flavia said to Artemis, "as are his for you. How will you prove that you have no bond?"

"If it existed," Garret said, "I think I would know it."

"Your word isn't good enough, human," the male Freeblood said. He looked at Kronos. "If you cannot convince your chief disciple to follow your path, why should *we* obey you?"

Kronos stared at his challenger, and Garret could almost feel the power emanating from him. This was a Nightsider accustomed to being obeyed, exile or not.

But these were Freebloods, not his vassals, and they were far from the hierarchical structure of the Citadels.

"I will prove that you are wrong," Artemis said, stepping in front of Garret. He moved to pull her back and stopped, realizing that the wrong action on his part could provoke the Freebloods into hurting the human captives as well as attacking Artemis. His need to protect her might set off an explosion that none of them could contain.

"Yes," Flavia said, "prove it." She pointed behind her into the woods. "We have fresh game. If you take your full share of the blood and your body accepts it, we will know there is no bond between you and the human."

Artemis's heart felt slow and sluggish. She knew she was much weaker than she should be; Garret had noticed it days ago, but each time he had chosen to trust her rather than question her about her condition.

This was the price he paid for that trust, to learn from hostile Freebloods what she had known of and tried so hard to ignore since they had left Coos Bay: the blood-bond that had developed between them in spite of all her efforts to prevent it.

Now she was caught, and Garret was in terrible danger. He had denied that any such bond existed, but she knew that he had only meant to protect her, with no thought for himself. His mind was steady and unshaken, focused on saving her, even though he must know there was nothing he could do.

"Will you release the captives if I satisfy you?" she asked Flavia.

The Freeblood nodded. "If you prove you are still truly one of us."

Battling nausea, Artemis stepped forward. She felt Garret's silent protest and focused on projecting confidence back at him, hoping he would sense it as well as he did so many of her other emotions.

It will be all right.

Pushing all awareness of Garret out of her thoughts, she followed Flavia into the thicket of small trees and bushes. Her mind was assaulted with the emotions emanating from Flavia and her two cronies, their hostility, their envy, their contempt for Garret. Their hunger. And she felt the humans' emotions, as well: fear, anger, the drive to escape at any cost.

She was raw and open to all of them, her mental shields fallen to exhaustion and illness. She deliberately dropped the last of her defenses, the ones she had built against herself. The ones that controlled her ability to project her feelings. The ones that kept her from becoming something she despised.

It would be easy to make Flavia see what Artemis wanted her to see, believe what Artemis wanted her to believe. Extending the control to the others would be more difficult, but far from impossible.

But once she gave in to the temptation...

You have no choice, she thought.

"Do you intend to do this or not?" Flavia asked, baring her teeth.

Artemis moved forward slowly, the scent of blood strong in her nose. She followed Flavia deeper into the woods. The game was fresh, and Artemis did her best not to flinch at the knowledge that there had been no need to kill the creature.

She did what Flavia expected, though it sickened her. Through the sickness, she imagined herself passing Flavia's test without difficulty, projected that image to Flavia and the others just out of sight.

When she was finished, she still didn't know if she'd succeeded. She wiped her mouth and met Flavia's gaze, concealing her disgust at what she had done. What she'd *had* to do.

Her eyes unfocused, Flavia blinked several times and nodded with obvious reluctance. "You have passed the test," she said.

Artemis remembered to breathe. "Set the humans free," she said.

"Surely Kronos will wish to question them first."

"He did not ask," Artemis said, "and you gave your word."

With a sharp sigh and a nod to her followers, Flavia began to untie the first of the human prisoners. As soon as the others were free, the male with the uniform markings that designated the highest rank prodded them from their stupor, and the three of them bounded off into the forest. The leader looked back once, briefly meeting Artemis's gaze, and then vanished.

Artemis was left with the aftertaste of Flavia's angry disappointment in her mind as she walked back into the clearing. Garret was on his feet watching for her, while Kronos stood at his ease, his hands clasped lightly behind his back.

"The humans are gone," Artemis said, meeting Kronos's gaze. "There is no question of any blood-bond with Garret Fox. This does not mean that I will cease to regard him as an ally who saved my life and set me free when he could have delivered me to Delos."

The remaining Freebloods muttered among themselves, but none seemed inclined to question her further. The crowd broke up, the Freebloods drifting away until only Garret, Kronos and Artemis were left.

"What did you do?" Garret asked, moving closer to Artemis.

"She convinced Flavia and her lackeys that she does not share a blood-bond with you," Kronos said.

Garret pulled Artemis aside. "Is it true?" he asked. "Is there a bond between us?"

She knew that no matter what she told him, it wouldn't alter the truth. He only wanted confirmation of what he already knew.

And he feared for her...feared the hold Kronos might have over her, worried about how she would deal with the need for his blood when the risk of exposure was so great.

Soon, even animal blood would be completely unpalatable to her.

"It does not matter if there is a bond or not," Kronos said before Artemis could speak. "Have you been breaking my laws?"

"No," Garret snapped.

"Then you must remain apart unless you are in full view of my followers."

"To hell with your noble philosophy," Garret said. "Do you think I'll let her starve?"

"There are ways of breaking such bonds," Kronos said. "It will not be easy or comfortable, but—"

"It's like breaking an addiction, but a hundred times worse," Garret said. "I've seen it. Artemis will be the one to suffer." He took her arm. "We'll go ahead on our own."

Artemis leaned against him, trying to clear her mind and get her ability under control again. She could influence the thoughts of others and cloud their minds, but she could not seem to think for herself.

"You do know what you have done to her, besides making her dependent upon your blood?" Kronos asked. "You have taken all choices from her."

"She has already made her choice," Garret said, his voice nearly a growl.

"Has she? Or have you made it for her?"

"I've never forced Artemis to do anything against her will," Garret said.

"Perhaps not deliberately," Kronos said. "But your emotions have constantly affected her. Your mere presence has influenced every move she has made."

"Even a blood-bond isn't that powerful."

"I am not speaking of something so simple." Kronos glanced at Artemis. "She is what you would call an empath. She can sense and even share the emotions of others. But surely you must know that by now, Garret Fox."

Garret stared into her eyes, and she felt him remembering times when he had almost believed he'd felt her emotions, even sensed her thoughts.

"Garret," she began, "whatever you may think—"

"I knew she possessed some degree of skill when I first saved her life by converting her," Kronos cut in as if she hadn't spoken, "but it was much enhanced by the change. In the years she was with me, she shared my emotions as well as my work, even when I believed I had lost all capacity to feel. She awakened a part of me that had long been dead."

Garret flinched, and Artemis caught a fleeting glimpse of Roxana. A part of *him* had been dead, too. He could feel the changes within himself—changes he had only begun to accept—because of her.

"Yes," Kronos said. "You and I have something in common, Mr. Fox."

"But it isn't just us, is it?" Garret asked Artemis, laying his hands gently on her shoulders. "Can you feel everyone? My God, how can you stay sane?"

"She can experience the feelings of anyone she comes into contact with," Kronos said. "She helped me understand the innermost needs and ambitions of the Freebloods we approached in the Citadels. When first I realized how much this made her suffer, I tried to shield her. As I should have shielded her from *you*."

"Shielded her?" Garret said. "My God. The War…"

"Indeed," Kronos said. "It is why I tried to keep her away from the battlefields. She was nearly driven mad by the savagery."

"I was not mad," Artemis protested, pulling away from Garret. "I am not as weak as he claims."

"True enough, my child," Kronos said, "it was your strength that enabled you to survive."

Garret's powerful desire to hold Artemis mingled with his fear of making things worse for her, but his pity was rapidly transforming into suspicion and anger—not at her, but at Kronos.

"So what happened in Oceanus, when you tried to spread your ideas?" Garret asked. "How was *that* protecting her from Opir savagery?"

"When Artemis and I were together, she was safe."

"Safe? You abandoned her."

"No!" Artemis said, moving to stand between them. "Kronos *did* help me."

"Help that obviously didn't last," Garret said.

Remembering how she had influenced Flavia's thoughts, Artemis tried to soothe Garret's anger. A dazed look came into his eyes, and Kronos cast her an inquiring glance. She realized what she was doing and stopped, horrified at how easy it was to reach for her forbidden talents just because it seemed the simplest course of action.

"I had to learn to manage my abilities," she said, trembling with self-disgust.

"Because anything less would eventually have destroyed her mind," Kronos said. "But you, Mr. Fox, must have fractured her armor and left her defenseless from you and everyone else."

"No, Kronos," Artemis said. "It would have happened sooner or later."

"Without the additional impetus of the blood-bond?" Kronos shook his head. "Mr. Fox knows I'm right."

Artemis recognized the precise moment when Garret began to accept everything that Kronos had told him. He tried desperately to mute his feelings—toward Kronos, toward the Freebloods who had attacked him, even toward her.

It only made things worse.

"How much do you care for Artemis, Mr. Fox?" Kronos asked. "Enough to leave her with me, so that I can teach her to master her abilities again?"

"P-please," Artemis stammered.

"Look at her!" Kronos said. "She is caught in your hatred of me, in the web of your irrational humanity."

"No!" Artemis said. "Garret, you must believe—"

"There is more," Kronos said, relentless in his honesty. "Artemis can also project her own emotions. She can share her feelings with others, cause them to experience her wishes and desires, even without conscious effort."

"And I refused to do it!" Artemis said. "Not in the Citadel, and not afterward."

"But you used that power on Flavia, did you not?" Kronos asked.

"Is this true, Artemis?" Garret asked, searching her eyes. "Can you manipulate what other people feel?"

His question felt like an assault, though he had every right to ask it. Could she have manipulated Garret in the past without realizing it, compelling him to save her from the militiamen and later "influencing" him into joining Kronos?

"I never did it when…when you and I were together," she stammered.

"Indeed," Kronos said, echoing her thoughts, "why should she try to influence your feelings, since, being such a very civilized human, you certainly needed no encouragement to save her life when you first met? And surely your devotion to her was reason enough for you to help her escape Delos and join forces with me and my disciples."

Artemis heard the stinging sarcasm in Kronos's words, the eagerness to sow doubt in Garret's mind. It hurt to know that he so badly wanted Garret gone that he would use any tactic to achieve that result. It hurt much worse to realize that Garret was now questioning everything he knew about her, weighing all their interactions, wondering if everything he'd done had been of his own free will.

"You're right," Garret said. "I didn't need any encouragement to get her away from the militiamen who wanted to kill her. I didn't need a blood-bond or any kind of push to help her escape from Delos, or trust her reasons for helping you get away."

Sucking in a sharp breath, Artemis went to Garret and leaned her head against his chest. He put his arms around her and held her lightly, his gaze never leaving Kronos.

Kronos smiled. The tips of his teeth were very white in the shadows. "I admire your loyalty, Mr. Fox," he said. "I'm quite certain that Artemis never abused her abilities. But she is still suffering because of them. And you."

Garret's face might have been carved from granite. "When we're alone," he said, "I'll ask her. And she'll tell me the truth."

"Unless she allows me to protect her as I did before, she will lose her sanity."

"You're wrong, Kronos," Artemis said, slipping free of Garret's arms. "I know you hate Garret. You would do anything to—"

"Your involvement with him has warped your senses," Kronos said. "I hold no hatred for him, or any human."

Perhaps, Artemis thought, her senses *were* warped, but Kronos was telling the truth. There was no hatred. Contempt, yes. Disgust that she had chosen the company of a human over that of her former lord and protector. And he emphatically wanted her by his side.

But there was something else. Something that floated just beyond her reach.

"Laying the blame upon Garret changes nothing," she said. She turned to Garret again. "I have no wish to separate unless it is your choice."

"It won't be that easy to get rid of me," Garret said, laying his palm against her cheek.

"Can you control your emotions, Mr. Fox?" Kronos

asked, speaking over Artemis's head. "Can you change the very nature of your being?"

"It is not *his* responsibility to change," Artemis said, taking strength from Garret's trust. "I can learn to master my ability again."

"Do you still require further proof?" Kronos asked Garret. "Artemis, come to me."

"She isn't your vassal now, Kronos," Garret said.

Before Garret could react, Kronos bounded toward Artemis, swift as a timber wolf, and embraced her. She stiffened to fend him off, but almost at once the tumult in her mind subsided. Kronos's and Garret's emotions—and her own—dimmed to a manageable pitch.

"Look at her now, Mr. Fox," Kronos said.

Chapter 19

Though Artemis did nothing, it was clear that Garret saw what Kronos wanted him to see. His pain was a distant thing to her now, but she recognized it in his eyes, in the way a muscle jumped in his cheek.

Once, she had simply accepted that something about Kronos helped to shield her from the worst of the side effects of her abilities. Now it came to her that she had never understood how he did it, just as she now wondered how Kronos had so quickly convinced Garret.

"We can still help you find your son," Kronos said to Garret, "but you must stay away from Artemis. I will help her break the blood-bond, and—"

"Let me go, Kronos," Artemis said.

"You heard her," Garret said. "You can't hold her against her will. If you try, I *will* stop you."

"I will not let you die for his sake," Kronos said, stroking Artemis's hair.

Instinct claimed victory over discipline, and Artemis acted almost without thinking. She turned her anger on Kronos, and he released her abruptly, his surprise almost comical.

Stunned by her own act, Artemis backed away. Garret was behind her, as solid as one of Delos's walls.

"We need to go," he said. "You have to take my blood, and we can't do it here."

"Think, Artemis," Kronos said, recovering from her emotional attack. "You and I understand each other as the human never will. Not because you are Opir and a Free-blood, but because you are beyond both."

His words made no sense to Artemis. But then again, right now nothing did. "If you think I will use this ability to win other Freebloods to our cause—" she began.

"I would never expect that of you," Kronos interrupted. "But I need—"

"Let's gather our things and get out of here," Garret said, grasping Artemis's arm. But when she looked at Kronos, she remembered the old days—his compassion for the Freebloods struggling to survive in Oceanus, his gentleness with her, his flawless logic.

What had changed him? Kronos had never been so possessive before, so determined to control her. How had she failed to see that Garret's concerns about her old master might have a basis in fact?

"Stay," Kronos said, extending his hand.

"Artemis," Garret said softly. "We'll find a solution."

She went with him. There had never been a question of that, though Kronos was clearly furious with her decision. Garret knew she was starving, and he would have physically attacked Kronos if the Opir had tried to hold her, with absolutely no regard for his own life.

But the intensity of his emotion was such that she couldn't separate it from her own. Once they had collected their things under the suspicious eyes of the other Freebloods and left camp, her desire for blood had become indistinguishable from his feelings for her. They traveled for a full mile, Garret half supporting her, before they found a place for her to take his blood.

At first, it was like surrendering to her most primitive instincts: Garret baring his throat, her teeth piercing his skin, the blood flowing into her mouth. But then she felt the joy, the contentment, the feeling of utter completion enhanced by the blood-bond. She realized how much she had been missing Garret's arms around her. The idea of cutting herself off from his emotions suddenly seemed unbearable.

"Garret," she said when they were finished, "you have no reason to fear what I can do. I will never—"

"Don't worry about me," he said, shifting her into a more comfortable position in the crook of his arm. "Is it true that I broke down your mental shields and left you defenseless?"

"No," she said sharply. "Kronos exaggerated. I did begin to feel your emotions soon after we met. At times I was uncertain, but I was never helpless."

"But you *have* been affected by my emotions, my humanity."

"Do you think that is such a terrible thing?" She grabbed his hand, feeling hard muscle, calluses, the way his fingers closed around hers. "I realize now... Kronos thinks he knows me. But I am not the same as I was in the Citadel, when I worked with him."

"Kronos recognizes your courage and your skill," Garret said, "but he doesn't seem to realize that you have qualities he can't comprehend." He stroked his thumb over her lower lip. "Kronos won't succeed in teaching Freebloods to change their way of life, because he wants to dominate too much. He'll never set an example they can follow."

Artemis couldn't meet his gaze. She had come to the same conclusion, and it hurt as much as Kronos's treating her like a vassal, bound to his will.

"Nothing he said could make me stop trusting you," Garret said, turning her face toward his. "The empathy wasn't only one way, Artemis. It also made me see you more clearly."

"Then you can forgive me for hiding this from you?"

"Humans and Opiri have another thing in common. They tend not to trust those who are different. You were protecting yourself by concealing what you could do, but you refused to rely on your other abilities to keep yourself safe." He looked at her very gravely. "I don't know if I can block my feelings from you, at least not quickly enough. You'll have to teach me to—"

"No." She smiled. "I don't want to be cut off from you ever again."

Garret took her in his arms and kissed her. His pride filled her to overflowing, and it was only their precarious circumstance that prevented them from following their most basic impulses.

"There is one thing I'd ask of you," he said when they had finally separated. "If your empathy will help us find Timon, will you use it?"

Jerked out of her drowsy contentment, Artemis played his question back in her mind. She had almost forgotten Timon in the drama of what had happened with Flavia and Kronos.

She felt a mingling of shame and anger, a part of her wondering why she hadn't thought of it herself, and another part—the old Artemis, who found it so difficult to trust—wondering if Garret found it so easy to accept her "talents" because he saw them as a means to get to his son.

Kronos had implied that Garret wanted to use her abilities, but Garret wasn't like Kronos. He wouldn't want her to use her mental powers to alter the thoughts and emotions of other beings.

Still, even after she had convinced herself of Garret's benign intent, she continued to feel uneasy. The first flakes of snow were falling as they broke camp and traveled side by side, moving quietly and without talking.

Near noon, when they paused to rest again, they had nearly reached the old Canadian border. The hilly landscape was only lightly dusted with snow, but the white-topped mountains of British Columbia—and the camp of the Master—still lay before them.

Artemis scouted ahead, heeding her sense that they were

being watched. Their pursuer's emotions were so muted that she didn't recognize him until she was nearly on top of him.

Pericles froze in place when she found him, a little nervousness seeping through the strange but familiar barrier around his mind.

"Artemis," he said in a flat voice. "Are you all right?"

"What are you doing here, Pericles?" she asked. "Spying for Kronos?"

There was no reason to be so hard on him, and she regretted it immediately. But Pericles seemed not to notice her accusation; she almost felt as if he were looking right through her.

"Kronos is in trouble," he said slowly.

Immediately Artemis was on her guard. "What kind of trouble?" she asked.

"The other Freebloods turned against him," Pericles said. "Flavia said that he trusted you too much and broke his own laws by letting you consort with a human. They attacked him and left him in a bad way."

Artemis's alarm quickly gave way to confusion. Pericles's words were stilted, almost as if he were reciting by rote.

And that barrier…

"When did this happen?" she asked, setting aside her troubling thoughts.

"Soon after you left," Pericles said. "He's alone. I thought maybe you could help him."

Artemis glanced over her shoulder toward camp. The last thing she wanted was to leave Garret now, and this could all be a ploy by Kronos to get her back.

If it was a ploy, he might not be injured at all. But she couldn't bring herself to take that chance. Whatever he had said or done, she couldn't leave him to die if she could find any way of preventing it.

Briefly, she considered her situation. She had fed well

not long ago. She carried the basic necessities in her pack, and she had her bow and quiver. She couldn't return to camp and try to explain to Garret why she was going back for Kronos, because he would surely try to stop her.

As long as she found him again in a few days, she wouldn't lose too much of her strength.

"Listen carefully, Pericles," she said. "I'll go back to find Kronos, but you must stay here and tell Garret why I've left. Tell him not to come after me. He needs to go on ahead. We have a good idea of where the Master's camp is located. Tell him I'll look for him there."

"I understand," Pericles said.

She gazed at him a moment longer, doubting both him and herself. But she had made her decision. Leaving Pericles to carry out her instructions, she set a fast pace southwest to Kronos's camp.

She found him alone and injured, just as Pericles had told her. Bleeding profusely, he had rolled under a clump of thick bushes, the dark red tatters of his clothes a testament to his injuries. But his wounds had closed, and he opened his eyes when Artemis knelt beside him.

"Pericles sent me," she said, gripping his hand. Pain and anger and shame came from his mind to hers through their touch. "He said the others attacked you."

Kronos choked on a laugh. "Yes. I confess to being surprised that they left me alive." He squeezed her hand. "I knew you would find me again."

She wetted a piece of cloth with her canteen and wiped his face. "You will need blood quickly," she said. "It is fortunate that they also left you your daycoat. Rest here, and I will find game for you."

"Don't leave me alone," he said.

His vulnerability softened her toward him in a way she wouldn't have believed possible, but she knew she couldn't give in to pity. "You must have fresh blood to recover," she said, "and I will only be gone a very short time."

As she rose to leave, he touched her leg. "Garret?" he asked.

"I sent him on ahead."

With a long sigh, Kronos nodded and closed his eyes.

Artemis returned an hour later with a deer slung over her shoulder. She stood over Kronos and forced him to take nourishment, even when he turned away in disgust.

"A pity that Flavia's captive humans are no longer here," he said hoarsely.

"But you would never break your own laws by taking blood from them," Artemis said.

"No," he said. "I wonder if Flavia and the others caught them again."

"I hope that Flavia's stupidity in attacking you carried over to her hunting ability," she said. "No, don't try to explain. You asked for more than they could give, and they turned on you for it."

"What have I done wrong?" Kronos asked, lifting his head. "Artemis, you who know me better than anyone… how have I failed?"

"You haven't failed," she said, her body aching with his regret and discouragement. "We knew this would never be easy."

He lay back again. "There is something you must know," he said, "in case I can go no farther."

"Of course you can," she said, alarmed by the thready sound of his voice.

"I know something of what this Master has planned," he said. "He is building an army."

"For what purpose?" Artemis asked.

"I do not know." Kronos coughed again. "But whatever that purpose may be, the Master will only bring harm to those you and I meant to save…the Opiri who know no other way but seeking rank through violence. And the end result will be terrible suffering for thousands of Opiri."

Artemis's breath grew short.

"What did you plan to do when you reached the Master's camp?" she asked.

"The Master has promised a reward to the Freebloods who bring the children and remain afterward. But, as we know, any leader can lose his followers, no matter how powerful he may seem." His laugh emerged as a bark. "I know that with so many Freebloods together in one place, some will have become disaffected and might listen to my words of peace. I had hoped to reach out to them in secret, with my own disciples to help me. But now…"

Artemis knew what he was going to ask, and she tried to harden her heart against him. But his despair and sorrow and hope had mingled so deeply with her own emotions that they overwhelmed the warmth and comfort she had felt with Garret.

"You want me to carry out your plan," she said.

"I cannot keep up with you now, and I know you will not abandon Garret Fox. But you can still be of great help to me. Once you arrive at the encampment, I would ask you to scout for any Freebloods who have come to oppose the Master and might be willing to listen to our philosophy. I would not expect you to act on what you learn, only to wait for me until I arrive."

"I will be helping Garret look for his son."

"You are resourceful enough to carry out two tasks at once. And it may be you can learn more about the children from Freebloods who are not completely loyal to the Master."

His words made sense, though Artemis wondered how he could draw so many conclusions based on relatively little information. All his assumptions might be wrong.

Still, she and Garret needed any information they could get.

"Can any Freeblood enter this encampment?" she asked.

"I heard that one must bring either a half-blood child or a human to add to their communal herd of blood-serfs," he said. "There may be other ways. You will have to determine what to do when you are there."

"Are you certain that you can travel on your own?" she asked him.

"I have recovered from much worse injuries."

"Then I'll do as you ask, if I can," she said. "I'll stay with you through the day and leave at sunset."

Kronos nodded and dropped off into the semiconscious state that served Opiri as sleep. Artemis went in search of game and water, and then returned to watch over her old mentor. By sunset, Pericles hadn't returned.

He's gone ahead with Garret, she thought. That was the only explanation that made sense. And yet she was left with that uneasy feeling she couldn't shake.

When she set out at last, all she could think of was being with Garret again. She only hoped that he understood why she'd gone back to Kronos, and that he would wait for her before he did anything rash in his eagerness to find Timon.

Garret looked down on the vast walled camp stretching across the river valley, turning to his field glasses again and again, wondering if Artemis had somehow managed to arrive ahead of him—as if he had any hope of finding her in the throng of Freebloods milling about like ants scouring the forest floor for their supper. A ridge of low hills formed a half circle around the camp, ending in the anthill—a cliff that towered over the sea of snow-dusted tents and awnings, surrounded by a royal guard of high mountains and topped with a structure out of some pre-War horror story.

A castle. That was what it appeared to be, anyway: all dark stone, massive gates and high turrets, a perfect home for a mythical vampire.

Or an egotistical, evil Nightsider who needed to make an impression on the thousands of Opiri who had been drawn here by the promise of reward for delivering the children. And maybe something worse yet to come.

These ants looked very much like an army. As a human, he would stick out like a sore thumb, even with the day-coat he had stolen from a small, untended campsite on the other side of the hill.

But he had to make his move soon, and he would much prefer to have Artemis with him when he did. He looked for her again. *She had to return to Kronos*, Pericles had told him. *She'll find you at the camp.*

Adjusting his pack, Garret began a careful descent down the hill. The moon was on the wane, but it was still close to full. Without it, he would have been nearly blind. His VS had disappeared from Kronos's camp before he and Artemis had left, and all he had now was a hunting knife, an ordinary handgun…and a well-trained but very human body.

When he was near the foot of the hill, he coated himself with a crust of snow and crawled low to the ground, pausing every minute to get his bearings. Now that he was close to the level of the valley, he could better see the scattered torches that indicated the presence of other night-blind humans. Here, they could only be serfs. Or prey, to be kept alive until they were used up.

Garret felt the burst of emotion before he could turn to face the Freeblood behind him.

"Garret," Artemis said. "I thought I'd never find you. I was afraid I—"

He grabbed her, pulled her down and kissed her hard. She melted against him, returning the kiss even though it was foolish and dangerous.

He didn't give a damn.

"Are you all right?" he asked, setting her back so he

could see her shadowed face. "Pericles barely told me anything. I was afraid that Kronos—"

"Would convince me to stay with him?" She kissed him again. "He was injured, and I had to make sure he was all right. But that's all, Garret. I'll never leave you again."

He held her close for a moment, feeling the slow beat of her heart against his chest. She flinched, and at first he thought he was holding her too tightly.

But there was pain in her eyes, and it was not physical.

"What is it?" he asked.

"So many emotions," she said, clenching her teeth. "All these Freebloods together, and humans… I haven't felt this since I left the Citadel."

"How can I help?"

"I don't…" She hesitated. "Maybe there *is* a way. Let me focus on your emotions. Perhaps that will allow me to block out the others."

"What do you want me to feel, Artemis?"

She looked into his eyes, and he knew. He gave her all the devotion and affection he had reserved for only a few people in his life: Roxana, Timon…and Artemis. She gasped, and though—like all Opiri—she couldn't weep, he could feel the reflection of his emotions cast back at him, filling his eyes with the tears she was unable to shed.

For a few brief moments there was no barrier between them at all.

"By the blood of the Eldest," she whispered. "It is working." She began to laugh, and Garret laid his hand across her mouth.

"I'll give you all the strength I can," he said. "But we have to find out where the children have been taken."

Artemis signaled that she was in control again, and Garret removed his hand.

"Kronos told me more about the encampment," she said, her voice still a little breathless. "He thinks the Master is preparing an army, but we don't know where or when he plans to strike. Freebloods can get inside the walls if they bring a half-blood child or a human."

"There must be two thousand here already," Garret said. He paused to listen to the constant hum of voices from the camp. "We have to get inside the walls to find out if the children are there," he said. "Our only plan is obvious."

Chapter 20

Artemis had known that there was only one way to get inside the encampment, but still she shook her head.

"There must be something else we can try," she said.

"I assume they're holding captive humans to feed the Freebloods. They probably won't let you keep me, so the worst that can happen is that I get thrown into a pen with the other humans. At least we'll both be inside." He gripped her hand. "We'll figure something out once we're there."

But Artemis knew that there was one other possibility: convert Garret into an Opir. It still left them with the problem of the "entrance fee" to the camp, and in all the time he had been with Roxana, Garret had never chosen to become like her. There must have been a powerful reason for him to reject immortality with the woman he had once loved, so Artemis could think of no earthly reason why he would do it for *her.* It was far too much to ask. She couldn't even bring herself to suggest it…especially since a part of her badly wanted to make him just like her. Make sure he could never leave her, even when this quest was over.

I love him, she thought. It was no sudden revelation but a gentle movement of a puzzle piece into its proper place. The feelings had been there for a very long time. She was no longer afraid of the words.

But she could not force her love on him any more than she could make him love her. And though she knew he cared for her deeply and held her in great esteem, that wasn't the same.

If ever he came to love her, she would know it. And even if he did not, she would never regret these feelings.

She would give Garret whatever he needed as long as both of them were alive.

"I must ask you to do one thing for me," she said. "Show me Timon."

His eyes caught the moonlight and glittered under his hood. "I've shown you what he looks like."

"Show me with your emotions. Perhaps, if we are any-where near him…"

Without hesitation, Garret closed his eyes and let her *feel* Timon. His image was not a physical thing with clear features and solid shape but was built entirely of Garret's love for his son, an aura of tenderness and devotion and fierce vigilance. Guilt and fear were there, too, but she refused to let those darker feelings taint the rest.

"I see him," she said, her mind overflowing with memories as fragile as spring ice and as powerful as love itself.

Garret opened his eyes. "Did it help?" he asked.

"If we find out where the children are held," she said, "I think I will be able to find him." *If he is still alive*, she added silently, glad he couldn't hear her thoughts.

While she kept watch, Garret concealed his pack behind a jutting boulder, along with his knife and gun, covering each of them with handfuls of dirt and small stones. When he was done, he pulled Artemis into his arms again and kissed her, pushing his tongue between her lips, groaning deep in his chest. She opened her mouth and met him with equal passion.

"Artemis," he said, his lips trailing kisses over her jaw and neck, "take my blood."

She broke free. "Now? Are you mad?"

"We've been apart for nearly two days. You need it. If you don't feed, you'll become too weak to fight if we have to."

Weighing the risk of discovery against her hunger, Artemis nodded. "We must be quick," she said.

Euphoria flooded through her at the first taste of his blood. She felt her emotions pour into Garret, a sharing not of pain but of ecstasy, belonging and wholeness that needed only one simple act to complete. He tipped his head back and gasped as she drank, and his sudden arousal triggered her own. She shifted to lock her thighs around his waist. He arched up, his body hard and insistent.

This was how the world was meant to be, she thought. This was *life*, and she never wanted it to end.

But neither one of them was stupid enough to give in, no matter how urgent their desire. The path they needed to follow now lay through the encampment and hundreds of hostile Freebloods. To Timon.

Garret released her, though his hands lingered on her waist. "Are you ready?" he asked.

"I have no way to bind you," she said.

"I know how to behave like a human among undomesticated Nightsiders," Garret said, taking the sting out of his words by brushing a bothersome strand of her hair out of her eyes. "Don't give yourself away, whatever you do."

"Only if you promise to do the same."

Taking care to make certain that no one else was observing them, Artemis rose first. A group of Freebloods passed by, arguing hotly, completely unaware of her or the human at her feet. Once they had moved out of sight, Artemis motioned for Garret to rise and pushed him ahead of her. He glanced over his shoulder, and she saw his entire body change. His expression became worn and defeated, his body slumped. Only his mind told her that he was the Garret she knew.

The stockade was built of tree trunks stripped from the forest covering the surrounding hills. Perched on the barren cliff at the opposite end of the valley stood the mysterious castle, its silhouette marked with high, pointed turrets, crenellated walls and an imposing bulk that suggested unassailable strength. During the era when Artemis had been born, such monstrosities had been the creations of writers who told tales of haunted strongholds and mad villains.

This castle, like the ones in the novels, had been built to symbolize power…and evoke fear.

As she and Garret approached the wall of the camp, they found themselves among packs of Freebloods crowded outside, forced to intermingle as they jockeyed for position. Artemis noticed that some of the Opiri approaching the stockade were half-blood adults—not prisoners like the children, but walking freely among the full-blooded Opiri. She concentrated on blocking the seething clamor of the thousands of contradictory emotions that radiated from the vast encampment.

She took firm hold of Garret's collar and made straight for the gate, a crudely wrought, lopsided affair made of the same rough-hewn logs as the walls.

There were five Freebloods manning the gate, along with a single Darketan, who appeared human but smelled Opir. She didn't let the gatekeepers see so much as a flicker of doubt on her face.

"I have brought a human," she said. "Let me in."

The Freebloods glanced at each other with obvious amusement. "Where is the rest of your pack?" the Darketan demanded.

"I need no pack to be of use to the Master," she said.

"Give the human to us," the Darketan said.

Artemis looked him up and down. "I take no orders from a Darketan."

"Give him up and we'll let you in," the tallest Freeblood said.

Garret stiffened, muscles tensing in preparation for a very one-sided fight.

"I will give him to the one in charge of the humans inside and to no one else," Artemis said quickly.

A low muttering started up behind her, restless Free-bloods who doubtless hadn't drunk much human blood in recent days. "Silence!" the Darketan shouted.

Amazingly enough, the Freebloods quieted. The gate creaked open behind the sentries. They turned in angry surprise as a pair of female Opiri walked out, unaware that they had interrupted an increasingly hostile dispute.

Several things happened at once. Two of the sentinels tried to close the gate, one of the females shouted in pro-test, and Garret charged through the gap between the door and the wall.

Artemis sprinted after him, barreling past the gatekeep-ers before they could react. There was another crowd of Opiri just inside the gate, possibly drawn by the scent of human blood. Some of them were already running along a central lane between rows of tents and canopies, giving Artemis a good idea of which way Garret had gone.

While Artemis had never been as strong as some Opiri, she was very fast. She hurtled by the pursuers, lashing out at them with arms and feet as she passed. She opened her mind to Garret, willing him to let her know where he was.

She found him quickly enough, alerted only a few sec-onds before by his mental cry of warning. Three Opiri were dragging him into a tent halfway across the camp. He was resisting, buying time to urge her to stay away.

Artemis went directly to the tent and stepped inside. Seven Freebloods were crowded into the space, and she recognized them at once.

Most of Kronos's former followers seemed surprised to see her; Flavia and one other were openly hostile, while one looked shame-faced, as if he realized that she knew what he and the others had done to Kronos.

"Let him go," Artemis snapped, gesturing to Garret.

To her astonishment, the ones holding Garret released

him. He straightened his daycoat with a sharp jerk and came to stand beside Artemis.

"It seems we've found old friends," he said with a curl of his lip.

"You betrayed Kronos," Artemis said to the Freebloods.

"It was Flavia's idea," one of the Freebloods—Mikohn—said to Artemis in a hurried burst of speech. "She thought Kronos was weak. She attacked him."

Flavia shot him a poisonous look. "We came here to look for the life Kronos couldn't give us," she said. "We knew his preaching would only get us killed if we came with him."

"And did you find what you were looking for?"

The Freebloods exchanged glances. "When we came here," Mikohn said, "we were told that we would become part of a new kind of life that the Master was making for all the Freebloods who agreed to follow him. We would share all the humans in common, no Opir getting more than another, and make raids on human colonies when we were strong enough. We would all be equals."

"As Kronos promised," Artemis said.

"You know what he made us give up," Flavia said. "He wouldn't have allowed any raids. We would have starved."

"And you were too afraid to leave Kronos without trying to kill him?"

Flavia opened her mouth but quickly closed it again. The rest were silent.

"How did you get into camp?" Garret asked.

"With your VS," Flavia said. "It seems that they can use weapons as well as half-bloods and humans."

"But we were wrong about this place," Mikohn said at last. "There aren't enough humans here to feed everyone. No one has seen the Master in many weeks, and some think he has abandoned the camp and his followers. A few Freebloods are trying to take over the camp as if they are

Bloodlords." He glanced toward the tent flap. "There's talk of a war. We don't want any part of that."

Rebels, Artemis thought. Only she hadn't expected to find them so quickly, let alone run across Opiri she knew.

But if Kronos's former disciples were discontented after only a day or two of being in the camp, there were undoubtedly others. Freebloods still remembered how they had been used as cannon fodder in the War.

Artemis leaned against Garret, grateful for his solid presence at her back. "Where are they keeping the children?" she asked.

"If we tell you what we know," Flavia said, "what will you do for us in return?"

Artemis laughed. "What can I give *you*?"

"You can help us get out." Flavia shifted from one foot to the other and looked away. "I know how you fooled us into thinking you didn't take blood from the human."

Garret started. Artemis gripped his arm. "I do not know what you're talking about," she said.

"When we got here, I remembered what really happened, what you did to me," Flavia said hotly. "You made me believe something that wasn't true."

"You're mad," Artemis said, striving to breathe normally.

Flavia bared her teeth. "Kronos made us all mad to follow him. Is he like you?"

"What?"

"Can *he* make people do what he wants and believe what he wants them to believe?"

Startled, Artemis remembered how oddly Pericles had behaved when Kronos was injured. She had thought it strange at the time, but to suggest that his behavior had anything to do with an ability like hers…

"I have known him most of my life," Artemis said. "He has no such skill."

"But *you* do," Flavia said. "And now you will use it to make the guards let us out."

"You can't leave?" Garret asked.

"Once you come in, you are not permitted to go out again without a pass. Some of the guards at the front gate probably work for the rebels, and they want to keep us in as much as the Master's soldiers do. If the Master is truly gone, they need Opiri to rule over."

"Why don't the rebel Freebloods overpower the Master's guards?" Artemis asked.

"The guards have human VS weapons," Mikohn said.

"Do as we ask," Flavia told Artemis, "or we'll throw this human out into the camp."

"And I'll tell them that you plan to sneak out," Garret said.

"They won't listen to a human."

"They'll listen to another Freeblood," Artemis said.

"Do you want to know where the children are or not?"

The war within Artemis's mind echoed in Garret's, and she knew he understood. She despised and feared her power to control and deceive others. She would do nearly anything to avoid using it—anything but abandon Garret. Or the hope of rescuing Timon.

"Tell us where they are," she said, "and I give my word that I'll help you, as long as it does not involve harming others."

Mikohn and Flavia looked at each other. "Agreed," Flavia said. "The Master has been keeping the children in the castle. The rumors say that he is treating them well, but no one knows what he wants with them."

"The castle," Garret said, exhaling slowly. "From the look of it, it's virtually impossible to approach from any direction. How can we get inside?"

"That is not our concern," Flavia said. "We have told you what we know."

"There may be a way," Mikohn said. "The Freebloods who are trying to gain power while the Master is gone…it is rumored that they intend to go up to the castle in force and demand to know where he is. If they can show the camp that he has disappeared, and that only his personal guards remain to defend his position, then—"

"Where are these rebels?" Garret asked.

"They have established themselves in the rear of the camp," Mikohn said. "They have the largest tents. You'll find them easily."

"We have to join these rebels," Artemis said to Garret. "We have a better chance of getting into the castle as part of a group."

"You'll have to prove that you're strong enough to be an asset to them, but also that you're not a threat to their new power," Flavia said. "But again, that is not our concern. It is time for you to get us out."

Garret laid his hand on Artemis's shoulder. "Can you do this?" he asked in a low voice.

She covered his hand with hers. "I will," she said. She addressed the other Freebloods. "We'll all go outside together."

After a brief hesitation, the Freebloods gathered behind her, Garret sandwiched between them to obscure his scent. The sun was rising, so Garret, Artemis and the Freebloods put up their hoods and made for the wall.

No one noticed them; there was some commotion at the gate that seemed to be occupying everyone's attention. As they drew nearer, Artemis heard Garret curse under his breath.

A dozen humans had apparently been captured, men and women in camouflage fatigues who stood with heads lifted and defiance in their eyes. They waited just inside the gate, surrounded by avaricious Freebloods who were obviously on the verge of grabbing any human within reach.

"These look like Enclave troops," Garret said.

"We cannot help them now," Artemis said. "We must—"

"Did you hear?" a young female Freeblood said, clutching at Artemis's arm. "A human army is coming, and the Master has deserted us!"

"Calm yourself," Artemis said, engulfed by the woman's very real terror.

"But now we will have to fight, and the Master is not here to lead us!"

"You should have considered that before you came here," Artemis said, fighting to separate the woman's feelings from her own.

The young female ducked her head and skittered away, hunched low and avoiding eye contact with any of the other Freebloods she passed.

"Stay close to me," Artemis murmured to Garret.

Garret did stay close, so close that he was nearly on top of her, ready to defend her from the slightest hostile gesture. His presence was a shield against the wildly fluctuating emotions of the Opiri around her, and she imagined herself in a position of authority, confident in her purpose. All she had to do was convince the distracted guards at the gate that she and those with her had to leave the camp on urgent business.

But as she felt for the minds of the guards among all the others, she felt sickness and revulsion surge up inside her, blurring her thoughts and making it impossible to focus. Garret caught her as she swayed, holding on to her under the cover of his daycoat. "You can't do this," he whispered. "When I yell, get the others out. Find Timon."

Before she could answer, he released her and stepped away from the group. "Human soldiers!" he shouted. "How many are coming? Hundreds? Thousands?"

As the human captives stared at Garret, other Freebloods turned toward him, their emotions swarming over

Artemis—hunger, fear and alarm—as Garret's words penetrated the growing chaos. Flavia's group pressed in around her, on the verge of panic themselves.

Garret continued to mock the Freebloods at the gate, asking them how ready they were to stand against a human army carrying Opir-killing rifles like theirs. Artemis couldn't seem to move. In a moment, she thought, the guards would overpower and silence Garret, possibly kill him.

Closing her eyes, she focused her thoughts and projected the terror of death, of becoming trapped, of being pawns in a game the Freebloods didn't understand. There was no safety here.

The number of Freebloods moving in the direction of the gate began to increase, while the gatekeepers made a futile effort to stem the tide.

"Go!" Artemis said, shoving Flavia forward. "Run. Now!"

Kronos's former disciples broke away and sprinted for the gate. They lost themselves in the crowd. Voices rose in warning, and there were gunshots, followed by fighting that rapidly overwhelmed the guards.

Artemis grabbed a handful of Garret's daycoat and hung on. "We must go back into the camp," she said hoarsely.

"You're sick," he said. "You aren't ready to deal with the rebels when they storm the castle. I'll find somewhere for you to rest."

"No." She grabbed his hand and tried to draw him toward the rear wall. Her fingers trembled, and racking pain hammered inside her temples. "Someone will surely come after us if we do not move while the fighting distracts the guards."

With a terse nod, Garret half carried her back the way they had come. She couldn't feel his emotions through the clamor inside her skull, but his warmth and strength wrapped her in a cocoon that no outside force could penetrate.

As they ran deeper into the camp, dodging between tents to evade any pursuit, the noise of the battle at the gates began to fade. Artemis peered through the glare of daylight, looking for the large tents Flavia had mentioned.

They had nearly reached the rear of the camp when Garret came to a sudden stop. Clustered against the wall stood several tents that had been decorated to suggest that their owners were Opiri of rank and power. They were painted with symbols of dominance and arrayed with crudely carved standards atop staffs reminiscent of those carried by Bloodmasters in the Citadels.

As Artemis and Garret watched, two Freebloods in thickly embroidered daycoats approached the tents, arguing in low voices. Their emotions were hostile and angry, like those of Opiri on the verge of challenge.

The rebels, Artemis thought.

"Find the nearest empty tent," she whispered. "Hurry."

Garret went straight to the row of tents perpendicular to the rebels', paused outside of one, moved on to the next and gestured to Artemis. Keeping an eye on the arguing Freebloods, she followed him inside.

The interior was very similar to the one Flavia's group had occupied: a few pieces of camp furniture, a folding table and little else. Artemis crouched by the tent flap and listened intently.

"What are they saying?" Garret asked, crouching beside her.

"They are speaking of the challenge to the castle and how many Freebloods they have recruited to follow them."

"We'll have to quickly prove ourselves of use to them if we're going to join their group," Garret said.

"You know you cannot come with me," she said. "You

will have to remain hidden while I am gone. I'll try to get you outside the camp, and—"

He met her gaze. "Did you think I came with you this far just to be left behind now?"

"Do you think they will allow a human to accompany them? They will simply seize you and keep you for themselves."

"They won't be able to," Garret said. "Because I won't be human."

Chapter 21

Artemis couldn't mistake his meaning. Her chest constricted, and she felt that, had she been human, she would have wept.

"It was inevitable," Garret said, holding her gaze. "We never discussed it, but you must have known all along. I can't go any farther as a human in this place. You have to convert me."

Struggling to quiet her own emotions, Artemis replayed that moment on the hill when she had considered and rejected this very option. "Do you know what you are saying?" she asked, spinning on her heel to stalk across the tent. "Do you understand that once this is done, it cannot be undone?"

"I understand," he said. "I've known it since long before I was sent to Erebus as a serf." He held out his hand to her. "I accepted all the ramifications long ago, when Roxana and I joined the colony and Timon was born."

She returned to him and knelt beside him. He stroked her knuckles with his thumb, as if she were the one about to sacrifice everything she knew.

"I chose to remain human because I believed it was important to set an example for others, to show that we could live on equal terms with Opiri without giving up our humanity," he said.

"But now you wish to surrender that humanity? You can accept the complete transformation of your very nature, becoming dependent upon blood for the rest of your long life, never able to feel the sunlight on your skin?"

He brought her hand to his lips. "I endangered both of

us, and Timon, by refusing to recognize the necessity of change." His fingers laced though hers, firm and unyielding. "I said we'd have to prove ourselves to these rebels. If it goes as far as a fight, the change will give me greater power and far better odds against any Opir."

"But do you know what else comes with the conversion?" she asked. "You will be my vassal, tied to me by a force even more powerful than the blood-bond."

"And once we find a way to join the rebels going up to the castle, you can claim the right to take your vassal with you."

"If these rebels had created vassals of their own, Flavia and Mikohn would have told us."

"They wouldn't have felt obliged to tell us everything. But once you've done it, Artemis, the rebels will have to accept it."

"If I can *make* them accept it."

"*We* will, and to hell with the rules of combat that forbid anyone from interfering in a challenge between Opiri. Getting into that castle is all that matters now."

So he thinks, Artemis thought. But would he feel the same when Timon was safe and he was faced with a world in which everything had changed? Would he come to resent her for holding power over him, even if she were to set him free the moment they had achieved their goal?

She saw that she had no choice but to play her final card. "I honor your courage," she said. "But courage will not save you if the conversion fails."

"I understand the risk."

"Do you? Are you aware that conversion by a Freeblood carries greater danger for the human than one carried out by an Opir of higher rank?"

"I know that some humans react adversely to conversion when it's done by a Freeblood," he said. "But it's not common for Freebloods to attempt it in the first place. I still believe it's a chance worth taking."

"You could die within minutes of my bite," she said, panic strangling her words. "You could become incapacitated, helpless."

"Nothing you've said changes my mind, Artemis." He cupped his hand around her chin. "Trust me."

She wanted to wail in protest. It shouldn't have been this way, done in haste and secrecy under conditions that would put him in far greater danger than almost anywhere else.

But he was strong. Strong and healthy and tenacious. His aura shimmered around him, red as flame, his determination feeding on his conviction and her faith in him.

"I will do it," she whispered.

"Thank you," he said. "Thank you for Timon's sake."

Surrendering to the inevitable seemed to take a weight off Artemis's shoulders. "The change is not immediate," she said briskly. "Your strength and speed will increase over time. You may even be able to tolerate sunlight for a few days, as your body adjusts. You should not require blood for at least twenty-four hours. But you must be very careful not to overtax yourself in the beginning, no matter how much you want to fight."

He nodded. "Do you need more blood before we begin?" he asked. "I know mine won't be as nourishing for you after I'm changed."

"I will receive some blood during the process," she said.

"Enough to get you through the next few hours?"

"We'll worry about that later. For now…"

She met his gaze. "Prepare yourself as best you can, and I will do the same." She took several long, deep breaths and began to focus her thoughts on what she must do. Garret let his body relax.

They sat facing each other, looking into each other's eyes in a last, wordless communication. Artemis's heart was so full that she was afraid she would broadcast her emotions all over the camp, so she locked her feelings away completely.

"Are you ready?" she asked.

In answer, he bent his head back. Opiri had no real religion, but Artemis sent a plea to the universe and gently pressed her lips to his skin.

"Do it," he said hoarsely.

She bit down. His blood rolled over her tongue, and she completed the adjustments to the chemicals in her body that would provoke the conversion. Her vision hazed. Adrenaline raced through her veins, activating her instinct to create a new Opir, a vassal bound to her until she chose to set him free.

Garret's head began to jerk, and his eyes rolled back in their sockets. His teeth snapped together, and the tendons in his neck strained under his skin. Artemis realized that he was seizing, swallowed her panic and tried to stop.

But the process could not be halted. She tried to hold him steady, imagining that she was giving him more than the modifications that would alter his chemistry and his very nature. She gave *herself,* as well—all the vitality she had to spare, all the will and determination to survive.

Still it wasn't enough. She let all the barriers fall and stepped *inside* him, carrying her love into the very center of his mind...the love that had become as real to her as the old dreams of Freeblood independence.

Gradually he began to respond. The tremors subsided, and the rigidity left his muscles. When she was certain she had finished her work, she closed off her emotions again and healed the wound, waiting for his body to accept what he had become.

Or for it to give up.

Sounds and smells passed in and out of her awareness.

Lassitude crept over her, a weakness she had felt before and knew only too well.

Had the work of conversion, the first she had attempted in her two centuries as an Opir, been more than she could safely manage? Would she now require more blood before she could fight?

She snapped back to full consciousness when Garret made a sound deep in his throat and opened his eyes. He stared straight ahead.

"Artemis?" he murmured.

She shifted to sit in front of him, and he reached for her blindly.

"I can't see you," he said.

The small amount of blood she had taken from him seemed to curdle in her stomach. "It will pass," she said.

He felt for her face. "The light," he said. "It's too—"

The tent flap opened, and a tall Opiri walked in. He was bristling with rage; his eyes were black with it, and his large teeth were on prominent display.

There was no question in Artemis's mind that this Freeblood was one of the rebels who had asserted dominance in the camp. He reeked of the confidence that set the strongest Freebloods apart from others, and his emotions and his arrogant thoughts were all of power.

"Who are you?" he demanded. "What are you doing in my territory?"

Artemis rose to stand between him and Garret. "My name is Nemesis," she said, "and I have come to join the Opiri who are going up to the castle. You *are* one of them, are you not?"

"I've never seen you before," the Freeblood said, taking an aggressive step farther into the tent. "How do you know about us?"

"The whole camp knows," she said. "I have a need to see the Master, if he is here."

"Why?"

"I have reason to hate him, just as you do."

"We want only to find out what has become of him," the Freeblood said, suddenly cautious.

"That would also serve my purpose," she said. "What are you called?"

"I am Brutus," he said, "and we do not trust strangers." His nostrils flared. "Who else is with you?"

"Only my vassal," she said.

"Vassals are forbidden here!" Brutus snapped. "How did you get into the camp with one?"

"Perhaps I am clever enough to be of use to you."

"Where is your pack?"

"I have no need of other Opiri to protect me."

He laughed scornfully. "Why do you think we will permit you to join us?" he asked.

"I will fight for the privilege."

Brutus tried to step around her. "Let me see this vassal of yours."

Garret rose up behind her, though she knew he wasn't ready. His emotions were chaotic, and she felt without looking at him that he still couldn't see.

"A new convert!" Brutus said with a sneer. "Still mostly human. Did you make him in this camp?"

"It doesn't matter," she said. "I am prepared to defend him and earn a place in your ranks. Will challenging you be sufficient?"

"You would challenge *me*?"

"Do you lack the authority to give me a place in your delegation when I defeat you?"

"My reputation is well known. If you truly seek death, I will give it to you."

"Then I offer challenge, to take place within this tent. You and I, alone."

"Without witnesses? What game is this?"

"Would you risk a formal challenge in full view of the camp, when you do not yet have complete control of this place?" She arched a brow. "If you are afraid to fight without witnesses, you can always summon *your* vassals. Oh, but they are forbidden, are they not?"

"I have already proven myself," Brutus snarled. "I accept your challenge. And when you are dead, I will kill the vassal. Slowly."

Brutus attacked without warning, throwing himself at Artemis with his mouth stretched wide to clamp down on her throat. She was lighter and faster than he was; she slipped sideways, and he barely caught his balance before he crashed into the tent wall.

Still, he was fast enough, and his reach was far longer than hers. If it hadn't been for Garret, she might have failed before she began.

But she was all that stood between him and Brutus's frenzy. That fact alone seemed to replenish her energy, feeding her body and pumping new life into her muscles. She feinted, drawing Brutus away from Garret, and danced across the tent with a derisive laugh. Brutus swatted at her, fingers curled, but she evaded him again and darted under his guard to strike at his privates.

She had hoped to enrage him into clumsiness, but she had miscalculated. She was too close to him, and he swooped down, seizing her neck between his long-fingered hands. She bit hard on his wrist, to no effect. His face descended toward her throat.

Garret slammed into him from behind, forcing him to release his hold. Artemis dropped to her knees and fell back, catching herself on her hands.

When she was on her feet again, Garret and Brutus were grappling like bears, the Opir snapping at Garret's neck. But Garret was holding his own, and it was clear that he was able to see well enough to focus on his opponent. His aura rose up in a halo around his head, scarlet tinged with purple, brighter than it had ever been.

Artemis didn't wait to find out how long his energy would last. She hurled herself on Brutus, grabbed a handful of his loose hair and bit his shoulder. With a howl more of outrage than pain, he reached back with one hand to dislodge her.

Moving with astonishing speed, Garret knocked Brutus's other arm aside and slammed his elbow into the Freeblood's gut. Artemis slid off Brutus's back, and Garret delivered a kick that caught the Opir in the middle of his chest and sent him flying across the tent. Brutus fell onto his back and lay there, stunned, like a turtle turned upside down.

Artemis and Garret reached the would-be Bloodlord at almost the same moment, Garret pinning him down with both hands while Artemis hovered over him, one efficient motion away from ripping into his throat.

"You're done," Garret said. His voice rasped and his arms trembled as he pushed down on Brutus's wrists, but Artemis knew he had passed the crisis.

In fact, he had done more than merely begin to change. His increase in speed and strength were only one sign, for when she met his gaze she saw that his green irises were ringed with vivid magenta, and his red hair was streaked with white. He smiled, and though there was no change in his teeth, she guessed it would not be long before they, too, revealed what he was becoming.

Brutus struggled to rise, heaving against Garret's weight. Garret hit him across the face with a clenched fist. Brutus subsided, blood trickling from his mouth.

"You...broke the laws of challenge," he croaked. "Your vassal..."

"Shall we tell the others that you were defeated by a

small female Opir and a new-made vassal, or will you let us accompany you to the castle?" Artemis asked.

Such was Brutus's pride that the threat worked. He agreed to allow Artemis to accompany him to a meeting with the other "emissaries," which was to take place in one of the large tents in two hours.

Once he had left the tent, Artemis had to do something she very much wished she could avoid. "You'll have to stay in the tent until I return," she said to Garret.

He met her gaze, the magenta circles around his irises expanding and contracting erratically. "Is this your first order to your vassal?" he asked.

"Do you think I would ever use that against you?"

"No," he said, shaking his head. "Not you." He ran his hand through his hair, plucking a white strand and examining it with interest. His aura was quiet now, his emotions calm and dangerous. Artemis had no doubt that he would become such a formidable Opir that he could challenge any Bloodlord and win.

"Is your vassal permitted to touch you?" he asked with a wry smile. Without waiting for her answer, he pulled her close and kissed her. It lasted only a few seconds, but when it was over she felt stronger than at any time since she'd taken his blood on the hill just outside the camp.

The last time she would ever do so. Their relationship would never be the same again. And she had no real idea what it would become.

The sound of a commotion outside shattered her reverie. Garret knelt by the tent flap and looked outside.

"Soldiers," he said. "Some are in daycoats, but there are half-bloods with them, all dressed in fatigues."

"The Master's loyal disciples?" Artemis asked, joining him.

"They're dragging the Opiri out of the big tents." His jaw

set. "It looks as if the Master, wherever he may be at this moment, has learned about the little rebellion in his camp."

Artemis clenched her fists. "I do not think we can escape unnoticed."

"They may not check this tent at all," he said. "But there are too many to fight." Unexpectedly, he smiled, and Artemis didn't think it was her imagination that his incisors were just a little more pointed. "If they do take us, maybe we can convince them to escort us to where we want to go."

Artemis was considering the possibilities when she recognized one of the invaders: Pericles, dressed in a daycoat and standing apart from the soldiers. She gasped, and Garret gripped her arm to keep her from running outside.

"He's with the Master's forces," Garret said. "Why?"

Before she could answer, one of the soldiers dragged Brutus over to Pericles, who asked the rebel a brief question. Brutus pointed at the tent.

"Get ready," Garret said, pulling Artemis to her feet. "If Pericles is a traitor to Kronos, we may have no choice but to fight."

Chapter 22

The soldiers came right at the tent, weapons raised. Garret and Artemis stepped back to give themselves room. He clasped her hand briefly.

"Before you do anything rash," she said, "let me try to talk to Pericles."

Two soldiers lifted the tent flap but didn't attempt to enter. Pericles came in, and Artemis cautiously tried to read his emotions. They were as close to blank as she had ever found in any human or Opir.

"Artemis," he said, pulling back his hood. "I'm glad I found you."

"What are you doing here?" Garret asked, stepping in front of Artemis.

Pericles blinked. "I work for the Master," he said.

He didn't sound like himself, Artemis thought. "What of Kronos?" she asked. "How long have you been a traitor?"

As if he were wandering through a dream, Pericles didn't seem to hear her. "The Master wishes to speak to you," he said.

"I thought he had disappeared."

"He has returned."

"You told him we were here?"

"Of course," Pericles said tonelessly. "He sent me to find you."

"But why would he want to see *me*?" she asked.

"He knows of your connection to Kronos and wishes to learn more of his philosophy. They want many of the same things."

"I never heard that Kronos wanted war," Garret said.

Pericles ignored him and continued to speak to Artemis. "The Master would prefer that you come willingly."

She glanced at Garret. He nodded slightly. This was their way into the castle, a more direct path than they could have taken with the rebels.

But if the Master knew about Kronos and had learned where to find his disciple, he might very well know *why* Artemis and Garret were here in his camp.

"We'll go with you," Artemis said.

"Good." Pericles ducked his head outside the tent and spoke to the soldiers. "We will leave right away."

The entire camp was nearly silent as the Master's soldiers escorted Artemis and Garret out through the gate. There were no more fleeing or fighting Opiri, though there were a few bodies scattered nearby, looking bleached in the morning sunlight. Other Opiri were dragging them out of the way as the soldiers strode past.

It was obvious that any open rebellion had been put down by the soldiers who now stood guard at the wall.

Once they had cleared the gate, the soldiers started up the narrow path that was the only direct approach to the castle on the cliff above, climbing a steep hill through the trees and then over bare scree where any attempt at attack could be easily prevented by a relative handful of defenders.

The path wound behind the castle and became a kind of narrow causeway, purposely designed so that only a few men or Opiri could approach at one time. The castle gate was high, wide and imposing, reinforced with massive sheets and hinges of steel that must have been salvaged from the remains of an old human town, dragged over some great distance along the river.

The castle itself was built, like the stockade far below, of heavy timber, but far more carefully worked and constructed. There were no windows except at the very tops of the four towers, and they were insignificant. But the painted wooden and metal embellishments and decorations above the gate and on the towers echoed designs from another time and place. A human time, long before the Awakening.

Unlike human-built fortresses, however, this structure was entirely protected from the open sky. The parapet walks were covered by heavy awnings, the rest by sloped roofs made to resist the snow.

As Artemis opened her mouth to speak to Garret, the gates swung open and a dozen of the Master's soldiers, dressed in fatigues and bearing rifles, walked onto the causeway, headed for the path below.

"More rebels to suppress?" Garret asked Pericles.

"There is much to be done," the young Freeblood answered cryptically.

Garret gripped Artemis's elbow, steadying her. The gates stood open, and their escort chivvied them into an empty, canopied bailey and forward toward the castle door.

The interior of the castle was as plain as the outside was imposing. The great "hall" of the keep was not the traditional large single room but a series of smaller interconnected chambers leading off into narrow corridors. Walls and doors lacked all decoration, and as Artemis and Garret moved deeper into the structure, it became more and more apparent that the castle had been built primarily to impress those outside it.

"Can you feel Timon?" Garret asked, his lips brushing her ear.

"No," she said. "And my sense of the others is dulled, as well. It almost seems as if something—or someone—is interfering with my ability."

Before they could discuss it further, they were ushered into one of the many small chambers, furnished with a recently upholstered couch and chair.

"You will wait here until the Master is ready to speak with you," Pericles said. "Do you require blood?"

Artemis met Garret's gaze. Considering the energy he had expended so soon after his conversion, he would need his first blood sooner than he might have otherwise.

But she was fairly certain their only option here would be to accept the blood of captive humans, and she knew that Garret would never consent.

"We need nothing," she said.

With a slight frown, Pericles studied her face a moment longer and then left the room.

"They didn't tie us up," Garret said, his gaze sweeping the room. "There's something strange going on here."

"Yes," she said. She reached for his hand, and he cradled it between his, his still-changing body almost feverish. "I wish I could see what it is. We may not have much time to find the children."

"What do you suggest?"

"I'm not sure. But perhaps…" She concentrated on Garret, and he started, his eyes widening.

"I heard that," he said. "I…*understood* you."

"Yes," she breathed. "We had a blood-bond before, along with an empathic connection. Now the bond is based upon something even more powerful."

"And you want me to help you with your empathy? By focusing on my emotions again?"

"I used that technique to block out the feelings of the Freebloods and humans in the camp," she said. "This time I need to draw on your mind to enhance my own ability."

"I don't understand how *my* mind can help you."

"You have great inner strength," she said. "Like the… the roots of a very ancient tree, sheltering the weak and drawing life from the earth. I can anchor myself to those roots and reach out in a way I could not risk otherwise."

"If I have that kind of strength," he said, "I came by it the hard way." He hesitated. "What do you want me to do?"

"Artemis!"

She and Garret looked up as Kronos entered the room, his bearing and his mind filled with concern and relief. "I am very sorry to see you here," he said.

Artemis shot to her feet. "Kronos! What are you doing here?"

He took a seat on the chair and gazed at her as if he wanted to make sure that she was still in one piece. "I was taken when I approached the camp to learn more of the Master's plans," he said. "Apparently I was recognized by someone who remembered me as a leader of Freebloods and had heard of my philosophy."

"Pericles works for the Master," she said.

"So I have learned."

"You seem fully recovered from your injuries."

"I was fortunate—in that, at least," Kronos said. "But I did not have the resources to fight when the Master's soldiers came for me." He smiled crookedly. "I was given the opportunity to attend the Master here in his dwelling, or…"

"We were given the same choice," Garret said, rising to stand beside Artemis. "The Master claims to want to speak to Artemis about your philosophy."

"There's been chaos in his camp," Artemis said. "Flavia and the others who abandoned you were trapped inside. We attempted to help them escape, but I do not know if we were successful."

"I saw Flavia fleeing the camp." Kronos lowered his voice. "It seems the Master is having trouble managing the Freebloods he lured here. But he is far from powerless." He glanced toward the door. "Under other circumstances I would be happy to speak to this Bloodlord and discover whether we share any common ground. Perhaps I might even have been able to persuade him to strike a more peaceful course."

"Not as long as the Master and his followers snatch innocent children from their homes," Garret said. "Do you know why he wants them?"

"Unfortunately, I doubt I know more than you. I assume it is still your desire to find them?"

"Yes," Garret said roughly. "If you have any ideas..."

"I do," Kronos said, addressing Artemis, "but first I have a confession to make."

"What confession?" she asked.

"About your gift of empathy."

She experienced a sense of foreboding so strong that Garret felt it and pulled her hard against him. "It has seldom been a gift," she said.

"It was what led me to you when you were dying two centuries ago."

"Because my mind called for help."

"Your emotions called me, yes. But why was *I* the one who came to save you?" He leaned forward, his hands clasped between his knees. "I, too, am an empath, Artemis. I learned early to control it, for such sensitivities can only hamper any Opir who wishes to rise to power. But I sensed your dying, and I recognized in you one like myself."

For a moment Artemis was too stunned to speak. Kronos's emotions were pouring into her now—not because she welcomed them, but because he was *making* her feel them. Pride, triumph, confidence, ambition. For the first time she could see his aura, a deep purple halo hovering around his head and shoulders.

"You saved me because I am like you?" she said.

"Because I knew that one day we could work together for the betterment of our people."

Artemis's foreboding increased. "Does your empathy include the mental strength to affect others?" she asked.

"It does."

"Blood of the Eldest," she whispered, remembering what Flavia had asked her about Kronos's abilities.

"Pericles was under some kind of spell when you were injured and he came to find me. Was that you?"

Kronos relaxed, as if he had no concern at all about what she might discover. "Yes. I found that it was easier to make him understand what he had to do."

Garret's face was a grim mask. "Did you control Pericles when you two were in the same jail in Delos, so that he could convince Artemis to see you?"

"I only encouraged him," Kronos said.

"But now he works for the Master," Artemis said, "and he's behaving just as strangely."

"I have no explanation for that."

Unless the Master has the same powers Kronos does, she thought. But the idea that she, Kronos and the Master should possess identical abilities was sheer madness.

"What about Oceanus?" she asked. "You were always so skilled at persuading the Freebloods we attempted to recruit, but I assumed—" Her blood froze. "You asked me to help you understand the feelings of those who resisted our message."

"And so you did, unaware that you sometimes pushed beyond merely sensing into encouraging, as you did with Flavia when you convinced her that you took the animal blood."

"So all along I was pushing undecided Freebloods to obey you?"

"You and I wanted the same thing. We were attempting to save our race."

"But you never told me. You never explained. And after you died…"

"You shut out your talents, because you needed me to guide you."

"But *you* couldn't keep Flavia and the others with you!"

"Ah, Artemis. I lack the focused power of your gift. I

can persuade, but not command. In this, I acknowledge you my superior."

"And now you want to use her again," Garret said, his voice a growl.

"What would you ask her to do in order to find your son?"

"I was going to ask him to help *me*," Artemis said.

"By employing your bond to enhance your empathy?" Kronos asked. He stared at Garret. "You are not far along, are you? Still not one of us. Your loyalty is entirely to the humans."

"He is my vassal," Artemis said, "but I do not control him. We work toward the same ends."

"Do you, Artemis?" Kronos held out his hands. "You wish to find his son. You wish to prevent a war, and lead Freebloods upon the right path, as we always did. If we can convince the Master—"

"By compelling him?" Artemis said. "Whatever you say, I have no such power."

"I can help you now, as I did in Oceanus." He smiled, and his aura lightened with something very much like joy. "Think of the good we can do here, my child. How many lives we might save."

"The children?"

"So much more than that, Artemis. Neither one of us can wield the power the two of us can when our minds and emotions join as one."

As she had proposed to do with Garret, Artemis thought, though on a much smaller scale. The idea of joining with Kronos disgusted her. He had already used her without her knowledge, deceived her for two centuries.

"I can see that the suggestion seems unpleasant to you," Kronos said. "But when we combine our abilities, we can change the world to match our vision."

Change the world. But she knew that he meant something more than improving the lives of beleaguered Free-bloods, saving the children, or even preventing another war. He had a grander vision.

Grand, and terrible. But she could only *feel* it, not see the specifics. She had no idea what he planned.

"How will you do this in the Master's house?" she asked. "For all we know his guards may have heard everything you just said."

"All the more reason to hurry," Kronos said. "We must act while we still—"

"Forget it," Garret said. He gently pushed Artemis behind him. "I never trusted you, and now you're talking crazy. Artemis's mind isn't a toy for you to play with."

"And what if I can save your son?"

"Not at that price," Garret said, though his voice nearly broke. "We don't need your help."

"Don't you?" Kronos said to Artemis. "Will you let the children remain captives of the Master, their fates unknown, because you are unwilling to try what I suggest?"

Fear washed through Artemis, quickly followed by anger. "I am prepared to try—but only for Timon's sake."

"No," Garret said. He turned her to face him. "I can't let you do it. I *won't*. We'll try it the way you suggested before. I'll be your tree, Artemis. Whatever you need to do, I'll give you everything I have."

"Artemis…" Kronos began.

She gazed into Garret's eyes. Their physical appearance was changing, but he was still Garret. Still strong-willed, courageous and resolutely set on protecting her.

"I must," she said softly. "I have to try, Garret, so that we can get the children out alive."

"And if Kronos is influencing you, even now?"

"Have I touched your mind in any way?" Kronos challenged. "Do you feel any compulsion?"

"No." Artemis laid her hands on Garret's arms. "Only for the children," she said.

Garret tried to dissuade her, not with words, but with the force of his emotions: his distrust, even hatred for Kronos; his driving concern for her; his certainty that Kronos's plan would end in disaster.

But through it all she could read his fear for his son and the other children, fear he couldn't conceal.

"Artemis," he said. "If you do this—"

The door opened, and Pericles entered with two of the guards.

"Kronos," he said, "the Master will see you now."

Kronos rose. "I am glad you are well," he said to Artemis. "I hope to see you again soon."

Shaking with anger, Garret turned to Artemis as the others left. "Kronos doesn't care about the children," he said. "He only wants a way into your mind, and then—"

"Garret," she whispered.

He turned toward the door. Pericles was still there, though his face remained as blank as it had been ever since Artemis had met him again.

"The Master inquires again if there is anything you need."

"Pericles," Artemis said, approaching him cautiously, "how did you come to serve the Master? You were with Kronos before. What changed? Or did you always work for the Master, even when you saved Beth and we took her all the way to Delos?"

"I don't understand," Pericles said, stepping toward her.

"Were you spying on us? Is that how the Master knew about me and Kronos?"

Expressionless, Pericles turned to leave. Artemis saw Garret near the door, opening it a tiny crack to check the hall outside.

"I don't think you are a spy," Artemis said quickly,

snatching at Pericles's arm. "Something's wrong. Let me help you."

Pericles flinched as if her hand had burned him, and she felt the first real stirrings of alarm.

"Look at me, Pericles," she said.

His clouded gaze met hers. Sharp pain sliced into her skull.

And she knew what she had to do.

Chapter 23

Artemis closed her eyes and, keeping a firm grip on Pericles, concentrated on all the things she had learned about him and admired when they had first met: his bravery, his willingness to change his way of life, his determination to defy his own people for the sake of a human child.

Then she looked for the invader in his mind. And found him, *part* of him, intertwined with the feelings that made Pericles what he was, corrupting them like spreading rot in a healthy grove.

Knowing that she had to work quickly, she tried to construct an image that would help her do what was necessary. She imagined the negative influence as a black thread entangled with a golden one, woven so tightly that only the greatest skill could pick the strands apart. She wove her own emotions into a third strand—crystalline blue—and searched for a weak place in the skein.

When she found it, she forced her thread between the other two, pouring her own emotions into it, all the compassion, trust—and love—that Garret had brought into her life.

Pericles moaned. His terror engulfed her. Her legs gave way, and she dragged him down with her. She lost all sense of herself as a separate being. Even breathing was agony. The black strand began to burn and shrivel.

She collapsed. When her vision cleared, Garret was crouched over her, and Pericles lay on the floor beside her. He opened his eyes. They were filled with bewilderment, but they were clear. He was himself again.

"Artemis," Garret said, supporting her head in his hands. "What in God's name did you do?"

"It's all right," she said, rubbing her temples.

Pericles sat up. "What hap—" he began. "Kronos." He covered his face with his hands. "He got inside my head."

"You freed him?" Garret asked Artemis.

"Yes," she said. *But if Pericles has been working for the Master...*

"Whose commands are you obeying now?" Garret asked Pericles, as if he'd heard her thoughts.

Pericles moved his head slowly from side to side, as if he wasn't sure that it belonged to him. "I don't know," he said. "But..." He looked toward the door.

"The guards aren't near the door," Garret said, suspicion rolling off him like waves of heat. "If they're listening, they're using a device, not their ears."

"What were you about to say, Pericles?" Artemis asked.

"I...think Kronos is working for the Master."

"Working for him?" Garret said. "How?"

"I don't know," Pericles moaned. "It's all mixed up inside my head."

"If Kronos is already involved with the Master," Garret said, "he's been deceiving us since you first met him at Delos." He looked at Artemis. "He wanted you here with him, and my search for Timon was only a convenient means of achieving his goal."

"But he can't support what the Master is planning," Artemis protested, nearly choking on the denial. "The idea of another war..."

"How can you know what's really in his mind?" Garret asked. "He can obviously hide his true feelings. He said he needs your help to influence the Master in some way. Is that really what he wants?" Garret forced her to look at him. "Why would he work for the Master in the first place, Artemis?"

"It's a trick," she said. "He heard of the Master's plans, offered his services to learn more..." She heard the pleading note in her own voice and tried to calm herself. "Even if he lied to us, he must have come to realize the Master was wrong. That's why he wants my help."

"He 'encouraged' Freebloods in the Citadel. He manipulated you. He made Pericles into a slave." Garret grimaced. "Do you remember what he said, Artemis? He said he learned to control his abilities because they would only hamper an Opir who wanted to rise to power. Isn't that what he's really wanted all along? Power? If he thinks he can get it through the Master…"

A grander vision, Artemis had thought when Kronos had spoken of changing the world.

Did he think he could destroy the Master, inherit his Freebloods and take command of a ready-made base of operations…all to establish the new way of life he had fought and nearly died for in Oceanus?

"Until I see proof," she said, "I cannot condemn him."

"Then be prepared to act quickly when you change your mind," Garret said.

They stared at each other, neither willing to look away first.

"Artemis?" Pericles said faintly. "Do you still want to save Timon?"

"Do you know where he is?" Garret asked, leaning over the young Freeblood.

"I…think…" With Artemis's help, Pericles got to his feet. "I think I remember seeing the place, but I'm not sure how to get there."

Garret sprang up and ran to the door. "The guards are still gone," he said. "It must be some kind of trap." He returned to Pericles. "If you're lying…"

"I don't sense the guards anywhere nearby," Artemis said.

"Are they so confident that we can't escape?" Garret

asked. "I saw that kind of arrogance in Erebus, when I worked for the Underground. But we can't count on it."

"If the Master means to kill us, will it matter if we remain in this room or search for the children?" Artemis asked.

"Pericles, will you show me what you *do* remember?" Garret asked.

"I'll try," Pericles said, meeting Garret's gaze.

"I want you to stay here, Artemis," Garret said. "If you find a way to escape, I want you to—"

"This is becoming tedious," Artemis said with a weary smile. "I will not remain behind, and you cannot compel me to. In fact, *I* could compel *you*, if I wished." Her smile faded. "We will go together."

"I had to try," Garret conceded with a look that made her feel hot and cold at the same time.

"Where do we start?" she asked Pericles.

Pericles looked around the room. "There are dozens of small chambers all through the castle," he said, "and just as many halls and corridors. If I could just figure out where we are…"

Artemis opened her memory, seeking the emotional imprint of Timon that Garret had left in her mind. The laughing, softly rounded face appeared to her inner vision, reverberating with all the love and devotion Garret felt for his son.

"I feel you," Garret whispered. He covered his eyes with his hand. "And I think I… I think I feel Timon."

She gripped his wrists. "Calm," she said.

"He's afraid," Garret said hoarsely. "My son. And all the others…so afraid."

Artemis closed her eyes. She caught the echo of what he was experiencing, the pain of feeling the suffering of the helpless and not being able to do anything about it.

The sickness of losing himself in the emotions of others. Of his own son.

If she let herself, she would be caught in the same trap. One of them had to remain clearheaded for the sake of those same children.

"It's all right," she said, rubbing his arm. "I did not know this would happen when I converted you. Perhaps I should have guessed."

Garret uncovered his face. "What *has* happened to me?"

"When I passed on the substance that provokes the change, I think I…also gave you a little of my ability. I am sorry."

Garret pressed his palms to his temples and sank to his knees. "How do I stop it?"

"I can show you how to protect yourself," she said, kneeling beside him. "But if I do it now, you may lose all contact with Timon."

Gritting his teeth, Garret shook his head. "Then I…don't want it to stop." Tears glittered in his eyes. "God, Timon."

"Can you feel where he is?" she asked gently.

"No. There's too much—" He broke off, and she was engulfed by his grief.

Roxana was there, his wife, with her sparkling eyes and undeniable beauty. Loss. Rage and the desire for revenge against someone he had never found. Devastating loneliness.

"I am with you," she said. "You are not alone." She rested her forehead against his. "Try to focus. There is a point where the feelings are strongest. We must find that focal point, because the children will be there."

"I'll find it," he said, struggling to his feet. He offered Artemis his hand and pulled her up. She knew that his pain wasn't gone, but there was that familiar determination in his eyes that rejected all obstacles. His fingers traced her face, as if he were committing it to memory. "We'll do this, Artemis."

A kernel of absurd joy burst in her chest. They were in accord again, fully aware of each other and of themselves. Garret squeezed her hand, pressed his lips to her fingers and then just as quickly let her go, moving to the door at the opposite side of the room.

"Pericles," he said, his voice calm and level, "don't reveal that you're free of Kronos's influence. Allow whoever we meet to believe that you're our prisoner."

He looked at him mournfully but nodded. Garret tested the door. It was neither guarded nor locked. With Garret leading the way and Pericles between him and Artemis, they passed into a similar room and then entered a narrow corridor, dividing their attention between watching for guards and following their inner senses.

Remarkably, they met no one at all, not even the servants Artemis imagined a Bloodlord like the Master would require. There were many rooms and halls, some furnished, but none felt as if they had ever been occupied. The emotional core of the building still lay ahead of them.

So did the danger.

They had just entered what appeared to be a small meeting or dining area when Garret lifted his head. Artemis knew at the same instant what he was sensing.

"Timon," Garret said. He whirled around and ran for a door on the other side of the room. Artemis and Pericles hurried to catch up, and they plunged into another corridor that ended abruptly at a flight of steep, descending stairs. Garret bounded down the steps, only pausing at the bottom to make sure that the others had negotiated the stairs successfully.

But now they were faced with a new dilemma. Three more corridors—little more than tunnels—branched out from the small room at the foot of the stairs, each smelling of damp, cold earth and stone.

"Underground," Garret said. "They're keeping the children *under* the castle."

Artemis took a deep breath. "Join with me, Garret," she said. "We can find them."

He took her hand again. Emotions exploded like fireworks and then receded to a distant hum. Auras mingled without resistance or discomfort, her abilities and his—the power she had given him—blending as one in full awareness.

Then they were off again, Garret squeezing into a space barely large enough for an adult, human or Opir. It was only the entrance to a maze of bewildering turns and reverses, stairs and dead ends, clearly built to hinder attempts at rescue or escape.

But the builders had not anticipated an invasion of empaths. Garret found the correct path, and they finally emerged into a long, narrow room furnished with a single ornate chair near the center.

To Artemis, it felt as if the entire room had been emptied of air. She sensed the crushing weight of mountain and castle above as if it might collapse in on them at any moment.

Garret swore. "They're here," he said. "Timon—"

"Yes," Kronos said, coming around a corner with eight Free- and half-blood soldiers at his heels. "They are all here, and safe. The Master…" He glanced at Pericles, and a flicker of doubt crossed his face. "The Master is temporarily disabled."

"By you?" Garret demanded.

"With great difficulty, yes. I cannot say how long his condition will last."

"The Master wouldn't listen to your proposals?" Artemis asked.

"He would not hear me at all. He is too far lost in his

dreams of power." He stared into Artemis's eyes. "I *must* have your help now. We can stop him before he goes any further."

Garret laughed. "Are you so certain you want to stop the Master, Kronos? Why didn't you kill him?"

"I am not a murderer."

"But if he's helpless, Artemis and I—"

Artemis silenced him with a gesture. An idea was developing in her mind, too terrible to acknowledge.

"Who are these soldiers?" she asked.

"I have brought them around to my way of thinking." Kronos looked at Pericles again. "Why is *he* with you?"

"He helped us find this place."

"Do not trust anything he says," Kronos said.

"Because he is no longer under your control?"

"His loyalties are suspect."

So are yours, Artemis thought.

Garret moved slightly so that Pericles was behind him. "Where are the Master's soldiers?" he asked.

"Most have left to deal with problems in the camp."

"What does the Master intend to do with the Freebloods?" she asked.

"Invasion of the Citadels with a Freeblood army, to ensure that Freebloods are granted the rights of full Opiri."

"Then why have so many of them rebelled?" Garret asked.

"The Master was away too long. There are too many Freebloods in camp to dominate easily, and his personal charisma was holding them together. They began to doubt, to fear."

"Then he's not going to have much luck managing them now," Garret said.

"Do not underestimate him, vassal," Kronos said. "You do so at your peril."

"But you still won't kill him."

Artemis trembled with the effort to keep her feelings hidden. All she sensed from Kronos was perfect control and a distant feeling of triumph.

"I am not a barbarian," he snapped. "But we can stop any possibility of his succeeding in his plans. If we work togeth—"

"Release the children," Garret said, "and maybe we'll help you."

"I need none of *your* help," Kronos said, with a twitch of his upper lip.

"Bring them out," Artemis said, "so we'll know they're all right."

"They're far safer where they are."

"You're lying," Garret said, trying to get past Artemis. "They're terrified. You've done nothing to help them."

Artemis touched his arm, projecting sympathy and patience. "What do you intend to do when the Master is no longer a threat?" she asked Kronos.

"Help the remaining Freebloods, of course. Organize them properly, and teach them as we always planned."

Artemis ached with wanting to believe him. But he could not easily have overcome a Bloodlord who had gathered so many Freebloods in a single camp.

"Garret has come all this way to save his son," she said.

"The children will only get in the way," Kronos said, his voice soothing and persuasive. "When the Master recovers, he could use them against us."

"I'll help you," Artemis said. "Show me what you want me to do."

"Artemis!" Garret said, reaching out to hold her back.

Without words, she tried to make him see what she planned to attempt. She had to make Kronos believe she trusted him, get him to let down his emotional guard.

Because if Kronos wanted so badly to join minds with her, there must be a way to use her empathy to stop him.

"Stay here, Garret," she said, avoiding his eyes. "Pericles, remain with Garret."

"Like hell I will," Garret said.

"Do not make me command you."

"No," Pericles said, pushing his way past Garret. "Don't believe anything Kronos says, Artemis. He'll do to you what he did to me."

"What *I* did to you?" Kronos said with a convincing display of surprise. "I no longer guide you. You serve the Master."

"Artemis freed him from *your* empathic influence," Garret said, taking a step toward Kronos.

"He didn't always try to control me that way," Pericles said. "I knew him long before he and I met in Delos." He looked from Artemis to Garret. "I lied when I said I lived in Oceanus."

"Be silent," Kronos growled.

"I was in the south of old California, near the Citadel of Angelus, when he came to the Freeblood exiles there with stories of a new life for us."

"When?" Artemis asked, unthinkingly reaching for the support of Garret's mind.

"About six and a half years ago," Pericles said.

Not long after Kronos's supposed "death" in Oceanus, Artemis thought, and around the same time as her exile. She felt Garret inside her mind, suppressing his rage at Kronos in order to help her. She grasped the mental lifeline he offered and shut out everything but Pericles's voice.

"Kronos said we could live as well as the lords in the Citadels," Pericles continued. "There were some mixed human-Opir colonies then, small and not very well protected. He said we should…" Pericles began to speak in a rush, as if fearing he would be cut off. "He said it wouldn't be wrong to take humans from the colonies, because we would only need them until we created a new society where all Opiri would be equal. Then we wouldn't keep running out of blood, and humans could have better lives in the Citadels." His eyes begged Artemis for understanding. "He *made* us believe him. We would raid the colonies and keep the humans for a while, but many of them couldn't survive in the wild. Then Angelus's agents drove us away, and we went north. We found more mixed colonies near Erebus and the San Francisco Enclave. Kronos tried to persuade the Opiri in the colonies to join us. Sometimes we fought them. Opiri and humans died."

"His memory is twisted," Kronos said. "The Master has warped his mind and would turn you against me."

"There was one colony where Kronos got to some of the Freebloods who were living peacefully with humans," Pericles went on, stumbling over his words. "They opened the gates to us. I tried to stay out of the way, but the others killed at least one high-ranked Opir before we got out." Pericles's eyes swam with misery. "After that, Kronos… couldn't control all the Freebloods who followed him. He decided to leave California, and a few of us went with him. He said he had to find a former vassal in Oceanus, and he sent us to find her. We found out she'd been exiled from the Citadel."

"Me," Artemis murmured. Garret moved up behind her, lending her his warmth as well as his emotional support.

"We split up and started searching the wilderness. But the group I was in broke up, and I…" He looked away. "I was too weak on my own. Chares took me in, and then they took Beth. I found out about other packs stealing children, carrying them north. And just before Chares decided to kill me, I heard a rumor about an exile in southern Washington who sounded a lot like Kronos. But after you saved me and I followed you to Chares's pack, I never thought I'd see Kronos again."

"I was looking for you when the Delosians captured me,"

Kronos said to Artemis, his voice beginning to rise. "These other things are fantasies, fruit from a poisoned tree."

"But it all makes sense," Garret said to Artemis. "He couldn't control the Freebloods in the south. He knew what *you* were capable of and believed he needed your help the next time he had to assert his dominance."

"Over the Master's followers," Artemis said. She stared at Kronos. "You allied yourself with him, always intending to take over when you found the means. But what were *you* doing for *him*, Kronos?"

"Nothing," Garret said, his aura sparking to brilliant life. "He isn't one of the Master's allies. He *is* the Master."

Chapter 24

Kronos sighed and sank into the throne-like chair. "Your vassal surprises me," he said to Artemis, "though it seems I underestimated *him* and overestimated *you*. All the time we spent together on the way here, all the many hints I gave you, and you never guessed."

"She believed in you," Garret said, somehow managing to put himself between her and Kronos again. "How much of that was your mind control?"

"I saw it not long ago," Artemis whispered, laying her hand on Garret's rigid back to keep from falling, "but I couldn't quite make myself believe. It seems so obvious now." She moved to stand beside Garret and met Kronos's gaze. "You sent me into the camp to look for traitors to the Master."

"And you found them for me," Kronos said, "though that was a small thing. I would far rather that you had continued to believe that I needed your help to dominate the Master and stop his 'evil' plans."

"Then you do admit to your own evil," Artemis said.

"Good and evil are limited human concepts," Kronos said.

"Why did you send Freebloods to steal half-blood children?" Garret asked, his voice very low.

"I assure you that they are safe," Kronos said.

"That isn't good enough."

"All will become clear in the future."

"But your army is defecting *now*. If you promised these Freebloods the same things you offered the ones in the south, it obviously wasn't enough to hold them when the 'Master' vanished."

"Yes," Kronos said. "I never should have left to find you, Artemis. But even that was not an irredeemable error on my part."

Garret's aura, no longer red like his hair but the color of old blood, seethed with dangerous anger. "You made a fatal error in thinking you could ever get Artemis to help you."

For the first time, Kronos let his anger show. "Surely you have more questions, Artemis, before we begin to quarrel in earnest," he said with biting sarcasm.

"Why did you change?" she asked, struggling to keep her voice level. "Why war and conquest instead of the separate, independent and peaceful existence you always wanted for our people in Oceanus?"

"After my supposed death," Kronos said, "I realized that what I had wanted would never be enough. There had to be redress for those who suffered at the hands of arrogant Bloodlords."

"So you plan to set your Freeblood hounds on the elite, steal their serfs and take over?" Garret said.

"A continuation of the old ways," Artemis said, "only with a new set of Bloodlords to replace the entrenched rulers. Do you truly think you can overthrow the Citadels with a few thousand troops?"

"It would not be difficult to rouse the disaffected Freebloods within the Citadels," Kronos said. "It would only be a matter of recruiting them. A handful of spies would be enough. And I have not entirely discarded the philosophy you and I developed in Oceanus. I intended to offer the aristocracy a chance to surrender. Their capitulation to my demands would give us the opportunity to rebuild our society along more equitable lines."

"This isn't about your concern for Freebloods," Garret said. "There's no idealism in you, Kronos."

"Vengeance," Artemis asked. "Your answer to the Bloodlords and Bloodmasters who tried to kill you for turning against your own rank and challenging the status quo. You've become just like them."

"If I wanted revenge, I could have taken it long ago. There can be no new beginning without tearing the current system down to its foundation."

"And you think that after unleashing an army of Freebloods to murder at will, you'll be able to control them afterward?"

"That is why I wanted your help, Artemis," Kronos said. "Why you *will* help me, because you know that without the proper guidance Freebloods are as savage as humans, and just as destructive."

Artemis's rib cage seemed to press in on her heart. "You will not stop with the Citadels. The violence will spread to the human settlements and Enclaves. Human troops were caught outside your camp. The abductions have already set the spark to the tinder."

Garret's strong hand found hers. "She isn't yours anymore, Kronos," he said. "She wouldn't help you even to save me or my son, so you can put that sick thought out of your mind."

"Such devotion," Kronos said, shaking his head. "But how strong is the edifice of your affection, Mr. Fox? You have every reason to hate her kind. Why did you let her turn you into one of us?"

"I knew I'd have a better chance of surviving to kill you," Garret said. "Where are the children?"

Kronos made a casual gesture, and one of his guards slipped away. Artemis turned to look for Pericles, but he had vanished.

"I believe you wanted to know what I planned for my little half-bloods," Kronos said to Garret.

Garret's aura burned so intensely that Artemis feared it

might do him some physical damage. "It won't matter once you're dead," he said. He lunged toward Kronos but didn't get more than two steps before Kronos attacked him with such a focused blast of contempt that Garret was utterly unprepared to defend himself against it. Artemis was too slow to help him. He fell to his knees with a sharp exhalation, as if Kronos had kicked him in the belly.

But there was a sudden, vital flush of fierce exhilaration in the emotions Artemis shared with him, and she realized what he had done. Garret hadn't run at Kronos out of a reckless loss of restraint. He'd meant to give her a chance to assess Kronos while he was distracted. And he hadn't given her warning, knowing that Kronos might sense his intentions.

And for a few seconds, Kronos *had* been vulnerable. He had been so focused on punishing Garret that he'd briefly let down his mental shield, and Artemis had been able to look inside him.

There was a chink in Kronos's armor. He was capable of uncertainty. He believed that she was more powerful than even *he* had guessed, and he was also desperately afraid of Garret. Of what he and Artemis could be together.

Garret pushed himself to his feet, then stepped between Artemis and Kronos, blocking the Bloodlord's line of sight. "Did you get what you needed?" he asked Artemis.

His dark maroon eyes narrowed in fury, Kronos shouted a command. Garret jerked, and Artemis felt another explosion of emotion from her lover, his aura reaching for someone she couldn't yet see.

Two soldiers walked around the corner with a red-haired child. A boy, dressed in a serf's tunic and pants, who walked with his smudged chin up and his eyes searching for the one he hoped to see.

"Timon," Garret said, his voice breaking.

"Dad!" the boy yelled. He started forward, and his aura,

the color of a monarch butterfly's wing, stretched to meet Garret's.

"Let him see his father," Kronos said, as the guards restrained Timon. They released the boy, and Timon pelted straight toward Garret. Their auras mingled even before they touched, and Artemis was swept up in a vivid outpouring of love that obliterated all hate and anger with a single embrace. Garret lifted Timon off his feet and kissed his cheek, murmuring words of promise and comfort. Timon grinned, his slightly crooked teeth gleaming in a face less like Garret's than she had expected.

At last Garret set Timon down. The little boy examined his father's face, a deep line between his ginger eyebrows. "You're different," he said. "You're becoming like Mommy, aren't you?"

"Yes," Garret said, sobering quickly. "I'm sorry I couldn't tell you before I found you."

"That means you'll live a long time, like me," Timon said.

"Yes."

"And you won't go away, like Mommy."

Garret's throat worked. He turned Timon toward Artemis. "This is Artemis," he said. "She came here with me just to find you."

"And I am very glad to meet you," Artemis said.

Timon was wary. "Did *you* make Daddy this way?" he asked.

"Yes, she did," Garret said. "But I wanted her to."

"All right," Timon said, unfazed.

His resilience surprised Artemis, but she was profoundly grateful. He, like Garret, was a survivor, brave and strong. If the other children were like him…

"Mommy would be very proud of you," Garret said, his voice and aura thick with emotion. "Listen, Timon. I want you to stay with Artemis, no matter what happens. She's still stronger than I am. When we—"

"Did I give you the impression that I was letting you take the boy?" Kronos asked, leaning back in his chair. "I was simply curious to see if such a reunion would meet all my expectations." He smiled at Artemis. "Not at all like ours, was it, my child?"

"I was never your child," Artemis said, resting her hand on the crown of Timon's head.

The Master gestured at the Opiri who had brought Timon. "Bring eight of the children, the ones marked as of least value."

Artemis reached out with her free hand to grip Garret's arm, half-afraid that he might charge at Kronos again, and Timon grasped his father's fingers. It was as if a broken circle had suddenly been made complete, a circuit closed by the most powerful of emotions. Timon and Garret became one, and as *they* become one with *her*, a shifting aurora of red, orange and blue light enveloped them.

Timon's eyes grew very wide, and Garret froze. He was about to speak when a group of half-blood children, a mix of boys and girls, filed into the room. The guards pushed them to stand in front of Kronos's chair. Eight pairs of eyes, brown and blue and gray and black, fixed on Garret, Artemis and Timon without comprehension.

It was as if they had been placed in some kind of trance, made incapable of resistance, and this time Artemis thought *she* might be the one to fling herself at Kronos. She dropped her hand, and the glowing circle broke.

"Let them go," Garret said hoarsely. "If they're useless to you…"

"Of little use to my program, yes. But I think in terms of decades, not years as humans do. Everything you said of my little Freeblood army was correct. I know they will not be reliable soldiers over the long term. Once they have what they believe they want, they will falter, lose their discipline, turn their attention to selfish pursuits. That is in their nature.

"That is why I realized, even in the south, that I would need more malleable and adaptable troops for the future, after the initial work is done and the Citadels fall. Troops that can fight in daylight as well as in darkness, and who have absolute loyalty to me."

"My God," Garret said. He reached behind him to touch Timon again. "And you think you can mold these children so easily, make them forget their families and their lives?"

"I have no doubt of it. But that is only one aspect of my plan. Eventually, I will breed my own half-bloods from humans and Opiri captured in the first phase of my program."

"Decades," Artemis breathed. Her disgust and horror were building into a rage that might make even Garret recoil. "You have truly gone mad."

"I am not mad, Artemis. What I envision is a world dominated by those who are *both* human and Opiri. A world in which wars will eventually cease, because there won't be enough full-blood Opiri and humans to destroy each other, and this earth along with them. All I need to do is encourage each race's present fear of the other, and they will do most of the work for me."

"Not decades, but centuries," Garret said. "Unless you…"

There were no words, Artemis thought, to describe Garret's emotions then. They were so clear that she could see the images in his mind: terrible pictures of slaughter on a massive scale, people killing other people because they were of a different culture or appearance, or simply because it was convenient to get them out of the way.

"Genocide," Kronos said. "You humans tried it first. You have a long tradition of such cleansing. Your San Francisco Enclave developed a lethal virus that would have killed nearly every Opir who came in contact with infected blood."

"And good people stopped it," Garret said, his voice shaking.

"For the time being. The project can be revived."

"You cannot begin to implement your program without vast quantities of blood to support your troops," Artemis said. "You do not have enough humans to—"

"I am working on that, as well. I did say that I still saw value in some aspects of our original plan. Relieving Free-bloods of their dependence on human blood is just the beginning, Artemis. There are dhampir half-breeds who do not require blood at all. I will have scientists working on this problem night and day, until we can extend those benefits to all Opiri."

"Will that matter to the Opiri and humans you have already slaughtered?"

Kronos leaned forward in his chair. "Just imagine, Artemis. A world of true peace. An earth permitted to heal. Is that not more important than the lives of a few thousand, even tens of thousands, of Opiri and humans?"

"You won't have peace," Garret said. "Eventually your half-bloods will turn on each other, just as Opiri and humans have always done."

"But they have me," Kronos said, spreading his arms wide. "With Artemis's assistance, I will become their true father." He dropped his hands and signaled to the soldiers. The guards moved to stand behind the children, one Free-blood to each child.

"No," Garret said.

"There is a simple solution," Kronos said. "I will permit all of you to live, even to remain together. But only if Artemis agrees to stay with me."

"I can't," Artemis whispered. "I can't help you destroy—"

"I will be generous, my child. I will not expect you to

work with me. I merely ask you to give your word that you will never use your abilities against me. If you were to break this agreement, then, of course, the boy and his father would die."

Garret looked down at Timon and then met Artemis's eyes. They both knew that Kronos was lying. He was still a powerful empath. If Artemis agreed to such a bargain, Kronos would find a way to coerce her into helping him. If she dropped her guard, and he got inside her mind…

Garret knelt before his son. "I'll need you to be very brave for a little while longer, Timon. Can you do that?"

"Yes, Daddy." Timon smiled and touched the tears on Garret's cheek. "I understand."

Garret rose and met Artemis's gaze. They didn't have to speak again.

"Do not harm the children," she said, bowing her head to Kronos. "I will do as you demand."

"Then come to me," Kronos said. "Release your vassal from your control, and he and the child will remain here as hostages, unharmed."

This, Artemis had not expected. Releasing Garret meant breaking the newly formed bond between sire and vassal, and she had no idea what that would do to him. What it might do to *them*.

"Garret has not fully turned," she protested. "If I release him so soon…"

"You have made your choice," Kronos said. "Now do what must be done."

So he is counting on something going wrong, Artemis thought. Garret could become gravely ill or mentally unstable. She sent him a clear picture of the danger, unable to separate her fear from her warning. Timon was staring at her.

"It's all right," Garret said, as if he was reassuring her

and Timon at the same time. But his gaze conveyed a far more complex message.

They would let Kronos think he had won.

"I must bite you again," she said softly. "But this time I will break the chemical bond that tethers you to me, and you will be free to do as you will."

"I understand," Garret said. He touched Timon's head. "Whatever you see, don't worry. Artemis is going to make me stronger."

"Okay," the boy said. But he grabbed Garret's hand again, and Artemis had to wait until Garret convinced his son to let go.

"Enough," Kronos said. "Artemis."

She expelled her breath and leaned toward Garret. "Listen to me," she said. "When it happens, drop all your mental barriers, even any you hold against Kronos. And give me all the strength you have."

It was obvious that he understood. He closed his eyes. She lowered her mouth to his throat and bit him quickly.

He stiffened. She tasted his blood and prepared to alter it yet again.

But more than merely his blood flowed into her. His emotions—so complex, so familiar—mingled with hers and, as before, became so much a part of her that she could no longer separate his from her own. His belief in her buoyed her up above all fear and uncertainty.

Acting purely on the power of those emotions, Artemis shaped them into an arrow, nocked a bow crafted of unshakable conviction and let the missile fly.

Kronos began to rise from his chair, only beginning to guess at the danger when Garret and Artemis attacked. They made a single, surgical strike at the weakness Artemis had sensed before—the fear—and broke through. Kronos fought to restore his barriers, but Artemis and Garret were already flooding his mind, replacing greed and ambition and hatred with love and trust and hope.

Kronos tried to speak, to order his solders to strike at the children. His Freebloods stared at him, waiting for a command that never came.

"Return…the children to their quarters," Kronos whispered. "Leave me."

The guards escorted the children out of the room, and Kronos slumped in the chair like a discarded doll.

It is done, Artemis thought, still floating on the currents of two auras, two minds, two hearts joined in consummate harmony. *He cannot harm anyone now.*

Kronos croaked like a dying raven, gave a strangled laugh and shaped his mouth into a death's-head grin.

"Impressive," he said. "But where is…that admirable human quality…forgiveness?" His eyes fluttered closed. "What of…your wife, Mr. Fox?"

Chapter 25

The arrow rebounded and flew toward Artemis and Garret. Emotion become memory. Kronos's memory, of a time when his new ambitions had begun to take hold.

Garret bent almost double, and his pain battered Artemis like a fist.

"Pericles...didn't tell you," Kronos said. "It was when I was returning north, abandoning my first experiment. The Freebloods who remained with me...were beginning to starve. I sent them to raid a colony that...had the misfortune not to consider defense a priority." His voice hitched. "There was a Bloodlady. Very beautiful. I had heard of her. She...fought for her adopted humans with great courage."

Garret sobbed. Artemis fell to her knees beside him. He tried to push her away. Timon ran to him and put his small arms around his father's shoulders, tears streaking his face.

"I did not know...that you were her mate," Kronos said, "until Pericles said that Artemis had told him about your high-ranked Opir 'friend' who had died at the hands of rogue raiders. Artemis told me much about you and your origins, and I was able to deduce the rest." His chin dropped to his chest. "What have you won, Garret Fox?"

No, Artemis said silently. *No. No. No.*

Garret didn't hear her. His aura darkened until all traces of red were gone, until Garret himself was shrouded in shadows even Artemis couldn't penetrate.

He lifted his head. This time *he* nocked the arrow.

She fought the dark impulse the only way she knew how: with her love for Garret, with Garret's love for Timon and his unshakable belief in her. But he had created a wall impenetrable to every emotion but rage, and not even all her power and experience were enough to pierce it. Soon she found herself sucked in by the very love she felt for Garret…lost, ready to strike out, to obliterate Kronos's mind completely.

Daddy?

A small, warm hand clutched at hers. Suddenly she broke into two pieces—Artemis and Garret, with Timon between them.

Timon was the bridge.

"No, Garret," she said. *It will destroy you.*

"No, Daddy," Timon said, tugging on Garret's arm. "Stop!"

Garret blinked. His aura wavered, leaped again, guttered like a flame doused with water and then rose up greater than before. Hatred became a weapon deadly enough to destroy not only Kronos but every living being in the castle.

She had given him that weapon.

Artemis looked into Timon's eyes. "Can you help me again, Timon?" she asked. "Can we show him how much we love him?"

He hugged her tightly. "He loves us, too."

She was afraid to believe it, afraid to rely on emotions that might not be real. But if she had to pretend in order to save Garret…

"Let's help him remember," she said.

If Garret had been in his right mind, he might have remembered that he had not always had this power. He might have realized that Artemis had given it to him when she changed him, when their minds and emotions had mingled and become indistinguishable from one another.

He might even have remembered that it was love that made it possible. But for him, now, there was no past, no future. Only the need to make *him* pay, the one who had taken Roxana and Timon from him.

Closing his eyes, Garret concentrated. The rage was a furnace inside him, a forge to create a weapon so powerful that nothing of his enemy would survive. And if the enemy's destruction reverberated outward, if it took the others of his kind down with him, there would be no one to mourn them.

The weapon took shape, red and black amid the seething flames. Garret seized it in his hands, but it did not burn him. It only grew larger, heavier, more potent. Its core began to hum with all the explosive energy of the world-killing bombs humanity had created during the War but never dared use.

Garret was not afraid to use *this* one. It began to vibrate, its shell no longer able to contain the energy of rage and hatred. He lifted it with his mind, positioned it, took aim.

We love you.

The words formed in his mind, distracting him from his purpose. He tried to brush them aside. They returned, more insistent than before.

We love you, Garret.

Love was a warm, soft light that wrapped around the weapon, dulling its radiance, seeping into his soul. Again he tried to reject it, and again it refused to dissipate.

Love. Memory returned: of Roxana, and laughter, and Timon a babe in his arms. Love that even death could not destroy.

And then other memories: Artemis, when he had first met her...before he had realized how quickly his heart would accept her even when his mind could not. Artemis taking his blood, giving him a part of herself she shared with no other living being. Lying with her, joining with her, beginning to recognize the truth.

Love.

The weapon in his grip began to cool. He tried to hold on to it, but the memories were too thick now, and he was filled up with Artemis and Timon and the emotions that were everything his hatred was not. Emotions he couldn't fight, because the darkness he had harbored for so long could not endure the light.

But then the new images formed in his mind. Ugly, distorted, unbearable scenes of death at the hands of savages.

See how your Bloodlady suffered, the enemy said. *See how she died.*

Light collapsed in on itself. Garret grasped the weapon again. Timon vanished. Only Artemis remained, a small, blue point of radiance nearly overwhelmed by the shadows.

He tried to push her out, but she resisted. The blue began to spread. It crept into the dark corners, invaded the crevices, exposed the monsters. And as she advanced, she absorbed the bitterness and rage and need to destroy. She took them into herself. The blue became a crystal, ever-expanding, threatening to crack with the pressure building inside it.

Too late, Garret turned against his darkness. Too late, he reached for the blue, strove to hold the pieces together.

The crystal exploded, hurling shards toward the source of pain. A roar deafened Garret, and he felt blindly for Timon. He wrapped his arms around the small body and curled himself over it.

Then the shadows were gone. He opened his eyes. Kronos lay on the ground before his throne, staring, mouth ajar. He was still breathing, but there was nothing behind his eyes. No emotion. No mind.

Artemis knelt a few feet away, rocking slowly, tremors working through her body. Garret swept Timon up and carried him to her side.

"Artemis?" he whispered.

Pericles ran into the room, panting heavily, and skidded

to a stop when he saw Kronos. He leaned over his knees, catching his breath.

"I… Is he…?"

"He can't hurt anyone else now," Garret said, crouching beside Artemis and lifting her chin.

Pericles straightened. "I just found out…that there's an army on the other side of the ridge."

"An army?" Garret asked, tearing his gaze away from Artemis's face.

"Soldiers from three Enclaves are here looking for the children," Pericles said, "and they've trapped the Freebloods who've been escaping from the camp."

"Human soldiers?"

"Not only humans," Pericles said. "Some Opiri, too, from the colonies, but they've all come for the same thing. They blame all of us for the kidnappings."

"You *are* to blame," Garret said coldly. "How many Freebloods are trapped?"

"Hundreds. I don't know how many are still in the camp, but the ones who escaped were trying to get out of the valley when they were surrounded. Kronos sent most of his soldiers to deal with the deserters, but the soldiers and refugees are outnumbered fifty to one." He swallowed. "Daniel is down there, too. He's trying to keep the humans from attacking, but it's only working because some of the humans and Opiri don't want to cooperate with each other."

Daniel, Garret thought. Somehow, he wasn't surprised.

"Artemis," Pericles said, moving toward her, "I know you came here to get Timon and free the children. But you care about our people, too. You know they're not all bad. You believed in me. A lot of them were misled as I was. You were, too. You can help us."

Artemis didn't answer. Garret cradled her face in his hands.

"What's wrong with her?" Pericles asked.

"I don't know," Garret said, stroking Artemis's temples with his thumbs. "She doesn't seem to hear us." He stared at Pericles. "She can't help you now."

Pericles backed toward the tunnel. With a low moan, Artemis stirred. Garret's attention snapped back to her, and he tried to feel her mind.

It was as if they'd never had any empathic bond at all. He remembered how she had tried to absorb his fury and hatred. He remembered a blue crystal of pure emotion, remembered trying to hold it together as Artemis struggled to control the forces he had unleashed within himself.

He had not defeated Kronos. *She* had. And she had paid a terrible price for her victory.

He glanced at Timon, whose eyes were shining with tears. "She's very far away," Garret said. "We have to help her until she can find her way back."

Timon nodded, biting his lip. "What should we do?" he asked.

"I want you to stay with Artemis. Take care of her." He kissed Timon's forehead. "You were very brave. Now be brave for her."

He left his son with the woman his rage had nearly destroyed and went in search of the children. Around the corner he found a long corridor punctuated by cell doors that seemed to stretch far into the distance. All the soldiers were unconscious, sprawled across the floor like puppets with cut strings.

The doors were unlocked. One by one he opened them and released the children inside. Nearly a hundred half-bloods of all shapes and sizes emerged, most under ten years old, frightened and hungry and bewildered.

With a few words of comfort and a promise that no one would hurt them again, he ushered them to the main room. They hesitated when they saw Kronos, but Garret showed them that the Master was unable to move or speak, and they scurried past him. With all the natural resiliency of children they began to talk in low tones, staring around the room as if to confirm the bewildering fact that they were free.

Artemis was on her knees, Timon pressed close to her. They both looked up at Garret as he went to them.

"Artemis," Garret said, dropping beside her. "Are you all right?"

"The children…are well?" she asked, ignoring his question.

She can't feel them, Garret thought. He suppressed his despair and smiled.

"They will be," he said. "Like you."

Her smile was a mask over a hollow space. "The empathy… it's gone," she said. "For so long I lived without it. I pushed it away. But now that I don't have it…"

"You'll get it back," Garret said, holding her gently by the shoulders.

"I don't know what you're feeling," she said.

"Don't you?" He pulled her close to his chest with one arm and hugged Timon with the other. "You don't need to see into my thoughts, Artemis. You saved me and defeated Kronos. You need time to heal."

"Can you feel *me*?" she asked.

He realized that he still registered some of her emotions: anguish and fear and a tiny mote of hope buried deep underneath.

"I know you're hurting," he said, "and that I'm to blame. But you will heal. I promise."

She touched his face. "I heard Pericles," she said. "About the army. He wanted me to help."

"There's nothing you can do."

"But they *are* my people, whatever they have done," Artemis said. "Kronos would have given them an evil purpose. They must find a better one."

"But it's not your responsibility to find it for them," Garret said, mastering his anger.

"A war is about to begin," she said. "The war we never wanted to see happen again. If it starts here with slaughter, it will not end here."

"But I know what Pericles would have asked you to do…use your empathy to influence the soldiers threatening the Freebloods. It would have been wrong then, and it's impossible now." He lowered his voice. "We're taking the children someplace safe until their people can reach them. That's all that matters."

Supporting her weight against his body, Garret helped her to her feet. Timon huddled close, shyly reaching for Artemis's hand.

She half turned to stare at Kronos. "We can't leave him here," she said. "What if he wakes?"

"He won't," Garret said. "Your empathy was damaged because of my emotions, but what *he* suffered went far beyond that. If he recovers at all—"

He stopped, thinking about the children. They'd suffered enough horror without knowing that a powerful man's mind could be broken beyond repair.

"The children," Artemis murmured. "You're right. We must get them away."

Together, they gathered up the children again and moved among them, speaking personally to as many as possible. Artemis was as easy with them as she had been with Timon, but Garret knew she was relying on her own natural goodness and not on what their feelings told her.

They were discussing what to do with the children when Pericles returned.

Artemis went to him at once. "Has the war begun?" she asked.

"Artemis!" Pericles said, flashing a grin. "You're all right!"

"Has anyone been hurt?"

Pericles's smile faded. "No, but—"

"Find Daniel," Garret said, sensing Artemis's plan. "Tell him to keep talking to the humans and Opir who have come for the children. Tell them that we'll bring the children to them by sunset, but that they must not attack."

"You don't understand," Pericles said, panic rising in his voice. "They're already coming. They're outside the castle *now*!"

Chapter 26

Garret listened. He'd become something more than human, and now he could hear what he'd been too pre-occupied to notice earlier: many voices and hundreds of marching feet. He smelled the dust kicked up by their boots, their perspiration, their fear.

It wasn't only the invading army approaching the castle. The Freeblood deserters were with them.

"They have prisoners," Garret said to Artemis. "If you want to save the Freebloods, we have to show the humans and Opiri that the children are all right."

"Can we go?" a dhampir girl asked from among the crowd of half-blood children. "Is it safe?"

Safe, Garret thought. Anything might happen with passions burning hot and humans afraid for the abducted half-bloods.

"I still look pretty human," Garret said. "I'll go ahead and find Daniel." He touched Artemis's cheek. "I need you and Pericles to stay and take care of the kids until I give the signal."

"Garret—"

"If the humans see you, they may act before they think. You must stay here, Artemis."

She met his gaze. "You cannot protect me from every-thing."

"No," he said bitterly. "Not even from myself." He dropped his hand. "Please look after Timon. I promise I'll return as soon as I can."

He turned to go.

Artemis called after him. "I am sorry about your wife," she said. "So very sorry."

Unable to find his voice, Garret entered the tunnel and retraced the route back to the bailey. The covered courtyard was deserted, as were the battlements. He paused to listen to the increasingly agitated voices outside the high gates. Someone was demanding that the hostages be punished if the Master did not appear. Others were debating an assault on the gate or suggesting scaling the walls.

Garret found several daycoats hanging along the wall inside the gate, thought about the sunlight and what it might do to him, and decided to risk exposure. The less he looked like a Nightsider, the better.

He took a deep breath, thought of Artemis and the children, and threw all his strength into opening the castle gates. He stepped out into the sunlight, wincing at the sudden discomfort.

"Daniel!" he shouted.

The human soldiers surged forward, weapons bristling, threatening to trample Garret beneath their booted feet. The Freeblood prisoners, many of them trapped among the forward troops, faced the same danger.

"Stop!" someone shouted. Daniel emerged from the packed line of men and women, and stood between them and Garret, a lone figure holding the wolves at bay.

"Garret," he said, gripping Garret's forearms and staring into his changing eyes. "Pericles told me what she'd done to you."

"Artemis did nothing but help me," Garret said. "We have the children."

"The Master—"

"—can't hurt anyone now."

"He's dead?"

"Even if he recovers, he'll never have the full use of his mind. Artemis made sure of that."

Daniel didn't ask any awkward questions. "Is Timon all right?"

"He's inside with Artemis and the other children." Garret peered over Daniel's head. "Get them to back off. I won't bring the kids out if there's any threat to them or Artemis." He met his old friend's gaze again. "Do you understand, Daniel? Whatever you may think Artemis has done, she's on our side. And she's not well."

"What's wrong with her?"

Garret closed his eyes. "She lost something," he said. "I'm not sure if it's permanent. But Timon and I will both be there for her."

"She was never your wife, was she?"

"Not yet."

Daniel nodded. "I'll get the human troops to back off so the children can come out."

"You'll need to do more than that," Garret said. "You have to persuade the armies to let the Freebloods go. They were under the influence of a Bloodlord who lied to them and backed up those lies with power you can't begin to imagine. Killing them will be murder, and there's still a chance they can change."

"How?" Daniel said. "No mixed colony will take them in. They'll go back to scavenging and raiding, as they've always done."

"No," Artemis said, coming up beside Garret. "I will see that they do not."

Garret looked at Artemis in her heavy daycoat, knowing he'd been a fool for thinking she would stay inside just because he wanted to keep her safe.

But it was her words he found most alarming. He didn't get the chance to ask her what she meant, because there was a great heave in the crowd on the causeway as Daniel passed on Garret's message about the children. The human soldiers dragged the Freebloods back with them, leaving a clear space in front of the gate. A moment later the children emerged, Timon in the fore. He ran to Garret and put his arms around his waist. The other children, blinking in the sunlight, drifted out behind him.

There were cries of recognition and relief scattered among the troops, and currents of movement as parents tried to shove their way toward the gate. Running feet, happy cries, weeping. Joy.

But there was also fear. Kronos's deserters were still trapped, and not all the anger was gone, not from the parents and kin who wanted revenge.

Revenge that would destroy everything it touched.

"Timon," Garret said, touching his son's soft red hair. "You were too young to remember my friend Daniel, but he came to help the children. He would very much like to talk to you about them."

Timon subjected Daniel to a grave, assessing examination. "All right, Daddy," he said. "Will you take care of Artemis?"

"I'm going to talk to her now." Garret nodded to Daniel, who knelt to Timon's level, and then left them to guide Artemis back into the bailey.

"Artemis," he said softly, "you need to rest. You shouldn't have—"

"I am not ill," she said. Her eyes were focused, no longer shadowed or dazed with loss. "My mind is clearer than it has been in a very long time."

"You're temporarily disabled. No one expects—"

"Not disabled," she said. "Only different. Better able to serve my purpose."

"Your purpose is to live your life fully," he said. "Live it with me, with Timon."

"No. I have a duty, Garret." She looked out the gate at a group of cowering Freebloods. Terrified and angry, remorseful and defiant, women and men. Those who had been

Opiri for many decades and others who had been changed only within the past year. They were, Garret thought, no more alike than any given set of humans.

"Look at them," Artemis said. "I searched for a way to help my people make a new life, and now that chance has been given to me. Kronos betrayed these Freebloods. They must have something to replace the false dreams he gave them. Peace is still possible, but only if they can truly learn another way. And now that I have lost my empathy, I will never be tempted to misuse it."

Suddenly Garret realized that he was truly on the verge of losing her. She had suffered a severe mental trauma with Kronos's defeat, and her convictions had been shattered by his betrayal of everything she had held dear.

If he couldn't make her see that they belonged together…

"Artemis," he said, "no matter how brave you are or how well you can lead, you're only one woman. You've done enough."

She met his gaze with deep sadness. "When you left your colony, did you truly believe that you would find Timon? Did you imagine that you would help free all the stolen children and destroy the Opir who caused so much suffering?"

"I didn't do any of it alone," he said. "You were there."

"But you would have fought to do those things even if you had never met me," she said. "If I let doubt stop me now, I will always know that I failed."

"No." He took her by the arms carefully, desperate to make her listen. "There are other ways you can make a difference. If you were to join a mixed colony, you could help Freebloods acclimate and understand how their lives will change as functional members of a peaceful society. Admittedly it would be on a smaller scale, but you would be contributing something truly valuable to our future."

"Our future," she said. "Kronos… *I* always believed that

the only safe way for Opiri and humans to coexist is to live separately, apart from corrupting temptation."

"Kronos was wrong. Living apart isn't a lasting solution. We have to find a way to exist together, Opiri and humans. Free and equal. As you and I have been."

He didn't have to feel her emotions to know how much she was struggling, torn by conflicting desires. But one of those desires was to stay with him.

To love him.

"Think, Artemis," he said. "You saw how Timon responded to you. I haven't seen him this way since his mother died. He needs you now, as much as he needs me."

"I want only happiness for you and Timon."

"Then you'll have to help us find it, Artemis."

"I can never be what Roxana was to you." She gazed across over the massed humans and Opiri to the mountains. Snow began to fall, settling gently on her hood. "Accept what must be, Garret. Return to your people."

"And who *are* my people?" he asked. "I'm a Freeblood now. I won't go back to Avalon, and I can't accept Daniel's way. I certainly won't join a pack and hunt humans. Timon and I have to make a new home. We can't do it alone."

"Of course you can," she said. "You are one of the strongest men I have ever known."

"Daddy?" Timon ran up to Garret and hugged his legs, pressing his face into Garret's pants. "I want to go." He held out his hand to Artemis. "Come on, Artemis."

She looked away.

Timon's lip began to tremble. "What's wrong, Daddy?" he asked.

Garret bent and lifted Timon to his shoulder. "Artemis has a hard decision to make. She wants to help people who don't have any place to go. I want her to stay with us."

"Me, too," Timon said.

Artemis clenched her fists. "You cannot coerce me, Garret."

"But I can and will use every means to convince you."

"I have heard your arguments," she said in a low voice.

"But not the final one." He set Timon down and turned her face toward him. "I love you."

Her expression crumpled, and he thought he'd won. But she was still fighting him, and he could think of only one reason why.

"You don't feel the same way," he said, forcing the words around the knot in his throat.

She shook her head. "I know how much you loved Roxana. No one can take her place."

"That's right. No one can. But I don't want a replacement. I want you, for as long as we live."

"It is not in the nature of Opiri to mate for life."

"It's not in the nature of Nightsiders to give up on human blood, but that's what you expect them to do." He ran the pad of his thumb along her cheekbone. "What proof do you need, Artemis?"

She didn't answer. Her gaze turned inward, as if she were seeking refuge from the pull of too many obligations.

"She's so sad," Timon whispered.

"Very sad," Garret said. "Are you feeling well enough to stay with Daniel a little while longer?"

"Will you make Artemis feel better?"

"I hope so, Timon."

The boy hugged Garret again and went out the gate. Fighting the need to pull Artemis into his arms, Garret could think of only one other way to reach her. He closed off the outside world—all the smells, the noise, the feelings—and reached inside himself, digging beyond the surface of his emotions, into their core, and then deeper still, where he had gathered the fragments of a shattered blue crystal.

Then he released his hold on the physical plane completely. Like a diver plunging into a lightless ocean, he swam so far beneath the surface that he could no longer even sense the presence of land.

But he was Opir now. He could see in darkness. He glimpsed the crystal and stretched his hand to grasp it. His fingers slipped. He tried again.

And caught it.

Jagged edges cut into his palm. He hurled himself up, fighting for breath, searching for a surface that seemed to have disappeared completely.

Artemis, he said.

No answer. He held the crystal close to his heart, hardened his will and hurled it into darkness.

Catch it, Artemis, he said. *It's yours. And mine. And Timon's.*

It is life.

The crystal shot through the darkness and vanished. Garret's lungs filled with shadows as thick and choking as mud. He continued to fight, reaching for the one thing that could draw him home.

Her hand caught his. She pulled him up and up, and his body regained its strength. The water was suffused with blue light, shot through with streaks of orange.

He broke the surface. Artemis's lips were on his, breathing life back into him, her love around and inside him.

When she released him, her emotions were as crystal clear and vivid as the waters of a pristine lake.

"I *felt* them," she said. "Your feelings, your—"

"Love," he said, lacing his fingers through her hair. "And I feel yours, Artemis. You can't run from it."

"I cannot run from my people. But I—" She searched Garret's eyes. "I won't leave you now."

Her anguish almost undid him. He thought of the new life he and Timon would have to make. He thought with pride of his son's courage and resilience, his ability to see a woman just like his kidnappers as a person worthy of love.

But could Timon adapt to a life completely unlike the one he'd always known, a life with the very people who had taken his mother, then taken *him*?

"I need to talk to Timon," Garret said, touching Artemis's hand. "Don't go anywhere."

He walked out the gate to find Timon. He drew him aside and talked with him, not at all certain of what to expect.

When the conversation was finished, he took his son by the hand and led him back to Artemis. She smiled at Timon, though Garret could see how much it cost her.

"Timon and I have talked it over," Garret said. "We think that what you have to do is important for the whole world. That's why we're coming with you."

Her eyes widened. "Coming with me?"

"To teach the Freebloods how to live in peace with humans. I'm one of you now. We can make a difference."

"But you—" She broke off. "I can't let you give up everything you know to help those you have regarded as your enemies for so long."

"I have no hate left in me, Artemis," he said. "You leeched that poison. You took my humanity, but you gave me new eyes to see with. Let me use them. Let me help you."

"Me, too!" Timon said. He puffed out his chest. "*I'm* not afraid."

Artemis looked down at him. "He has been through so much. As brave as he is…"

"It's the children who will make the difference in the end," Garret said. "Timon is an ambassador to the future." He laid his hand on his son's head. "If he finds it too difficult, we'll do whatever we have to. Until then, let him try."

A voice Garret recognized carried over the murmur of

shuffling feet, shifting bodies and low conversation. Pericles was speaking with Daniel. He glanced toward Garret and Artemis, turned and slipped away into the crowd.

"What about Pericles?" Artemis asked. "He is not an innocent."

"Kronos mocked us about forgiveness," Garret said, watching the young Nightsider disappear. "I can't forgive the Freebloods who killed Roxana, but eventually I'll have to accept the ones who took the children. I can try to start with Pericles."

"That is all any of us can do," she said. "Try to begin again." She looked into his eyes. "Thank you," she said. "Thank you for believing in me. For this sacrifice."

"Where is the sacrifice?" He gathered her into his arms. "I love you." Their emotions mingled, and Artemis flung back her head and laughed.

"I love you," she said. "I *love* you."

"Me, too!" Timon said.

They pulled him close, and they all laughed together.

* * * * *

MILLS & BOON®
n○cturne™

AN EXHILARATING UNDERWORLD OF DARK DESIRES

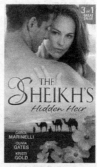

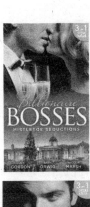
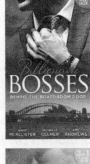

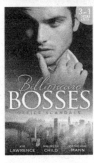
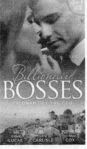
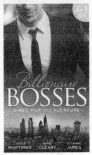